Bethan's Identity

Jessica Hopson

Content Note

To everyone who has ever wondered if what they have done
determines who they are.

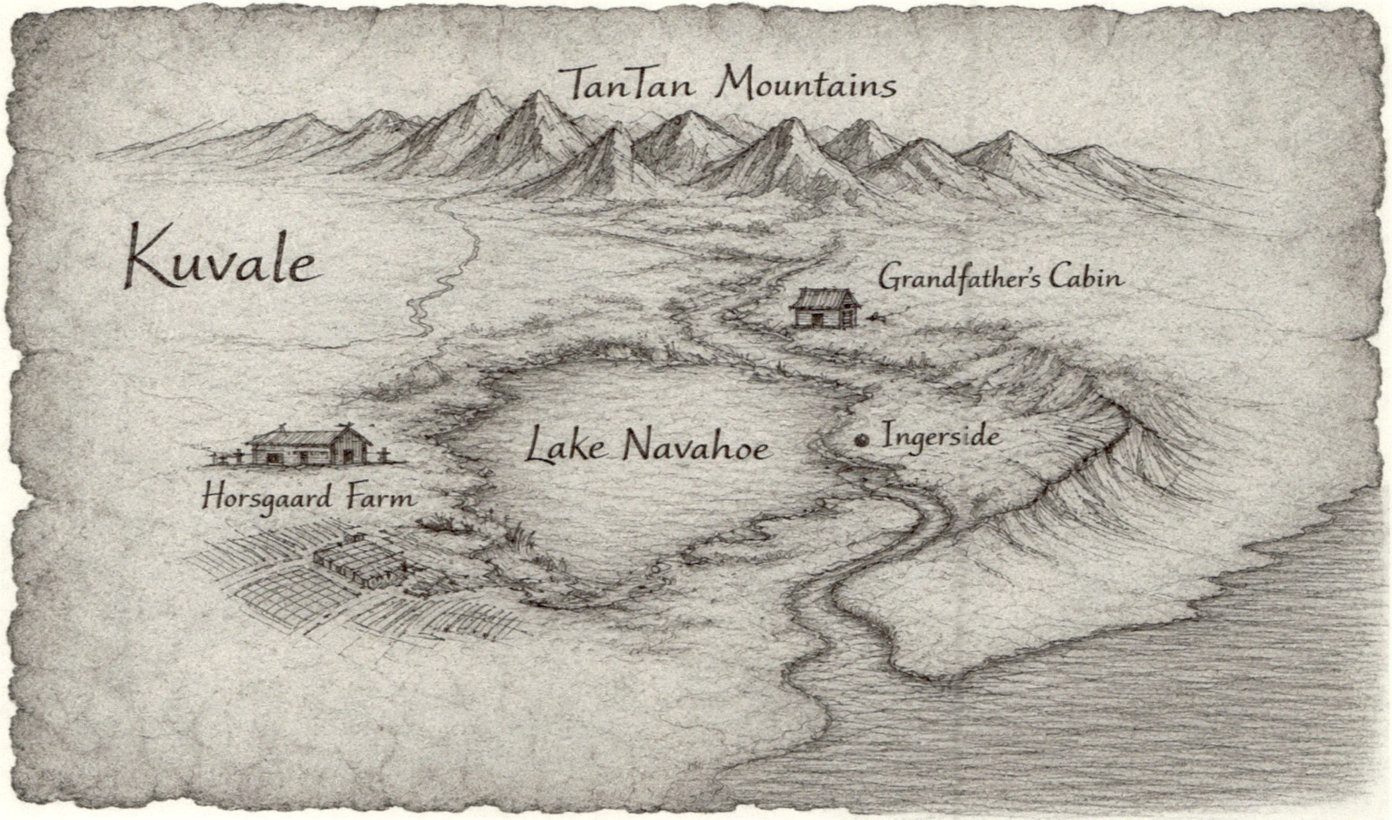

TanTan Mountains
Kuvale
Grandfather's Cabin
Horsgaard Farm
Lake Navahoe
Ingerside

Regnum
GERSHAN
Northern Houses
The High Keep
Crown Lands
Caerdis
Southern Trade Coast
Nobelgrae
Vershan Antiquities
Western Marches
Southern Marches
N
E
S
W

Act 1

1

Chapter 1

Bethan Horsgaard stood outside the family stall in the market, staring at the official seal pressed into the bottom of the eviction notice. The wax was still glossy, the sigil sharp. It caught the light like something proud of itself.

Her father, Cal, tore the parchment down. The sound split the air, dry fiber ripping from the nail. His brown eyes moved back and forth over the words as his jaw tightened, nostrils flaring. The icy set of his shoulders didn't match the warm spring sun resting on Bethan's back. The air smelled of crushed herbs and citrus peel. Someone nearby laughed.

"Is it bad?" she asked tentatively, her voice barely above the street noise.

Cal looked at her, then at her mother, Valaya.

"We had ten days to take the Oath," he said quietly. "We did not. Now we're fined. Until we pay ten thousand yadri, we are not permitted to buy or sell here."

The words sat between them like a blade. Valaya's face paled, freckles standing out against drained skin. "Our harvest?"

Cal shook his head once slowly "We'll have to sell or barter privately. The tax is too high. And we will not take an Oath that splits our allegiance."

His hand tightened around the parchment until it bent.

Bethan swallowed, her eyes finding Quinn's. Her older brother by two years and her best friend. He returned her look, but there was fire behind his, sharp and unapologetic. Not peaceful anger. The kind that waited for the right spark and hoped it came soon.

He shook his head once. *Not here. not in front of everyone.*

But Bethan knew the moment they were away from watching eyes, he'd give their father an earful. Quinn burned hot. Cal burned cold. Both were dangerous in different ways.

Bethan watched a beggar wearing a Talsian amulet, lift his cup to a man in the fine regalia of the counsel. The man turned away, and she narrowed her eyes.

"Those who have taken the Oath seem not much better off than we are." She said with scorn.

Cal looked at down at her and then to the beggar, and finally at the council member.

"Hush now, others can hear." Her father admonished.

Bethan frowned and opened her mouth to reply, then thought better of it. Instead she reached up and smoothed the notice where Cal had ripped it away. The crease of the parchment lined perfectly with her palm, the fibers rough against her skin. It felt like a mark. Like the city was pressing its thumb against them.

Branding them.

The Horsgaards were on their own.

~

Bethan tossed another crate onto the wagon bed, brushing dirt from her palms onto her skirt. The field stretched behind her, earth rich, ready, stubbornly theirs. Furrows dark from last week's rain.

"Careful," Quinn called, swinging another crate beside hers with a thud. "If you break the eggs, I'm telling Mother."

Bethan rolled her eyes at him. "You'd blame me if the sun exploded."

"Because you'd probably be poking it with a stick." He retorted.

She snorted.

Cal emerged from the barn with a coil of rope slung over one shoulder, his steps steady in the dust. He smelled faintly of hay and leather, sleeves rolled, forearms lined with old sun. He didn't have to raise his voice; his presence alone smoothed the air. Even the mule flicked an ear and settled.

"We'll take what we can sell door to door," he said. "Yah-Roi will provide."

Valaya stepped onto the porch, arms crossed against the light breeze that tugged at her skirt. Her voice was soft, yet firm. A warning wrapped in tenderness.

"He provides," she agreed. "But He will not be sending any angels to help sell these turnips."

Quinn stiffened. A muscle jumped in his jaw.

"Or any help at all." He muttered just loudly enough for their father to hear.

Bethan felt it, the spark hitting flint. Quinn's jaw set hard; Cal's settled into calm steel. The mule shifted, leather creaking.

"We don't take oaths to men," Cal said. "Not when we belong to another King." His voice was low and the words fell heavy and certain.

Bethan blinked, confusion pulling her brows together.

"We love Kuvale," she said. "It's a good country."

Wind skimmed the field behind her and blew wisps of fine light hair into her eyes.

Cal's expression softened. Not patronizing. Patient.

"We love Kuvalians, daughter," he said.

Bethan wrinkled her nose. "Are they not the same?"

Cal smiled softly and squeezed her shoulder, calloused thumb warm through the fabric. "Only in the way chicks are eggs."

She paused. Considered it. Then grinned. "You always do that, Papa. Make us think."

Cal's mouth twitched. Almost a laugh. "It's good for you. Come along. Your mother is right."

Bethan climbed into the wagon, the wood warm beneath her palms. Her father's answer felt close enough to be true, yet not enough to stop the riddle rolling in her mind like a pebble in her shoe.

The smell of roasted roots and pan-seared pheasant filled the Horsgaard home, warm, and comforting. However, the mood at the table was anything but. Bethan watched her father break bread with calm hands, the loaf steamed gently. His eyes were distant and prayerful. She mirrored his posture, though her movements were sharper, more restless. Selling their harvest had been difficult today. They were all tired.

Cal said grace, his voice firm but gentle, and the moment his final "amen" passed, Quinn leaned back in his chair, arms crossed.

"We could've just said the words, you know," he said, his tone respectful but edged. "Just the words. Would've kept the stall. No one really means them." He pressed.

Cal didn't look up from his plate. "I meant every word I ever spoke before Yah-Roi. I won't start lying now."

Quinn arched an eyebrow. "And starving's the better choice?"

"Better to starve free than live chained," Bethan snapped thinking of the beggar in the market stall, then glanced at her father, softening. "Isn't that what you always said?"

Quinn gave a quiet scoff. "Easy to say when you're sixteen and righteous."

Bethan glared. "And you're nineteen and jaded?"

Valaya set her hand gently on Bethan's, her eyes like tempered steel. "Enough, both of you. There's room at this table for questions, not division."

Quinn sighed, and his jaw tightened before he picked up his fork and resumed eating.

Bethan looked down, chastened.

Cal finally lifted his gaze, sweeping it across the table. "This won't be easy. But Yah-Roi never said it would be. He said He'd be with us. And that's all I need."

Valaya's hand slid into his under the table. "Then that's all I need too."

Bethan stared down at her plate. Quinn brooded and said nothing. She dared risk a look at him, but his eyes were stony.

"He is good," she pressed softly.

The words sounded small in her ears. Quinn huffed and sopped his gravy with his biscuit. The rest of the meal passed in silence.

The Gathering occurred in the barn of the Travalian farm.

A circle of forty men, women, and children came together to pray, to sing, to glean from the Book the words pertaining to life, and the Way of Yah-Roi.

Bethan peered at the ring of faces, lantern-lit and yellowed at the edges. The smell of hay tickled her nose, dry and sweet, clinging to wool and skin alike.

The Gorsas were missing this week. Word in the town, and whispered through the Gathering, was they had taken the oath to sustain their butchery.

Elder Ronan stepped forward. "Hear us, Yah-Roi," he prayed, his voice steady but worn. "You see the hardship of our country, and the way our people have abandoned You. Forgive those among us who have chosen the wide way. Keep those of us on the narrow path. Deliver us from the temptation to step off it. Help us to catch the brothers who have stumbled."

A low murmur rose behind Bethan. Not assent. Not quite dissent either. Something sharper.

The Richters were still here, though they had taken the oath just before the expiry, their place in the circle now uneasy, their shoulders stiff beneath the weight of knowing eyes.

Bethan raised her head slowly and sang the opening song louder than normal.

~

When the service was ended, and the families had sat down for a communal meal. Bethan cradled her cup of mulberry cider, the steam curling faintly against her fingers. Around her the adults spoke in lowered voices, numbers, consequences, futures weighed and found wanting. Her father's fine alone amounted to three months' wages. No one was paying that. Not unless they were wealthy. And the fine was only the beginning. Access to trade and medicine. Protection from the security forces. All of it specifically denied to non-Oath takers.

Cal stood a little apart, his voice calm but strong as he spoke into the circle that had formed around him. He argued that this stripping away was not only loss, but release.

"It gives us clarity," he said. "We can establish trade with others who refuse the Oath. We can take in doctors who will not bow. We can begin patrolling our own farms. Take responsibility for our neighbors."

Nells Richter shook his head, cider sloshing darkly in his cup.

"Do you know how hard that will be?" he said. "And we don't even know if the sheriff of our parish will allow us to patrol our own lands."

Cal turned to him, not sharply, quietly.

"I am not arguing that it will be easy," he replied. "The Master never promised easy. But hard is not the same thing as bad."

The barn had gone still. Even the children sensed it. Bethan's grip tightened on her cup.

"Now is the time for community," Cal continued. "Not winter, when everyone is starving."

Bethan watched the faces around him. Some fearful. Some thoughtful. Some already pulling inward, calculating cost.

And she realized, with a sudden chill sharper than the cider's heat, her father was already living as if the line had been crossed.

Chapter 2

The wagon wheels creaked in rhythm with the horses' steps, the air crisp with the scent of pine and moss. The Gathering had left their spirits stirred, but the road home was long and treacherous.

Valaya sat upright beside Cal, her eyes scanning the narrow forest pass ahead. Cal's hands rested steady on the reins, though his jaw worked like a man chewing through a thought. Behind them, Bethan sat turned backward on the buckboard, facing Quinn, who leaned across a bale of wool. They were mid-argument again.

"You're not hearing me," Bethan insisted, her voice low but forceful. "We can't play by their rules and claim we're still free. It doesn't work like that."

"I'm not saying we sell out," Quinn shot back, his arms crossed over his chest. "I'm saying there's a difference between strategy and surrender. Maybe we pick our battles instead of dying on every hill."

Bethan narrowed her eyes. "And when do you decide which hill is worth it? After it's too late?"

Quinn opened his mouth, but Cal's hand suddenly shot up.

"Quiet." His tone procured instant obedience.

Everyone stilled. Even the forest.

Then they saw it. The fallen tree sprawled across the path, too clean a break to be natural, too well placed to be coincidence.

Valaya stood, instantly alert. "It's an ambush."

Cal's eyes flicked back, sharp. "Quinn, stay down."

Quinn froze. "What?" His voice came out strangled.

Cal turned slightly, his tone steely but low. "You're not the one they want. Stay hidden. That's an order."

Bethan saw the fire rise in her brother's face, saw his jaw lock and his shoulders tighten. His hand hovered near the blade strapped beneath the wagon seat. Then, with visible effort, he dropped it. A beat of silence passed.

"Yes, sir," he said through clenched teeth.

Bethan searched the shadows between the trees as Cal climbed down, slow, and deliberate, his hands empty, his posture nonthreatening but unyielding.

From the brush, seven figures emerged, bandits in the muted colors of the wild. One stepped forward, half his face covered, the other smirking.

"Well now," the man said, eyeing the wagon. "A family of Oath-breakers if the market talk's true. Shame."

Cal didn't flinch. "We've broken no law."

"You broke the law of survival," the bandit sneered.

Bethan's heart pounded. Her tongue felt dry, her palms slick with sweat. Valaya hadn't moved from the bench, one hand wrapped quietly around the hilt of her dagger. Behind the bales, Quinn watched, his shoulders coiled like a spring.

"We are no lawbreakers," Cal repeated, his voice steady, deep as the earth. "The Laws of Yah-Roi guide our path. Always have."

He paused, and there was something in his eyes, something soft and fierce and unbearably tender.

"And He desires you, too," Cal said, his voice thick with sorrow. "Even now, He longs for you to follow Him."

The bandits shifted. The leader spat, his eyes full of scorn.

"Your Yah-Roi is a corpse on a cross. And you can meet Him yourself."

The cudgel moved faster than reason, a blur of wood and rage. Bethan screamed, pure, raw terror, as the blow landed. Her father dropped. Just dropped. Like a tree felled in the woods. A groan escaped him, then nothing. But they weren't done. The bandits closed in, clubs and boots and fists. Blow after blow, raining down. Again and again.

Bethan's scream dissolved into frightened sobs as she threw her hands over her face, shielding her eyes. The sound of bone breaking, mixed with her mother's screams, begging them to stop, filled the clearing. Her mother didn't move. She just sat, the plea never ending, one hand on Quinn's shoulder, holding him down with strength far deeper than muscle.

The beating went on long past reason. By the end, Cal was unrecognizable. A man who sowed and tended and prayed over his fields, now broken on the very road he had traveled to worship. The bandits turned toward the wagon Bethan's breath caught, her fingers digging into her thin shawl. Valaya started to rise.

But then, through the trees, came the sound of a bugle and hoof-beats The sound of cavalry approaching from the southern road cracked through the clearing like lightning. The bandits stilled and exchanged sharp glances. And just as quickly as they had come, they scattered, melting back into the forest, like shadows retreating from the dawn.

Bethan didn't move. No one did.

The horses had barely stopped when the lead cavalry officer stepped down from his mount. He was a sharp man, too sharp. His eyes swept over the scene with the precision of someone used to cataloging carnage without flinching. He took in the wagon, the huddled women, the teenage boy stiff with rage, and the torn flesh that had once been Cal Horsgaard.

Bethan did not breathe, it was as if she could not. The officer said nothing at first. He simply observed. Evaluated.

Then Valaya found her voice, barely a whisper, cracked and raw. "Please, officer. Will there be justice for my family?"

She had reseated herself when the unit had ridden into the clearing, returning her grip on Quinn's shoulder. Her face was streaked with dirt and tears and blood that was not her own. But her spine was straight. She spoke like a woman who had held her husband's hand through births and storms and famine and now had been unable to halt his end.

The officer finally looked at her. His expression did not change. His tone was crisp. Cold.

"Have you taken the Oath?" He asked flatly.

Bethan froze.

The words rang through the clearing like a death knell, louder than the beating that had left her father dead, louder than the cries of her mother that still echoed in her ears. Her eyes darted to her mother, still steady, still silent. To Quinn, his jaw clenched. Back to the passive face of the man who was supposed to represent justice. She swallowed, as the courage she had felt just moments ago was replaced with an ache in her heart. Allegiance had a cost.

The officer stared at Valaya long and hard and Bethan could feel the silence stretch, taut and waiting. But her mother did not flinch. Valaya Horsgaard squared her shoulders. A simple woman. A mother with no weapon, no armor but her faith. Her voice cracked at first, no louder than a breath. Then it grew steady and strong, echoing like a song passed down through generations.

"Hear, O people," she said. "Our Yah-Roi is One." Valaya quoted from the Book.

Bethan's hand shot up to hold her mother's, fear worming its way into her heart.

"Thou shalt have no other gods before Him," Valaya continued, her voice rising like fire. "And thou shalt love Yah-Roi with all your heart, and all your soul, and all your might. Beside Him, there is no other."

The words rang like steel in the stillness.

The officer's jaw clenched. His eyes flashed and his lips twitched.

"Much good has that done you," he said, his tone icy. "Your family is in danger of extending yourselves past the deadline to comply."

He let the words hang, baited and pressured.

Bethan's stomach twisted, as the man's gaze briefly met her own.

"Unless," he added slowly and deliberately, "you take the Oath. Here and now." His eyes swept across them all. "All of you." "My hands are tied." The officer went on, each word a thinly veiled threat. "I cannot interfere in this matter. I would advise you to do so, because the protection of the state will not apply to those who fail to obey." He leaned slightly forward. His voice dropped. "I do not see Yah-Roi here. Do you?"

A beat of silence.

Then, "Please, ma'am," he added, "consider your children. And do what is right."

Bethan's eyes followed her mother as Valaya stood.

"And let their father's death be in vain?" She whispered.

A muscle ticked in the officer's jaw.

"Ma'am," he began.

Valaya held up a hand. "We will consider what you have said. If you could be so helpful as to assist my son in loading my husband's body, we will be on our way." She had already reached for the reins. Bethan knew that tone. Her mother would not be considering anything other than an honorable burial

The officer sniffed and stepped back. His demeanor was cold as ice.

"Very well, Followers," he said.

The word was tight between his teeth. It was what they were called. Now it was a slur coming from his mouth. He flicked two fingers toward his sergeant, who dismounted to help Quinn.

Bethan flinched.

When her father's remains had been lifted and covered, the officer remounted, his voice hard with warning.

"Consider quickly, ma'am," he said, flicking the reins of his horse. "Before it's the blood of your children staining the ground."

Then he wheeled his horse. A curt signal from his hand. His men moved with trained precision, clearing the tree from the path as if it were no more than a fallen branch.

Bethan stood frozen in the wagon, staring at the blood-soaked earth where her father had lain. he cavalry passed them by, indifferent. One rider leaned low as he passed, sneering at Quinn.

They didn't look back. Not once.

~

They buried Cal on the hill overlooking the fields he had tended with his own hands. No carved epitaph, just a stone, weather-worn and unadorned, set deep in the earth above the man who had loved them more than life itself.

Bethan spent long hours beneath the elms, knees in the soil, eyes on the sky, whispering to Yah-Roi between broken sobs and long stretches of silence. She was not angry. Not truly. She was confused, and it gnawed at her ribs like a hungry thing. Her father had said Yah-Roi would provide. And He had. In ways that defied logic. The rains had come. The wheat had broken through the earth. The garden bloomed with reckless generosity.

But none of those miracles brought her father back. Nor did they stop the flow of time. In just three days, the Horsgaards would be declared felons, marked as threats to the very world Cal had died trying to redeem.

On this day in mid spring, Bethan had climbed the hill, sitting with a parchment and pencil. A warm westerly breeze stirred her hair as she sat down and began to draw.

"Papa," She said, like he could hear her.

"You told us that Yah-Roi is always here, but I-" Her voice cracked. "I miss you, and everything feels upside down."

A tear splattered on her hand, and she swiped at her nose with sniff. Behind her a twig snapped and she turned. Quinn stood against the apple tree, arms crossed.

"What do you want?" She snapped.

His jaw tightened, "You feel it too." He said pointedly.

She frowned. "Feel what?"

He huffed. "How unfair it all is. Yah-Roi is with us, but He took Papa? Is that what a good God does?"

Bethan's brow furrowed. "He is good, He brought the rain, and the wheat."

Quinn shook his head. "Never mind, you're too young to see it yet."

"Don't call me young," She snapped. "I am only two years younger than you."

Quinn shifted, turning to walk down the hill. "Two years is enough."

She picked up a dirt clod and threw it at him. "You miss him too, Quinn, just admit it."

Quinn turned then, walking back up the path, his eyes angry.

"Of course I miss him. Now it's on me, Bethan, me. The food and the farm and the law." He gestured with his finger for every point.

Bethan sat back. "I'm-"

He held up a hand. "Don't say it. I don't need your pity."

She reached for him. And he stiffened, before stepping back.

"Go back to talking to Yah-Roi, or Papa, they are better company than I am." He said gruffly.

And with that he turned and stalked away. Leaving her with the birds, the breeze, and the unmarked stone.

~

That night, the air inside the farmhouse felt heavy, like the sky pressing down.

The hearth crackled behind them, sap popping in the logs. Wood smoke hung low in the room, sharp and familiar, clinging to wool and hair. Bethan felt the heat of the fire warm her cheeks while a thin draft slipped under the door, cold against her ankles, as if the night itself were trying to get inside.

Quinn stood at the center of the room, jaw tight, voice firm. He spoke like a man full-grown, like someone trying to fill a pair of boots that had barely cooled beneath the earth. They needed a plan. A way to defend the land. Already, word traveled fast. Soldiers were sweeping through the countryside, seizing homes, and arresting those who refused to bow. His fists clenched as he spoke. The firelight jumped across his face, throwing sharp shadows along his cheekbones, making his fear and fury flicker in uneven turns.

Valaya said nothing as he raged. She simply sat, her hands folded in her lap, her posture still as stone. The fire did not seem to touch her. When he finished, when the heat drained from his voice and silence hovered over the table like smoke, she looked at him. And said only one word.

"No." Soft. Final. Unshaken.

Bethan watched her mother with wide eyes, the firelight reflected in them, bright and unblinking. Valaya stood then, tall, and rooted.

"We will do as your father would have done," she said, her voice steady like the ground beneath them. "We will wait. And we will pray."

Bethan's heart ached. The warmth on her face felt suddenly thin, fragile, like it could be taken away with one more opened door. She wanted to believe those words. Wanted to find comfort in them. But as Quinn turned away, silent and seething, and Valaya crossed the room to light the lamp by the window, Bethan felt the edges of her faith fraying, the cold from the door creeping closer. Even she was no longer sure if prayers were enough.

~

The soldiers came on the morning of the fourth day. They rode in with purpose, metal flashing, hooves thudding against the earth that had once been tilled by Cal's hands. At their head rode the same cavalry officer who had stood beside Cal's broken body. His posture was perfect. His eyes sharp and cold. His voice was sharp with authority, caring not that these were a widow and her children.

"You are in violation of the Talsian Alliance," he declared, his voice carrying through the crisp morning air.

Bethan stood beside Quinn. He trembled with rage, barely held in place by her grip on his arm.

"As criminals," the officer continued, "your land and livestock are forfeit."

His gaze moved over them. Valaya, firm and still. Quinn, barely contained. Bethan, her chin high, eyes narrowed, too much like her father's had once been.

"You may take the Oath now," the officer said, slow and deliberate, "and remain. You may even farm this land. But you will do so as servants to the Alliance."

He paused, letting the words settle. Then, as casually as a man announcing the weather, he added,

"Or your home will be burned. Your buildings torn down. And you will be cast out. Outlaws. Refugees. In a country that no longer tolerates dissent." He finished the speech in monotone.

Quinn's breath hitched. Bethan tightened her grip on his arm. Valaya did not flinch. Her voice rang out, calm and clear, like a bell sounding truth against stone.

"We will not bow." She answered with a voice of steel.

The officer did not argue. He did not bargain. He turned to his men with a flick of the reins and gave the order in three words that would follow Bethan for the rest of her life.

"Burn it all."

Quinn surged forward, teeth bared, fury breaking loose at last. But two hands held him back. Bethan's first then Valaya's firm and steady. He stood between them, trembling his jaw locked, eyes wild.

The soldiers moved with practiced efficiency. They trampled the new wheat. Tore the garden up by the roots. Slaughtered the animals with unnecessary force, laughter carrying as blood soaked into the soil.

The barn went first. Dry hay caught quickly, flames climbing fast. From the house smoke rose thick and black, the smell of their life curling into the sky. No one spoke as they were marched to the edge of the road.

A young soldier pressed a small sack of feed corn into Valaya's hands. He did not meet her eyes.

"That's mercy," he said.

Bethan felt nothing, it had happened so fast her mind was still trying to catch up. Behind them, flames consumed everything they had known. Ahead lay only the road. Valaya drew her children close, one arm around each of them. She looked forward. She did not look back. Bethan followed, ashes clinging to her skirts, the heat of her father's dream dying behind her.

Chapter 3

The smell of smoke clung to Bethan's hair and clothes, sharp and bitter in the back of her throat. Ash dusted the hems of her skirts and streaked her hands. Quinn had taken the bundle of corn from his mother's hands. Valaya was shaking, the tremor running through her arm, and Bethan slid her own beneath it, lending warmth where she could. Three shadows stretched long before them as the sun sank low in the west, the light thinning until the road ahead blurred into gray.

They were not the only ones walking. A family with a wagon passed them, wheels creaking softly. Then the Prangers, heads down, carrying little more than the clothes on their backs. Their footsteps faded quickly. No one stopped. No one looked.

Quinn halted them at last. "We must stop for the night."

The forest pressed close on either side of the road. Bethan heard it then, the rustle of small animals, the distant call of a night bird. He did not need to say that bandits roamed freely. The memory still sat heavy in her chest.

Bethan led her mother toward a stand of trees where the ground dipped slightly and the wind was weaker. Valaya sank onto a bed of thick clover with a sound halfway between a sigh and a sob.

"I will take care of supper, Mother," Bethan said softly.

"Mind our rations," Valaya whispered.

Bethan swallowed. The danger was no longer just the road or the law. It was quieter now, hunger, cold and thirst. The slow, patient work of being worn down.

"Yes, ma'am," she answered. There was nothing else to say.

Quinn returned with a bundle of damp tinder, pine needles and bark clutched tight in his fists.

"This will have to do for tonight. You and Mama stay here. I'll get water." He commanded.

Bethan opened her mouth, but his look stopped her. The firelight had not yet reached his eyes. She huffed and said nothing. Not tonight. Not after the farm. Not after the fire.

She poured each of them a small handful of corn onto a flat stone. Her fingers ached as she ground it, the grains resisting, slipping away. She added water sparingly, shaping the coarse meal into rough cakes and setting them close to the fire. The flames licked unevenly. One cake cracked apart. Another burned along the edge. The last sagged into mush.

They ate anyway, chewing slowly, listening to the pop of sap in the logs and the wind threading through the trees. When they finished, hunger still gnawed at them, dulled but not gone. Bethan pulled her cloak tighter as the heat faded and the cold crept in. She and Quinn began to settle near the fire when Valaya spoke.

"We will pray." She said calm and insistent.

Quinn's head snapped up. "What? Mother—"

Bethan flinched at his tone. Valaya raised her hand, steady despite the shaking that had not fully left her.

"For every night of all your nineteen years, we have sought Yah-Roi. We have thanked Him for His goodness and beseeched Him in hard times. We will not stop now." She admonished gently.

The fire cracked loudly. Quinn snorted. Bethan felt the space between them stretch thin and sharp.

"And where did all that beseeching get us when the soldiers came today?" His voice came angrily.

Valaya's eyes narrowed. Bethan stared at the ground, the clover crushed beneath her knees.

"Quinn Austin Horsgaard," Valaya said quietly, "you do not take that tone with me."

Quinn's jaw tightened. A vein throbbed at his temple, visible in the weak, flickering light.

Valaya's shoulders sagged. "Would you only love Him when life is good?" Her voice was tired and sad.

The forest answered with silence.

Bethan felt very small between them. "Please, Quinn," she whispered.

He let out a long breath, white in the cooling air, and finally moved closer.

"Very well" He sighed heavily, "But I won't be the one beseeching or saying thank you tonight."

Valaya said nothing more. She bowed her head. The fire burned lower. The night closed in.

When Valaya finished praying, she curled onto her side, exhaustion finally claiming her. The fire popped, sending a brief shower of sparks upward, and Quinn nudged Bethan with his foot.

"You want first watch?" He asked.

Bethan frowned, not understanding at first. Then it settled into her bones.

"We're in danger out here," she whispered. She hated the edge in her own voice.

Quinn's hand curled into a fist. "This isn't our nice parlor anymore." His tone was flat. Cold.

Bethan's brow tightened. "You don't have to be cruel."

"I'm not being cruel," he snapped. "I'm being real."

Bethan almost snapped back but was too tired for the fight. Somewhere in the dark, an owl hooted. A cold breeze slipped through the trees, lifting the fine hairs along her arms and carrying the damp scent of earth and smoke.

At last she sighed. "Fine. I'll take first watch."

Quinn did not answer. He rolled onto his side, pulling his cloak close, turning his back to her as sleep claimed him.

Bethan watched the fire burn low, listened to the night settle around them. She could hear Quinn's breathing, uneven at first, then slow. He was not trying to be unkind, she told herself.. She had never seen him look so old. So she sat awake, back straight, eyes scanning the dark beyond the firelight, doing what she must to protect him in return.

Even if it meant being afraid alone.

~

Two hours later, Quinn touched her shoulder to relieve her. Bethan startled, then nodded. She curled into the warmth he had left behind in the clover, drawing her cloak tight. The fire had burned low. The night air pressed cold against her back.

Sleep did not come. She lay awake, eyes fixed on the slow, patient drift of the stars. *Will we ever rest? Is there any place left for us to go beyond the reach of the alliance?* The full weight of exile had not settled yet. But she could feel it gathering, low and heavy, like a storm building beyond the hills. She missed being so sure.

The horizon began to pale. Stars faded one by one. Then the sun rose, dull and red, filtered through haze and ash and low clouds. The light did not warm her. Bethan pushed herself to her feet and walked toward the tree line, joints stiff and muscles aching.

"Yah-Roi," she whispered into the morning.

The Name felt small to her ears.

"Are you there?" She asked.

She stood in the growing light, the world waking around her. And still her chest felt hollow, and dark. As if the night had never truly ended.

Bethan heard her mother stir behind her, and she turned to tend the fire. Valaya smiled thinly at her daughter.

"We will sleep better tonight, we have a long way to walk." The woman's voice was far too cheerful for the circumstances.

Bethan's brow furrowed as she set the gnarled stick aside that she'd used for a poker.

"Where can we go that will not arrest us or cast us out?" She pointed out.

She hated to doubt her mother, but their prospects felt more than bleak.

Vayala stretched her hands toward the coals, Bethan tended.

"There is a place." She answered confidently.

Bethan swallowed. "It is far?."

Valaya did not deny it.

Bethan sighed. "Quinn will not be happy."

"Your brother's happiness is not the issue. Safety is." Valaya said, taking up rock to grind more corn.

The rising sun caught Bethan's eyes as she met her mother's gaze when the woman stood.

"Safe?" Bethan asked slightly confused. "Is there such a thing, anymore?"

Valaya tilted her head, still grinding, the stone knocking against the rock, dry kernels snapping in the cold air.

"Safe enough." Valaya answered patiently.

Bethan's breath frosted in a plume in front of her. She watched her mother's face, but Valaya was giving nothing away.

When Quinn emerged from the trees with fresh water, Valaya smiled up at him.

"Thank you for looking out for us." She said, reaching for his hand.

Quinn's eyes met Bethan's and she raised a brow.

"Mother says she knows of a safe place." Bethan added.

Quinn's own brow furrowed, and his mouth tightened. He turned back to Valaya,

"Is it far?" He asked warily.

Valaya shrugged, "It is in the Tantans." She said calmly shaping the cakes.

Quinn nearly stumbled back, "The Tantan's? Mother, that is a wagon journey of three weeks, and we are on foot."

Valaya stared at him blandly. "I am aware," she answered flatly.

Quinn snorted throwing up his hands before running fingers through his already unruly hair. "Bandits, food, water, shelter, what if one of us gets sick? What if we have a late snow?"

Valaya listened to his words with settled calm. Setting the cakes near the fire. She did not answer for a time, just gently turned the meal as it roasted. Finally she pulled them from the heat and handed them to her children and bowed her head.

"Yah-Roi, we ask for provision for our journey, and the strength to bear today."

Then she ate and let her prayer be her answer.

Days of travel blurred into a week, then two. More strangers joined them on the road at first, families walking in tight clusters, heads down. Whenever Quinn spotted the amulets of the Oath-takers, he steered them wide around, adding miles to their journey. The detours slowed them, but he never hesitated. They were not the only refugees. But with each passing day, they saw fewer of them.

On the sixth day, the corn ran out and they went to bed hungry. Bethan lay awake, listening to crickets begin their thin chorus in the woods. The night air was warm against her skin, carrying the scent of dry grass and dust. Summer was coming. She could feel it in the air, the way the earth held heat longer after sunset. But she wondered if it would come soon enough for them to find food in the forest.

Morning brought quiet groans from her mother as Valaya pushed herself up from the bed of pine needles. Her movements were slower and more careful now. Bethan rose from her own mat and scanned the glade for Quinn. He was nowhere to be seen. She opened her mouth to call out, but the sound of footsteps reached her first. Relief washed over her. . Quinn emerged from the trees carrying a rabbit, freshly butchered, its blood still dark on his hands. The sack that had once held their corn now bulged with sweet nuts.

Valaya clapped her hands. "Thank you, Yah-Roi," she said, stepping forward to take the bounty. "See? He has not failed us."

Quinn looked away. Valaya did not notice, but Bethan did. She saw the tightness around her brother's eyes, the way his jaw set. Her stomach sank.

The smell of fresh meat hung heavy in the clearing as Valaya set to work preparing the rabbit.

"Bethan," she called, a little breathless, "start cracking the nuts." Then she turned to Quinn. "Were there berries where you caught it? It's the season for stalkberries."

Quinn's jaw tightened. "No," he said quickly.

Valaya frowned, then waved it away. "Never mind. We'll find some soon enough."

Bethan stared at her brother. Her eyes narrowed.

He shot her a look that said *not now.*

They ate. For the first time in days, their bellies were truly full.

Valaya set the pace afterward, walking with an energy that belied her fifty-five years and the long days without proper nourishment. Bethan slowed just enough to pull Quinn back beside her.

"You didn't snare that rabbit," she said. It was not a question.

He sneered faintly.

"You and I both hunted with Papa. You know how hard that is." His voice full of vitriol.

She did not let it go.

"So you stole it?" The word tasted sour in her mouth.

Quinn's eyes flashed. "What would you have me do? Let you and Mother starve?"

"But stealing," Bethan pressed. "You could have been caught." She hissed.

"But I wasn't." He sighed, the sound edged with impatience, the way he used to sigh when she was younger and slow to understand. She hated it.

Without answering, he stepped ahead and took Valaya's arm.

"Come on, slowpoke," he called back to Bethan, his voice light, almost playful. As if everything were still right in their world.

The Horsgaards did find stalkberries. That evening, Valaya spotted them along a narrow side road where they had turned off into a freshly harvested wheat field. The stubble scratched at Bethan's ankles, the cut stalks sharp and dry beneath her feet. Quinn slowed, his eyes scanning the field.

"We could glean," he said. "Just the edges."

Valaya shook her head. "We will ask first."

Bethan's eyes flicked to Quinn as he shifted, his shoulders tightening.

"Mother," he said gently, though his gaze had gone flat, "you know they cannot permit us to harvest even the corners."

Valaya tilted her head. "Perhaps he will allow what is right, even if he has taken the Oath."

Quinn let out a short breath and stared across the field. "Forgive me for not having the faith you do."

Valaya reached out and squeezed his arm. "I will ask. You two stay here."

A bolt of alarm ran through Bethan. She stepped forward without thinking. Quinn reached for her, grabbing her arm and keeping her back. They watched from the road as Valaya walked up the lane to the farmhouse. The door opened only a crack. Valaya lifted her hand in greeting.

A moment later, the door shut, firm and final. Their mother walked back toward them, shoulders drawn in tight, her steps measured. She said nothing. She only shook her head.

Quinn pulled her close. "I'll find something," he said quietly.

That was when Valaya saw them.

A scraggly vine of stalkberries, half-hidden along the roadside, leaves dusty, berries dark and ripe.

"Thank you," she breathed.

They picked as many as they could. The juice stained their fingers and lips, sweet and sharp on their tongues, but fruit was poor substitute for anything filling. That night, on watch, Bethan sat with her back to a tree and thought about it.

Quinn's choice.

Her mother's.

Both had ended with food. Only one had filled their bellies.

~

The next morning, Bethan had little time to worry about where their food came from. As dawn rose and turned the sky pink, then gold, then blue, Valaya did not. Bethan jolted upright when she heard a low groan from her mother and scrambled across the ground to her.

Valaya's lips were cracked and dry, her eyes shadowed and bruised as if she had not slept at all. Panic surged, in Bethan's heart,

"Mother," she cried, her voice sharp enough to bring Quinn running.

He dropped to his knees on the other side of Valaya and pressed a hand to her forehead.

"She's burning up," he hissed.

Bethan scooted closer and lifted her mother's head into her lap.

"I'm right here, Mama," she said.

The old name slipping out without thought.

Valaya moaned. "We need to move on."

"No," Quinn said gently. "You will rest. I will forage. Bethan will care for you."

Valaya tried to wave him away, but her hand fell limp at her side. At last she nodded, her breath shallow.

"One day," she murmured. "We will rest one day."

Bethan looked at her brother. Quinn swallowed hard, the sound loud in the quiet clearing.

"One day," he echoed, as if the words themselves might hold.

Dread crawled up Bethan's stomach and lodged in her throat. She brushed damp hair from Valaya's face with a shaking hand. Heat radiated from her mother's skin, too much, too fast. Valaya's eyes fluttered closed, her breath quick and uneven, the pulse in her throat pounding so hard Bethan could see it.

"She was fine yesterday," Bethan whispered.

Quinn's jaw tightened. He stared into the trees.

"She hasn't had enough water," he said. "None of us have."

He did not need to add that boiling and filtering water had been more work than three starving people could manage.

Bethan frowned. "But we aren't sick."

Quinn shrugged. "We're young."

Bethan sucked in a breath. "Mama isn't old."

Quinn's shoulders sagged. His gaze dropped to the ground. "She didn't used to be."

After that they said little. Quinn left to forage and Bethan stayed with Valaya. He returned before dusk with more stalkberries, a small bag of cornmeal, and six eggs. While he was gone, Bethan had set up a crude still, a skill their father had taught them on a hunting trip years ago. The work was slow and she was careful. Filtering and purifying water took most of the afternoon. Valaya was not worse, but she was not better either. Bethan did not ask her brother where the food had come from.

"How is she?" Quinn asked quietly, setting his bundle down.

Bethan crossed to her mother and pressed her palm to Valaya's forehead.

"Still burning," she said. Her voice sounded very small.

Quinn nodded and crouched beside them.

"Mama," he called gently. "I have food."

Valaya stirred. Her eyelids fluttered, unfocused, then fell shut again.

Quinn met Bethan's eyes. She tried to hide her fear, and failed He took the cup from her hand and lifted Valaya's head, tipping the water carefully to her lips. She swallowed some, but most of it spilled down her chin and soaked into the ground. Bethan wiped her mother's face with the hem of her filthy apron. Only then did she realize her own face was wet. A breeze brushed across her skin, cooling the tears she hadn't known she was crying.

She would not leave Valaya's side that night. She hummed softly. She whispered psalms. She spoke to her mother about nothing and everything. Quinn kept watch at the edge of the clearing, arms crossed, eyes fixed on the dark. Near dawn, Valaya stirred and called his name. Quinn crossed the clearing in three strides.

"Your great-granddaddy's cabin," she rasped, her breath coming in short, painful pulls. "You remember it."

Quinn paused, searching his memory, then nodded. "Yes, Mama."

"Go north at Lake Nevahoe," she said. "Follow the drinking gourd. The cabin is tucked into a valley on the western side of Roder Mountain." The effort cost her. Her chest hitched.

Bethan leaned forward. "You need to rest, Mama."

Valaya looked at her. Then past her. Toward the paling sky. "Oh, I am going to rest, Beety."

Bethan swallowed hard at the sound of her childhood nickname. "You can't rest yet. Mama, we need you."

A single tear slid from Valaya's eye, tracing a slow path into her hair. "Your Papa is waiting."

A sob tore loose from Bethan's chest. "No."

But Valaya had already closed her eyes. The sun climbed higher. Valaya's breaths grew farther apart. Shallow. Uneven. Then there were no more.

Bethan and Quinn clung to one another, kneeling in the quiet clearing.

They were all they had left.

Chapter 4

Bethan and Quinn scooped dirt with their bare hands over the shallow grave where they buried their mother. They stacked stones until their fingernails split and bled. By the time they finished, the sun was sinking in the west, the light thinning and dull. Neither of them wanted to stay another night here. Not with the cairn rising where none had stood the day before. Bethan looked back once more at the pile of stones. She pulled the hood of her cloak over her head and choked on a dry sob. The tears were gone. All that remained was the ache in her chest, heavy and unrelenting.

They walked until Bethan stumbled in the moonlight. A dog barked somewhere up the road. Quinn stopped short and caught her arm, steadying her. His grip was tight.

"We can't stay here," he said quietly. "They'll come looking."

Bethan's breath caught. "Who is they?" Her voice was guarded.

Quinn didn't answer. His face tightened in the pale light.

Understanding hit her hard. Her heart stuttered. "You stole," she whispered. "And someone saw you."

Quinn ground his teeth. She heard it, felt it in the tension of his arm. "It's not like the forest is full of food," he hissed.

Bethan grabbed his sleeve. Her tone suddenly urgent. "We'll keep walking. But no more stealing. Please." Her voice shook. "I can't lose you too."

"You don't understand," he said. His breath was hot against her cheek.

Bethan leaned in. "No. You don't understand." Her words came fast, too loud in the stillness of the road Her voice was hard. "I can't survive on my own. And if someone catches you, you'll be arrested, or worse."

The image of her mother's grave flashed behind her eyes.

"Please, Quinn," she said, forcing her voice lower. "There's food. Now I can stay with you. One of us can watch the road while the other forages. Please."

Quinn looked down at her. Bethan held his gaze, refusing to look away. At last he let out a breath.

"All right. We'll try it." His voice was tight. "But if we can't find enough to keep our strength, we reassess."

Relief loosened Bethan's shoulders. She exhaled, surprised by the breath she hadn't known she was holding. Tears burned but did not fall.

"Thank you," she said.

Quinn turned and started down the road.

"Keep up," he said. "We'll stop at daylight." He glanced back once. "We travel at night now."

~

Quinn pushed them hard that night, only stopping when one of them stumbled over stones or roots. By the time the sun broke over the horizon, Bethan sank gratefully into a bed of clover. They slept until afternoon, and when the light began to lower, they gathered what they could find. They did not say much to each other.

By nightfall, Quinn led the way once more down the road. The pattern set quickly. Night proved safer. They saw few travelers, and both preferred it that way. At first, Bethan remembered to pray each night, even after Quinn stopped joining her. A week into their journey, Bethan groaned as she sat down to pull off her shoes.

"We rest here for tonight, then we try for another seven markers." Quinn stated gruffly.

Bethan moaned. "My feet are blistered."

"So are mine." He retorted, snapping at her complaint.

She glared at him. "Aren't you just a ray of moonlight."

He snorted derisively. "You're not much better."

She ground her teeth, and rolled into her cloak, Too tired to argue, or pray, she fell asleep nearly as soon as her head laid down.

The next afternoon, she and Quinn rose to find food. Summer brought forage, though never easily. Apples lay bruised beneath a lone tree, their sweetness already turning. Wild barley bent low in the fields. Tubers had to be pried from damp soil. Mushrooms and bitter lettuces filled out what they could gather from shaded glades. Most days it was enough to keep moving. Some nights they stumbled on, their stomachs echoing a hollow chorus.

After that, the world narrowed.

Measuring each day by the rumble in her stomach, the search for water, the slow burn in her legs. Survival took more than strength. It took attention, thought, and planning. They could not afford to bypass a stream or cut around a wild meadow. Ignoring bugs in the dirt was not an option.

Bethan walked along slowly, pulling rocks up to expose the grubs underneath, when she smelled it, smoke. Someone was close. She stilled as she listened closely. Quinn was knee deep in the creek trying to catch a trout.

She whistled in a signal, and his head came up. They both listened intently, a bird chirped and then a dog barked. Bethan's grip tightened on the stone. *Please, Yah-Roi-* She thought. Her heart gave a squeeze. It was the first time she had called on Him in days.

The dog's barking grew distant, and the smell of smoke wafted away on the breeze. Bethan offered up a shaky thank you and then returned to her task.

Two weeks after they buried their mother, The rolling hills gave way to steep climbs. Broad leaves thinned into pine straw, then to boulders and loose gravel that shifted beneath their boots. That night Quinn found a tall evergreen, its fallen needles thick on the ground. Their first soft bed in days.

The next morning. She eyed the strip of leather Quinn had found at the base of tree days ago. "You really think you can kill something with that?" Her voice betrayed her lack of confidence in his skills.

He ignored it, taking a few practice swings. The leather whipped through the air, cracking in the stillness as he flung a stone thirty paces.

"You had better hope I do." His voice was serious. "There isn't much forage up here otherwise."

Bethan swallowed, he wasn't wrong.

She followed him as he stalked the bushes around their camp. She had learned how to hunt silently behind him. The last time she had scared off a crow, and they had gone to bed hungry.

Rustling in the bushes brought her head around, her heartbeat faster, hoping for a rabbit. A couple of chipmunks wrestling over a pinecone burst from the shrub and she froze.

Quinn wound up and took his shot, Bethan was not sure if her brother had been lucky or if his aim was true, but both animals flew apart, and landed in the dirt, stunned. The siblings rushed forward and grabbed the rodents.

"You are either incredibly lucky, or better at that than you ever were with a bow." She said as she skinned the animals with her knife.

Quinn speared them and they roasted them over the fire, barely waiting for them to cook before tearing into the meat.

Only after they had finished and licked the bones clean, did Bethan look up at the stars and the fleeting thought that she had not given thanks whisked through her mind, before she fell asleep.

~

They had arrived at grandfather's cabin, as the days grew shorter and the nights even cooler. Bethan stood at the edge of the clearing, her arms wrapped tight around herself as the wind tugged at her tangled hair and slid cold fingers down the back of her neck, causing her to shiver. The old retreat was more ruin than shelter, half-buried in leaves, log walls scratched and sagging with time, the scent of damp rot rising where moss crept along the seams. It would have to do. Her hazel eyes traced the shape of it with quiet resolve. Not safety. Not yet. But maybe it could become something like it.

"At least it still has its roof," she said, to herself, Quinn having gone to forage. Her voice was thin in the open air, already kneeling to shove aside the worst of the fallen branches. Dry leaves rasped beneath her palms, brittle and sharp.

Bethan pushed open the door and took a look at the inside as it creaked against her palm. the roof leaned in one corner, dark with old water stains, and something had definitely nested inside it recently. The faint musk of animal lingered. She rolled up her sleeves anyway, the fabric stiff with grime.

She cleared debris until her arms burned and her shoulders trembled. Hauled what dry firewood she could scavenge, bark flaking into her hands. Found a rusted pot half-buried in the dirt that might boil water if they scrubbed it clean enough. The work was cold and thankless. Her fingers numbed, then ached. Still, she welcomed it. If her hands were busy, her mind couldn't spiral into the dark. If she kept moving, maybe she wouldn't think about how little Quinn had spoken that morning. Or how long he'd been gone.

The sun was already bleeding out behind the trees by the time she heard his footsteps, slow and careful, leaves crunching softly underfoot. He stepped into the clearing with the gait of someone who had moved quietly for too long. A small pouch hung from his hand. His coat was damp at the hem, darkened with creek water. No meat. Just a few roots, dirt still clinging to them, and some hard berries that wouldn't keep for more than a day. He didn't say anything when he stepped inside the cabin and dropped the pouch near the fire she'd managed to coax to life. The flames snapped weakly, smoke stinging her eyes.

Bethan sat across from him, arms wrapped around her knees, the chill of night seeping up from the ground of the dirt floor through her skirts. She watched him with something caught between worry and gratitude.

"I made a dry corner to sleep in," she offered softly, as if it might help. "I swept it out. It's not perfect, but—"

"I know it's not perfect," Quinn snapped. His voice wasn't loud, just sharp enough to cut. "Nothing about this is."

Bethan blinked, the words landing heavier than she expected. She let out a slow breath, then reached into the pouch, her fingers brushing grit and shriveled skins as she divided out what little he'd brought.

"You were gone a while," she ventured another try at conversation. "Did you find tracks?"

He didn't answer right away. He lowered himself onto a bench on the wall and stared into the flames. Sparks popped and drifted upward, dying almost as soon as they were born.

"Yeah," he said finally. "I'll hunt tomorrow. Set some snares." His voice was tired now, flattened. "You'll have to look for more tubers. We're not in the low country anymore."

Bethan nodded and handed him a few of the berries. They were cool and firm in her palm. "You're doing your best."

Quinn snorted softly. His eyes drifted over the interior of the cabin, the sagging roof, the dark corners where the firelight didn't reach.

"If one of us had taken the oath, we wouldn't be here." He said it like it was an afterthought.

She stared at him, the crackle of the fire suddenly too loud. "You think Papa made the wrong choice." It wasn't a question.

He sighed and poked at the fire with a stick. Ash lifted, warm and bitter in the air.

"I think taking care of your family is harder to do on ideals than paperwork." He finally admitted.

She didn't know what to say to that. Or even what it meant. So she stared into the fire, letting the heat warm her shins while a draft slipped through the open doorway and cooled the sweat on her back.

"We're together," she said finally. Her voice was quieter now. "We still have each other."

His jaw tightened. Then he reached out, hooked an arm around her shoulders, and pulled her in. His coat smelled like smoke and creek water, the stiff wool was rough on her cheek.

"Yeah," he said finally. "We do."

~

They did not stay awake much past the meal. Bidding one another a good night before retiring to their respective spaces on the floor. Bethan didn't sleep well that night. The high country was alive with unfamiliar sounds: something skittering through brush, a distant cry that rose and fell on the wind, the constant rush of air moving through the pines like breath through a great chest. Her stomach rumbled loudly enough that she felt it along her spine. Quinn's answered it from the other side of the cabin, a hollow echo in the dark. The door creaked as the wind worried at it, wood complaining against its age. But none of that was what kept her awake. It was Quinn's words.

If one of us had taken the Oath. She stared into the dying embers of the fire, watching them pulse and fade, red collapsing into gray. Tonight, she lay still and tried not to think about her brother's certainty that Papa and Mama had been wrong. She sighed and turned onto her other side. Cold pressed through her cloak as she turned away from the fire. She faced the trees beyond the open window, their dark shapes shifting as branches swayed. There was no answer there. No sign. No comfort.

"Yah-Roi," she whispered, the name barely more than breath.

But the prayer died before it could take shape. What was she supposed to say? What could she say? She hadn't prayed in weeks, not really. And even when she had, heaven had been silent. No warmth. No reassurance. Just the slow grind of hunger and the long road north. Her eyelids finally slipped shut, exhaustion dragging her under. And with it came the thought she hadn't dared finish before. *Maybe Quinn was right.*

~

They had arrived too late in the season to plant, not that they had any seed. Game was still plentiful but snaring it in unfamiliar terrain proved frustrating. Rabbits slipped the snares as if they knew better. Quinn tried to fashion a bow, but curing the wood took time they did not have. In the meantime, they subsisted on chipmunks he managed to kill with his slingshot, berries Bethan could find, and fish pulled from the creek with numbed fingers. Winter was coming. Their foraging prospects thinned with each passing day.

Bethan watched Quinn's frame grow gaunt. He moved more slowly now, conserving energy. Lines settled into his face, the kind that belonged on much older men. Every morning she went out to forage. Each day she had to go farther, climb higher. The deeper she pushed into the forest, the harder the return became. She had no mirror, but she could feel it. Her skirts hung looser. Her strength burned away faster. She was starving too.

On a night, a week after their arrival, Quinn came into the cabin and set his bag down with care.

"I found a patch of barley," he said. His voice carried a thread of relief.

Bethan's head came up sharply, she shifted from the fire where she was stirring a thin soup of mushrooms, berries, and pine needles. She faced him fully.

"Where?," she asked, her voice full of new urgency.

Quinn sagged onto a stool he had fashioned from what remained of his grandfather's sideboard. The wood creaked under his weight.

"It's a hike up the west ridge." He answered.

Bethan nodded, her excitement growing.

"Eat then, we'll need our strength to gather tomorrow."

They both knew time was not on their side and saying it aloud would not change that. Bethan ladled the pungent broth into the last two unbroken bowls her grandfather had hidden in a cupboard. The steam carried a sharp, resinous scent. Quinn sipped slowly. She did the same. The watery meal dulled the ache in their bellies just enough to let them sleep.

At dawn, Quinn led the way into the forest. He slowed his pace to match hers, making sure she could keep up. They had walked for an hour when he stepped into a clearing on a south-facing slope, and Bethan stopped short behind him. An entire acre of wild barley waved in the wind, green-gold and alive. She gasped and stepped forward, and reached with hesitant fingers, stopping herself. Finally grasping an ear and pulling it free, chaff and all, she bit down. The taste filled her mouth, warm and green and bitter. She chewed slowly, closing her eyes and savoring the bite. It reminded her of days spent in the late summer sun on the farm. It reminded her of Papa. She opened her eyes then, the memory too heavy for her to carry.

Quinn smiled at her, his first real one in weeks.

"It's good?" He asked.

She nodded "Better than good. It's a miracle from Yah-Roi."

Quinn neither agreed nor disagreed, just moved off to pick barley and Bethan followed suit. When their sacks were full and the sun sank low, they walked back to the cabin. They ate well that night and for the first time in weeks they both fell into a dreamless and deep sleep.

The following morning Bethan opened her eyes to see her breath curl above her in the light of the sun streaming through the window.

The tip of her nose burned with the sharp cold. Her first instinct was the curl into her cloak and nestle deeper, and the thought hit. *Frost.* She bolted from her pallet of pine boughs and dashed to the window. The sight that met her gaze made her stomach turn. Snow covered the ground. Dread made her heart sink. The barley would be flattened.

Chapter 5

The snow melted by afternoon, but the following day, when Bethan and Quinn climbed back to the barley slope, they found what Quinn had feared. The stalks lay wilted and blackened from the freeze, trampled into the mud by animals that had grazed through in the night. What remained was bent low, grain scattered and half-rotted into the earth.

Bethan had never imagined she would cry over food. Her throat tightened and her knees hit the mud and slush, soaking through her skirts, and a sob tore from her throat before she could stop it. Her hands shook so hard she could scarcely pick the kernels she could see in the slush from the saturated ground, fingers numb and shaking. Quinn said nothing. He only knelt beside her and gleaned what he could, his movements slow and deliberate.

Runoff soaked their clothes. Melt water seeped into their boots. The cold bit into their fingers until feeling dulled into ache. When the sun dipped behind the ridge, Quinn stood.

"We camp here tonight," he said. "I'll try to make a fire. We won't leave the patch until we've saved everything we can."

5Bethan ground the barley into rough meal. Quinn found enough dry wood to coax a fire from damp earth. They settled into an uneasy camp beneath a sky already hardening with cold.

"How much do you think we can save?" she asked softly.

Quinn bit carefully into his hot cake and chewed. Then he shrugged. He did that a lot now. He used to tease and banter. Now he carried the world on his shoulders.

"Maybe enough for the next few days," he said at last.

Bethan swallowed hard against the sudden lump in her throat. She nodded and looked out over the ruined slope beyond the dark line of trees, blinking away the sting in her eyes.

"Then we gather what we can," she said.

Quinn nodded tossing a stick into the fire. Bethan looked into the darkness, swallowing the last of the bitter barley grains. *I wish we had help.* Then she sighed and curled into her cloak.

"Goodnight Quinn," She said as exhaustion overtook her. He did not reply.

~

They camped there two more nights, gleaning everything they could salvage from the field. By the third day, another icy wind swept down the slope, sharp enough to sting exposed skin. Quinn straightened slowly and stopped working.

"We go back to the cabin now," he said.

Bethan didn't argue. She stood, her skirts stiff and damp from days in the mud, swaying on her feet.. The hike back was slow, and she leaned heavily on Quinn when the ground pitched or the trail narrowed. She didn't speak. It took too much effort. When they reached the cabin, the fire had burned down to cold ash. Quinn set to work re-igniting the flame. Bethan opened the jar holding the barley they had gathered before the snow. She counted it with her eyes. Four meals, if they rationed.

Quinn coaxed the fire back to life while Bethan made gruel. The thin porridge steamed faintly, smelling of earth and smoke. They ate in silence, then sagged down in front of the hearth and slept where they sat, exhaustion pulling them under without ceremony.

Quinn was gone when Bethan woke. Fresh snow lay on the ground, an inch, maybe two, just enough to matter. She stood in the doorway, the cold biting at her bare ankles. Snow like that would push game to lower elevations. It would cost him time and energy. She went down to the creek instead. The air was sharp with frost, the water dark and fast. Bethan crushed the last of the spoiled barley into a paste and clumped it onto her hook with numb fingers.

She caught one mountain trout and a spiny fish her grandfather had once called a charky. She killed them quickly with a rock, then carried them back to the cabin, listening for Quinn with every step. The woods gave her nothing back. She seared the fish as the sun slid low. The fat crackled in the pan, sharp and mouthwatering. She ate the charky and set the trout aside for her brother.

Quinn did not return. paced until her shins ached, her stomach twisting with fish and worry. Quinn hadn't said he would be gone overnight. She tried to believe his absence meant he was tracking. Tried to tell herself he was fine. That he would come back. The sky thinned toward dawn. She had worried the edge of her lip all night long. Now it was raw and bleeding and Quinn had still not returned. She swallowed against the fear pressing in on the edges of her mind. *I wouldn't know where to look.* She realized, that though made her stomach clench.

~

.The sun rose higher and Bethan's eyes flicked toward the door each time the wind stirred it. Every hour Quinn stayed away pressed harder on her chest.. A panicked, gnawing dread that she might lose the only person she had left. By the time the sky bruised with twilight, she heard it. Boots crunching through snow. She raced to the door. For one brief, flickering moment, hope sparked in her chest. Then she saw his face.

Quinn's hands were empty. His shoulders slumped, his jaw clenched tight against failure. He didn't speak. He brushed past her and dropped onto his cot, as if the weight of the world had finally won. Bethan stood frozen, breath shallow, her heart pounding so hard it hurt. She couldn't lose him. Not Quinn. Not after Papa. Not after Mama.

When night fell and the wind moaned through the trees like a mourner, Bethan rose. She moved quietly, wrapping her threadbare cloak tight around her thin frame. The cold struck her like a slap, biting through wool and skin, but she welcomed it. It kept her awake. It kept her focused. Her boots crunched over frozen ground as she stepped into the dark. Moonlight spilled across the snow, turning the world silver and strange. Her breath clouded in front of her face, sharp and shallow. There was no plan. Only desperation. And one unyielding thought. *Do something. Anything.*

For Quinn.

For the dead she couldn't bring back.

And for herself before the silence swallowed her too.

Bethan started pacing outside the cabin, forcing herself to think through their options. Even with the hunger slowing her thoughts she still knew they did not have many. The stream would freeze. The snow would fall, and any game they might track would be looking for predators.

She needed to find another source of food. Ingerside was close. The town sat squatted on the banks of Lake Nevahoe. *A town meant people. People meant food. Food meant . . .* She cut off the thought lest she lose herself in hope. Her hands shook as she used charcoal to scratch a note to Quinn.

Gone to Ingerside, will return with food.

And with that, Bethan slipped into the night.

~

Bethan stumbled down the mountain trail, the world narrowed to snow, rock, and the sharp burn in her lungs. Her cloak snagged on branches that reached like fingers, tugging and tearing at the fabric. She didn't stop to fix it. Roots caught her boots. Gravel slid beneath her feet. More than once, her knees slammed into frozen earth hard enough to scrape skin. Her palms were raw, slick with blood and dirt, but she barely felt them. The cabin lay somewhere behind her, quiet and cold, heavy with absence. Quinn too. Silent. Fading. Like everything else she had loved.

Her breath tore in and out of her chest, fogging the air. Each step jarred through ribs made brittle by hunger. Her stomach clenched around nothing, a hollow ache that never eased. *I asked him not to steal, he didn't. Now I must take care of him.* Bethan's heart hammered as she pressed forward, something feral brightening her eyes. The trees thinned. The sky widened. Cold wind cut across her face, sharp enough to sting tears loose.

Chapter 6

The smell of salt met Bethan's nostrils long before she reached Ingerside. The town squatted in the marshes of Lake Navahoe. Wooden buildings on stilts emerged through the gloom, their warm yellow lanterns glowing in defiance of the icy fingers of fog that crept along the shoreline. Beyond them, she could make out the quay and a handful of shallow-bottomed boats tied low in the water. A town of rough reputation. She and Quinn had avoided it on their journey to her grandfather's cabin.

Her feet found the gravel road that sloped down the hill into the town proper. It had looked smaller from above. A dog barked somewhere up the street. A baby cried from one of the hillside shacks, thin and desperate. Bethan kept to the shadows, moving carefully, making herself small. She wove through the clustered residences, past doors patched with scrap wood and windows fogged from breath and smoke. Ingerside was a way-faring town, a stopping place for merchants heading into the interior of Kuvale. Most of them would winter here now, waiting for the high mountain chain she and Quinn called home to loosen its grip.

As she drew closer to the industrial quarter, the town changed. Houses gave way to taverns and public halls. Raucous laughter spilled into the street, along with tinny music and the high, false gaiety of women pressed close to rough men. Bethan kept her eyes down. Her boot came down in something wet and yielding. The smell hit her a moment later. Her stomach lurched, empty and tight. A man staggered out of a tavern to her right, his hand reaching blindly. She pulled away just in time, his fingers closing on air where her wrist had been. She didn't stop.

The wind cut sharply off the lake, threading between the buildings. Bethan pulled her shawl tighter and moved deeper into the town. The sun was still hours from rising. She glanced at the shuttered fronts of closed shops as she passed, judging doorways, measuring shadows. At last she found one that would do. She slipped her narrow body into the shelter of the frame. It offered little protection from the cold, but it blocked the worst of the wind. She looked out over the street. Lanterns burned in paper globes, casting weak halos of light that reached only a few yards in either direction. The road lay empty. So did her stomach. Bethan folded her arms across herself and leaned into the wall, forcing her thoughts away from the mountains behind her. Away from the cabin. Away from her brother. . She stayed where she was. Waiting.

~

She did not sleep and as morning came on and shopkeepers and hawkers came to sell their wares, She left her shelter and moved cautiously through the shadows toward the market end for the farmers. Bethan wrapped her threadbare cloak tighter around her shoulders, shivering as a cruel winter wind sliced through the decaying town. The air reeked of unwashed bodies, rotting fish, and the acrid bite of smoke from makeshift fires. People huddled in small groups, thin and hollow-eyed, their faces illuminated by flickering flames.

A woman caught her eye. Fat. Bethan blinked. No one here was fat. Not a soul. Not in a village starved half to death. But this woman — round-faced, thick-necked, arms soft and full beneath her heavy cloak—stood behind a cart laden with dried goods and tins of something that looked suspiciously like real meat. That alone should have sent Bethan turning back. But she didn't. Couldn't. Because the woman smiled a smile too tight. Too knowing. Too cold to be anything close to kind.

Bethan hesitated. Just long enough. The woman lifted her hand in a slow wave, fingers tipped in chipped green polish, beckoning her closer. And Bethan, desperate, hollow, broken down to her bones, stepped forward. The woman's eyes swept over her. Took her in. Saw everything. The hunger. The grief. The emptiness carved into her soul.

"You poor thing," the woman said, voice syrupy sweet. "You've been out in that wind too long."

Bethan tried to speak, but her lips were cracked and dry, her throat burning from the cold. The woman reached beneath the cart and produced a flask.

"Here. Drink. Just a little. It'll warm you up." The woman offered.

Bethan hesitated. The woman's smile deepened, her voice lowering, soothing, like a lullaby meant to quiet a child before the knife.

"I'm not going to bite," she said softly. "Wouldn't offer if I couldn't spare it. I take care of girls like you."

Bethan took the flask, hands shaking. The liquid burned on the way down, but it brought heat back into her limbs. Enough to keep standing. Enough to hope.

"You here alone?" the woman asked, already knowing the answer.

Bethan said nothing. The woman clicked her tongue and shook her head.

"World's a cruel place to be alone, love. But it doesn't have to be." She leaned closer. "My brother runs a place just up the street. Stone house. Yellow door. Keeps a warm fire going. Food on the table. Real food. None of this dried boot leather they're hawking down here."

Bethan stiffened. Her fingers tightened around the flask. The woman's voice dropped, soft as ash.

"You've got the look of a girl who could earn her place. Pretty thing, you are. Strong, too. I can see it. He likes strong ones. Gives them better rooms. He's fair, my brother. You do your part, you eat well, sleep warm. No more wandering. No more starving." The woman smiled again. "Better than freezing to death on that mountain. Or digging another grave, yeah?"

Bethan's throat closed.

"Go on," the woman said, nodding toward the narrow street veering north. "Tell them Mave sent you."

The woman's eyes glinted, her voice dropping to a whisper.

"You've already buried too many, haven't you, love?" "Don't go joining them."

~

Bethan's mind raced. This wasn't stealing. But it wasn't right either. She thought of Quinn's shaking hands. Of the way his breath had sounded thin in the cold. Her jaw tightened and she turned in the direction Mave had pointed.

"You can't miss it," Mave called after her. "Stone house. Yellow door. Just up the road."

Bethan didn't look back.

Each step felt like something being taken from her. Shame crept up her spine, hot and raw, but she kept walking. Because Quinn was starving. And she had asked him not to steal. This was the price. And she would pay it.

The house with the yellow door looked warm. Too warm. Light spilled from the windows like honey, soft and golden, pooling on the frozen step. It felt out of place, like it belonged to another world. Not this one of hollow cheeks and broken shoes. Bethan hesitated. Then she knocked.

The door opened with a lazy creak, and a woman answered. Older than Bethan. Lips too red. Powder too thick. A shawl hung off one bare shoulder, as if she couldn't be bothered to fix it. Her eyes skimmed Bethan once, then curled into a sneer.

"Another one," she muttered.

Bethan flinched. The woman looked her over again, slower this time. A quick up and down. Disappointment followed.

"What do you want?" Her tone was sharp, edged with mockery, like Bethan's presence was a waste of breath.

"Please," Bethan whispered. "Mave sent me."

The woman rolled her eyes and sighed, like she'd just been asked to scrub the floor. "Fine. Come in. Sardon'll want to see you."

Bethan stepped inside. Warmth hit her like a slap. Thick. Perfumed. Almost sweet. A narrow foyer stretched before her, modest but deliberate. Beeswax candles glowed in brass sconces, casting soft shadows along the paneled walls. A bowl of fruit sat on a polished counter. Real fruit. Not bruised or half-rotten, but full and ripe. Golden apples. Blushed pears. Fat purple grapes. Bethan stared.

Another girl passed through the hall. Younger. Painted like the first, but her slip was thinner, almost sheer. She paused when she caught Bethan's gaze on the fruit.

"You can have some, if you want," she said. Her voice was tired, but kind.

Bethan startled, then nodded once. Her fingers reached before she could stop herself. She took a pear and held it like it might vanish.

The first bite was soft. Sweet. Spiced. Juice cooled her tongue. She swallowed carefully, afraid to waste even a drop. Luxury, wrapped in suffering. The contrast twisted her stomach. This was wrong. This was survival. She had never fallen so far and still, some quiet part of her whispered, she hadn't reached the bottom yet.

The painted woman returned. She did not speak. She only jerked her head, signaling for Bethan to follow. Down a hallway. Deeper into the brothel's belly. The scent changed here. Still warm, still perfumed, but darker now. Musk. Smoke. Sweat. Bethan's stomach tightened with every step.

They stopped at a heavy door. The woman knocked once, then pushed it open. The room beyond was decadent to the point of mockery. Velvet draped the windows from floor to ceiling. Gold-threaded tapestries covered the walls, clashing in color and design. A crystal chandelier hung too low overhead, its light fractured and dizzying. A fire crackled in the hearth, making everything too hot. Too bright.

A man sat in a cushioned chair like a king, though he looked more like a toad. Sardon was just as round as his sister. Rings crowded every finger. Grease darkened his collar. Two women attended him, one massaging his shoulders, the other refilling his goblet with wine so dark it looked like blood.

Bethan's breath caught. Her sensitivity, scraped raw by everything she had endured, flared painfully just standing there. Sardon saw the flush rise in her cheeks and laughed. A deep, rumbling sound, like something breaking. "Well now," he said, his voice thick and slick.

"A modest little something. Haven't seen one of those in a while." His eyes dragged over her. "Not my taste, but there's a man... a client... who appreciates innocence."

Bethan flinched. She did not speak.

Sardon waved the girls away and leaned forward, resting his elbows on his knees.

"Tell me your story, girl." He waved to her.

She shook her head.

"Come now. It helps to know what I'm selling. And I do intend to sell you." He smiled like a butcher surveying livestock. "What's your name?"

Her eyes flicked to the floor "...Bethan." She said so softly she might have missed it herself.

"Mm." He nodded once. "And what brings little Bethan to my door? Mave said you looked like you'd crawled out of the river. You running from something?"

She shook her head again, eyes still fixed on the floor.

He sighed, long and dramatic. "No family?"

Bethan clenched her jaw. "...a brother."

"Ah. The picture sharpens." Sardon chuckled. "You and your brother starving. No coin to your names. You thought you'd trade a little virtue for supper. How quaint." Her shoulders tensed. "Well," he said, slapping his knees as if the matter were settled. "An hour of your time. That's all. You and your brother will eat for a week." His grin stretched wide and grotesque. "And believe me, that's generous."

The painted woman had returned. She stood quietly near the door, not looking at Bethan. As if this part always played out the same way. Bethan's body remained frozen. She tasted bile. Shame rose, hot and thick in her chest. She hated this Sardon. She hated herself more. She hoped Quinn would forgive her. Hoped Yah-Roi would forgive her.

"...yes," she whispered.

Sardon studied her for a long, grotesque moment. "Can you remember directions?"

Bethan nodded once, stiffly.

He did not wait for more. "Good. He doesn't come here. Too high and mighty, our mystery man. Always has me send the girls to him."

He leaned back, the chair creaking beneath his bulk.

"You'll go up the eastern road until you see the second stone marker. Half-buried. Looks like a lion. Turn left there. Cross the stream. You'll see a red door behind a thicket of blackthorn. That's the place."

Bethan repeated the words silently, like a prayer. Eastern road.

Stone lion. Left. Cross the stream. Red door. Blackthorn. Her breath caught, but she forced herself to nod again.

"Don't be late," Sardon said, already bored. "He doesn't like to wait."

The painted woman slid aside as Bethan turned toward the door. Her eyes did not meet Bethan's. They did not need to. Bethan pulled her shawl tight around her shoulders, her thin arms trembling. The warmth of the brothel clung to her like a lie. She stepped out into the chill. The wind sliced through fabric and resolve alike. Eastern road. Lion stone. Stream. Red door. *It's only an hour.* . Her heart did not believe it. But her feet moved anyway.

~

The cold slapped Bethan in the face as she left the stone house. She kept to the edge of the road, footsteps light, body hunched against the wind. The shawl did little to hide her. Nothing could. Shadows were her only allies now.

When she saw the lion stone, cracked and moss-ridden, her breath caught. Almost there. She turned.

"You there!" The shout cracked across the cold like a whip.

Bethan stopped, then she turned slowly, too slowly, to see a man in a black Talsian uniform moving toward her, boots crunching through frost-bitten grass. Her eyes flicked left. Trees. Right. A ditch. No cover. Nowhere to go. Before she could move, his hand closed around her wrist, hard and fast. She hissed, biting back a cry as pain shot up her arm.

"What's your name?" he demanded.

Bethan stared at him, her voice caught in her throat. His grip tightened.

"I said—name."

"Bethan," she managed.

The word sounded small, like it belonged to someone else.

"Where's your Alliance amulet?" He interrogated.

Her mouth opened. Closed. Dread tightened her chest. Finally she managed to squeak out. "I don't have one."

He stared at her like she'd grown a second head.

"What do you mean you don't have one? You're out here alone, after curfew, without an amulet?"

She shook her head, pulse hammering.

"Have you taken the Oath?" His voice dropped but somehow grew sharper.

Bethan looked at him, wide-eyed. Her shoulders crept up, in shame and fright.

That was all he needed. The officer grinned. Not with humor. With the satisfaction of a man who'd found something broken and was now free to destroy it.

"Then you'll come with me," he said, yanking her forward by the wrist. "Tribunal'll want to hear why a little rat like you's sniffing around the hills without protection."

Bethan stumbled, breath trapped behind her ribs. The yellow door. The stream. Quinn. All of it vanished behind her as the road she'd chosen twisted into something darker. .

Chapter 7

The officer marched her back past the stone lion, past the stone house, past the cart. They turned toward a more established quarter, where government buildings rose in the gloom, stone, and imperial. His heels clicked sharply on the flagstones. His grip on her arm was firm enough to bruise as he yanked her toward a side arboretum sheltered in the shadow of the tribunal.

Another guard looked up from her table. Her gaze traveled over Bethan coldly before shifting to the officer.

"What's she in for?" she asked, sounding almost bored.

"No amulet," he answered flatly.

She raised an eyebrow.

"It's been a while since we brought in an Oathbreaker. Put her in the corridor. I'll send a runner for Morwyn."

He didn't speak again as he marched Bethan down the long stone passage. His grip never loosened. When they reached the small holding structure, he shoved open the iron door and motioned her inside. Bethan's heart pounded, but she moved.

Inside, the air was damp and thick with the scent of mildew and old blood. A lone torch flickered in its bracket, casting long, crawling shadows across the stone floor. There were no other prisoners. No guards inside. Just her.

"Empty your pockets," the officer said.

"I don't have—" She started.

"Now." He interrupted, with a raised hand.

She opened her shawl and let it fall. Her fingers trembled as she revealed the inside of her dress, threadbare and empty. He checked anyway. Rough hands. Impatient. It was brief, but enough. Enough to make her flinch. Enough to turn her stomach. Enough for her to understand that whatever she had been prepared to trade, her body, her dignity, it had already been taken in some form. Just not the way she had expected.

He said nothing. Just nodded toward the corner cell and gestured her inside.

"You'll wait here," he said. "Until the tribunal decides whether you're worth the time."

Then he was gone. The door clanged shut, the sound echoing far longer than it should have. Bethan stood in the silence. Then she sat. Slowly. Her legs barely working. The stone beneath her was wet and cold, seeping through the thin fabric of her dress. She pulled her shawl around herself again, but it didn't help.

She thought about Quinn. About the yellow door. About the taste of the spiced pear. Her chest ached. Her throat closed, but no tears fell. It was as if a part of her had turned to ice since she had started on the road to the stone lion.   She had been ready to give it away for a crust of bread. *Even Yah,* she thought, *must be disgusted with me.* She didn't pray. She just sat. Cold. Aching. Alone.

Bethan lost track of time. The cold stone of the cell pressed in from every side, leeching heat until even her thoughts felt brittle. She had not moved since the guard shoved her inside. Her body had folded inward, conserving what little strength remained. Hunger had stopped being pain. It had become distance. Her stomach growled, low and hollow, like an animal rooting through refuse. Her mouth was dry. Her tongue felt thick. Every breath took effort. Even holding her head upright felt like work she might not be able to finish.

The scrape of iron on stone cut through the fog. Bethan's head jerked up as the door opened. Light spilled in, harsh and white. Footsteps echoed closer. Two figures entered. A man and a woman.

The man wore a pressed Talsian uniform. The woman was older, her expression sharp and precise, eyes assessing Bethan the way one might assess spoiled meat.

"Up," the man said.

Bethan didn't move. He grabbed her arm and hauled her to her feet. Pain shot through her legs and she gasped, swaying. The woman watched with detached interest.

"How long has she been without food?" the woman asked.

The man shrugged. "Long enough."

The woman nodded once, satisfied. She stepped closer. "You were detained without an amulet," she said.

The air thick with accusation.

Bethan hardly dared breathe.

"You are outside Alliance protection," the woman continued. "That leaves you with limited options."

The man tightened his grip to keep her upright. The woman gestured toward the corridor beyond the cell.

"The tribunal will hear your case. Eventually." The woman said crisply.

Bethan understood the word eventually. It meant time. Time she did not have. The woman's gaze softened just enough to be cruel.

"There is an alternative."

Bethan lifted her eyes.

"You may take the Oath," the woman said. "Here. Now."

The man spoke next. "You'll be registered. Fed. Given shelter."

Food. The word landed harder than anything else. Bethan's stomach clenched. Her vision swam. She thought of Quinn's hollow cheeks. His shaking hands. The way he had tried not to look at her the last night. She could not die here. Not like this.

"What... what do I have to say?" she whispered.

The woman smiled. Not kindly. Efficiently.

"You repeat the words," she said. "You sign your name. And this ends. There will be bread." The woman finished, her voice falling soft and coaxing.

Bread. To her shame Bethan's mouth watered. She could nearly feel it, warm. Soft, chewy. Yeast on her tongue. She nearly groaned from the idea.

"Okay, okay, I'll take it." Her voice was desperate.

The enforcer straightened, her false sweetness gone, she nodded once sharply. "You've agreed. We'll make it official."

Bethan's thoughts slid past one another, unfocused. Surely Yah-Roi would understand. She was dying. This was the only way. She barely registered leaving the cell, only the cold biting her skin, the scrape of stone beneath her feet, the weight at her ankles keeping her upright. The corridors narrowed, then opened again as they crossed the square.

The tribunal chamber rose from the gloom, stone, and shadow, heavy enough to feel alive. Inside, three men sat behind a long table, black-robed, faces impassive. Well fed. Every one of them. The enforcer shoved her forward.

"Kneel." He said harshly.

Bethan dropped to the floor without thinking. Her legs trembled, useless. The stone was cold, but hunger drowned everything else.

Silence stretched. The judges watched her as if waiting for something already decided.

"She admits to sedition," the enforcer said flatly.

Bethan's head jerked up. She hadn't—

"But she agrees to take the Oath," the woman continued. "In exchange for food."

The words tangled in Bethan's mind. Save Quinn. Live. That was all that mattered. The central judge leaned forward. His voice was calm. Certain.

"Do you swear fealty?" He asked, his voice almost grandfatherly.

Bethan breathed through the ache in her chest. There was no room left for fear.

"I do," she whispered.

"Repeat it." He demanded. Waving the clerk forward to oversee her oath.

The words scraped her throat as she spoke them, foreign and bitter.

"I swear fealty to the gods of the Alliance, and to its sacred order, forsaking all other loyalties, for the sake of stability and continuity."

For a moment there was silence in the room. Bethan's head started to swim, then a crust of bread landed in front of her, skidding across the stone.

She dropped to her knees, and the smell hit her first. Yeast. Salt.

Her hands shook as she reached for it. She didn't hear the murmurs of approval. Didn't hear the scratch of ink or the closing of ledgers. Only the sound of her own chewing. fast, desperate.

"Congratulations," the judge said without interest. "You are now under Alliance protection."

Relief flared, but it was thin and fragile.

"However," he continued, "your oath comes late. Penance is still required."

The word penance landed heavy in her stomach alongside the bread. But she scarcely had time to think about what it meant before hands seized her arms. Shackles closed around her ankles.

"You promised," Bethan gasped, bread still in her mouth. "You said—"

"We spared you," the enforcer replied, already turning her away. "You'll serve in another capacity."

The chamber receded. The stone swallowed her footsteps. Bethan clutched the last of the bread as they dragged her down the corridor, understanding settling too late. She had survived, nothing more.

~

Bethan was dragged through the narrow streets toward the docks, boots slipping on slime-slick stone. The air stank of salt, rot, and human waste. Lantern light clung to the cracked buildings like mildew, illuminating faces that didn't look twice at suffering anymore.

The docks were worse. Here, misery had been organized. Corrals lined the quay, wooden pens reinforced with iron. Inside them, people stood packed shoulder to shoulder. Men. Women. Children. All stripped down to the same thing: bodies waiting to be claimed.

Bethan's stomach turned as she was shoved into a pen with girls her age. Hollow-eyed. Sharp-boned. Silent. The cold gnawed through her dress, but hunger burned hotter. She wanted to call on Yah-Roi. Wanted to beg. But the words wouldn't come. She had pledged to the Alliance. Forsaken all others. The thought lodged in her chest like a stone.

Time passed, hours, maybe. Buyers drifted past the rails. Some leered openly. Some touched. Others inspected with flat, professional eyes, as if selecting tools. Bethan learned to stand very still. A thick-armed man with a scar down his cheek stopped in front of her. His gaze crawled over her. He motioned her forward. Her feet wouldn't move. His hand reached out. And stopped. Another hand had closed around his wrist. Iron-hard.

The man snarled and turned, but whatever he saw made him recoil. He yanked free and disappeared into the crowd without a word. Bethan looked up. The man who stood there did not belong to the docks. His coat was dark blue, trimmed in gold. Tailored. Clean. He carried himself with an economy of movement that drew space around him without effort. His eyes were cool. Assessing. His jaw was tight.

"Stay near the middle," he said. Not loudly. Not gently.

Bethan nodded without thinking. Her head dipped instinctively. For a moment, his gaze lingered. Then he turned and was gone. She obeyed, and no one else attempted to touch her.

When the auction began, she barely felt herself moved to the front. Chains clinked. The auctioneer's voice rose and fell, oily and loud.

"Five."

"Ten."

"Fifteen."

The men laughed. Bethan stared at the ground.

"Fifty."

The word cut through the noise like a blade. Silence fell. The auctioneer looked up, startled. At the back of the crowd, the man in the navy coat stood with his hand raised. He didn't repeat himself.

"Sold," the auctioneer said quickly.

The chain was pulled. Bethan stumbled forward. As she was led away, she looked back once. The man met her eyes. Nothing softened in his expression.

~

The man kept her bound. He didn't speak at first. He didn't need to. He moved like something dangerous and contained, every step measured. His black hair was pulled back from sharp, controlled features. A single gold hoop gleamed in his left ear like a warning. Nothing about him was careless.

Bethan struggled to keep pace as they reached the cashier's box outside the auction hall. The heat of the crowd still clung to her skin. The noise still rang in her ears. He had not looked at her once. Until now. With a sudden jerk of the rope, he pulled her close. Too close. She caught the scent of leather and spice and cold authority.

"Keep up," he said quietly. "Or I'll drag you through the streets to my vessel."

Her breath caught. She nodded. His hand moved without warning. Fingers closed around her chin, sharp and precise. Not brutal. Controlled. Enough.

"When I ask you a question," he said, his voice low, "you will answer, 'Yes, Master, or Yes Captain.' Do you understand?"

Her lips parted. A flicker of resistance sparked in her chest.

"Yes, Captain," She would not call this man Master.

A faint smile touched his mouth but never reached his eyes.. "Good."

He released her and turned away. The rope snapped tight as he strode forward. Bethan stumbled, the rope biting into her wrists. He did not look back once.

~

He led her through the streets, but Bethan saw nothing. Stone and smoke and shouting slid past in a gray blur. She moved as if caught in a current, pulled forward by a force she could not resist. The rope stayed taut between them.

The docks rose out of the fog, the smell of salt and rot thick in the winter air. The quay yawned wide at the lake's edge, planks slick with damp. Shallow boats rocked against their moorings broad, wooden vessels, more wagon than ship beneath the pale sky.

He drew her down the gangplank and onto one of them. A sharp tug on the rope shoved her forward, pressing her in among the others. Six captives in all, two men, a girl, a boy, and a woman older than Bethan, her face worn thin by years of hunger and fear.

Her owner barked an order in a foreign tongue. One of the boys on deck sprang to obey, casting off the lines. Along the sides of the vessel, a dozen slaves in loincloths leaned into their paddles. A massive beam set at the center of the deck began to turn, the wheel at the stern creaking as the boat eased away from the dock.

Bethan stared as Ingerside slipped backward, the town shrinking into fog and smoke. She turned once, searching the shoreline. Her chest tightened at the thought of Quinn, alone, starving, searching the mountain paths. He would come looking for her, she knew that as sure as she knew her name. He would likely die trying.

I will be dead to him now. The singular thought cracked something in her chest. A single tear slid free, tracing her cheek before falling into the dark water below, the vast lake oblivious to her suffering.

Act 2

Chapter 8

The shallow boat creaked as the paddle wheel thumped into motion, carrying them downriver. The farther they drifted, the thicker the fog grew, pale tendrils curling along the banks and swallowing the shoreline whole .An icy wind blew down from the northern mountains, biting into Bethan's skin. She was still in her shift, the cloak gone, stripped away during her preparation for the auction. She drew her knees to her chest and shivered, teeth chattering uncontrollably, the sound loud in her own head.

The man who had bought her came to stand over her. He looked down at her without expression. Cold. Assessing. He reached out and brushed his thumb along her cheek. She felt only the pressure, her skin too numb for anything else . He clicked his tongue once, then turned and opened a chest at his feet. Something flew toward her. She flinched hard, arms coming up instinctively. It was a blanket. The heavy wool was course on her skin.

She fumbled for it with stiff, clumsy fingers. Her joints felt ancient, reluctant to obey as she tried to pull it around herself. The woman beside her lunged, clawing for the fabric. Bethan nearly lost it. At the last moment, she tightened her grip and dragged the blanket in, curling around it, wrapping herself tight. The woman snarled. Bethan snarled back. The sound shocked her. She blinked, revulsion washing over her as she realized what had come out of her mouth.

The woman surged forward. A wooden baton cracked through the air and struck her across the head. She dropped with a cry, collapsing into the boards. The man stood over them, baton in his hand. He glanced down at Bethan and chuckled, low, and amused.
"You'll do." He said with satisfaction.

The words landed flat. Final. As if she had passed some test she hadn't known she was taking.

Do for what? Bethan pulled the blanket closer, hands shaking, and he turned away, already speaking again in that foreign tongue. She risked a glance at the woman, now groaning and dragging herself backward. The other slaves stared at Bethan with open wariness. Bethan tucked her head beneath the blanket and pretended she didn't see.

~

They drifted down the river through the night. Bethan was the only one given a blanket. When the sun rose behind them, the other slaves sat huddled together for warmth, shoulders pressed tight, breath fogging in pale clouds. The older woman glared. Bethan ignored her.

Marsh and reeds slid past in slow silence. A flock of herons burst into flight as the boat rounded a bend, white wings flashing against the gray sky. Then the river widened, and she saw it for the first time. The Great Fire Sea. On land, moss- and vine-covered towers reached upward like skeletal fingers. Narrow inlets cut between them, channels of dark water threading through stone. A city they called Sasfriska. Her parents had never come here, this place belonged to pirates and scavengers.

The riverboat slowed as the sun tore free from the horizon. When they reached the docks, the scent of salt and rot thickened in the winter air. Chains clinked. Wood groaned. Gulls screamed overhead. Downriver, toward the edge of the sea, the harbor opened before them like a mouth. Ships rocked in place, tall and proud beneath the pale morning light. But one stood apart. It was a dark vessel. Almost black. The sails had been charred or dyed or both. She couldn't tell, but they bled shadow even in daylight. A black flag snapped sharply overhead. No crest. No sigil. Just defiance.

From the riverboat, they were herded into a dinghy. The pirate took the helm. No one spoke. The oars dipped soundlessly into the icy water as they crossed toward the waiting ship. As they drew near, gold lettering glinted against the dark hull. Unreadable. Her stomach twisted.

The prow bore the carved figure of a woman, torso bare, breasts swathed in twisting seaweed, her head tilted back, mouth parted in a silent wail. Her hair was sculpted wild, frozen in imagined wind. Her arms were nowhere to be seen. Bethan shivered and dropped her gaze.

The dinghy bumped softly against the larger vessel. The pirate stood, reaching for the rope ladder that hung over the side of the ship. Waited. Then beckoned to her. She hesitated only a moment. Then she scrambled to her feet, brushed past him, and began to climb.

The deck of the vessel creaked beneath her bare feet. Bethan stepped up, blinking against the sudden brightness, the cold salt wind biting through her shift. She half-expected jeers. Whistles. Laughter. but the crew said nothing. Dozens of eyes turned her way. Some furtive, others lingering. Not a single voice broke the silence.

Men stood with ropes in hand, knives at their belts, muscles straining beneath worn linen and leather. Scars cut across jaws. Ink crawled up necks. They watched. Afraid. Not of her. Of him.

The pirate stepped onto the deck behind her, and the tension snapped taut like a bowstring. Every man went back to work as if the order had been barked. Lines were coiled. Buckets lifted. Voices rose in song, but only after he'd passed. Bethan's breath fogged in the cold. She felt her shift whip around her thighs in the breeze and flushed deep, but no one reached for her. No one dared. Just a dark sea stretching wide around her, and his shadow at her back. The pirate didn't look at her. He didn't need to. He merely gestured, once, toward the stairs leading below deck. And she followed.

The cabin was bare. No comforts. No warmth. Just a cot against the wall with a thin wool blanket, a water basin, and a single lantern casting long shadows. One door led in. The other, thinner, and darker, led straight to whatever lay beyond his quarters. Bethan did not ask.

He stood at the door, arms crossed.

"I am Tarren," he said, his voice cold and low. He gestured toward the spartan cabin. "You can walk in," he added, his tone careless, "or I can carry you in."

Bethan swallowed and stepped inside. The door shut behind her. She flinched. "What do you want from me?" she whispered.

His voice came flat. "Plenty of things. But we will start with obedience. Turn around and look at me."

Bethan's pulse pounded. She stiffened. Her breath caught. Slowly, she turned halfway and dared a glance.

A slow, dangerous smile touched his mouth. "Good," he murmured. "I prefer a challenge."

Then he was gone. The lock clicked into place, leaving Bethan alone in the dim, swaying cabin.

~

Bethan sat on the narrow cot in her cabin, her wrists still raw from the earlier bindings. The ship rocked gently beneath her, the distant sounds of crewmen working above deck. She had spent the better part of the evening here. After testing the locked door, she had sat and waited for the next order.

Then, just before dusk, a knock came at the door. She tensed as it creaked open, revealing a young cabin boy no older than fifteen. He carried a bundle of fabric over one arm and a neatly folded note in his other hand. Without meeting her eyes, he set them on the cot and quickly retreated, shutting the door behind him.

Bethan hesitated before unfolding the note.

Pet,

You will dine with me tonight. Wear the dress. You may refuse, but I will not ask twice.

*—*Tarren

Her fingers tightened around the parchment. *Pet*, she thought. He had never asked her real name, and now he had given her one. Her gaze dropped to the bundle on the cot, and with reluctance, she unfurled it. A gown of deep crimson spilled over her hands, the fabric finer than anything she had touched in years. It was soft, smooth, and too fine for a prisoner. With a sigh, she changed into the gown, leaving her own tattered clothes folded on the cot. It fit too well, as if it had been made for her. The bodice hugged her ribs, the skirts flowing to the floor like liquid fire.

After a time, the cabin boy returned, escorting her down the dimly lit corridors until they reached the captain's quarters. He knocked once before stepping aside. Tarren stood inside, waiting, wearing a fine dark vest over a white shirt, the sleeves rolled just high enough to expose his forearms. His lips twitched as he looked her over, eyes gleaming with something unreadable.

"You clean up nicely," he remarked.

Bethan watched him closely. She did not say thank you. The room was larger than she expected, lined with shelves of books and maps, a broad mahogany desk pushed against the far wall. In the center stood a polished table set for two, golden candlelight flickering over gleaming silverware and a meal that smelled far too good for a pirate's ship.

Tarren flicked his finger toward the seat across from him. "Sit."

Bethan hesitated, but obeyed, keeping her posture rigid. The moment she sat, a crewmember entered to pour wine into their goblets before vanishing again. She refused to touch it. Tarren, however, sipped his with ease. He carved into his meal, taking a bite before watching her expectantly.

"Eat," he said. "We have much to discuss."

Bethan's stomach twisted. Taking a slow, shaky breath, she picked up her fork and ate in silence. She tried not to show how hungry she still was, but it was all she could do to control the pace at which she consumed her food. It was delicious and she hated that it was.

For a time, the meal passed in unsettling quiet. Tarren made no move to speak further, content to watch her between bites. Finally, he set his utensils down and leaned back in his chair, his piercing gaze locking onto hers.

"Do you know why I bought you?" he asked.

Bethan forced herself to meet his gaze.

"Because you wanted a slave." She answered.

Tarren chuckled, shaking his head. "No, Pet. If I wanted a slave, I could have taken any desperate girl off the docks. But you." He tilted his head. "You're different. You carry yourself like someone who has everything to lose, yet you've already lost it all, haven't you?"

Her fingers clenched around her fork. "I bought you because I want something from you," he continued. "Loyalty. Willingness. Submission."

There were his terms, again. Tarren's smirk faded slightly. He studied her, as if weighing her worth. Then, slowly, he rose from his chair, circling the table until he stood beside her. He reached down, his fingers lightly brushing the back of her chair.

"I don't need to force you, Pet." His voice was quiet but laced with something dark. "I have time."

Bethan stared at the candle flame. She could feel the heat coming off him, her heart thudding, her mouth dry. For a long moment, Tarren simply looked at her. Then, to her surprise, he smiled, a slow, knowing curve of his lips that never reached his eyes.

"And you are mine now." He said again, his voice grounded in contentment.

With that, he moved away, returning to his seat.

"Finish your meal," he said smoothly, as if the conversation had never happened. "I have no intention of letting my investment wither away. "Bethan forced herself to breathe, her heart still hammering in her chest.

Chapter 9

Days passed, yet Tarren did not push her. He did not take. Rather, he demanded. It was in the way his voice deepened when he spoke her name. The way his presence filled a room, leaving no space for her to ignore him. He demanded nothing yet expected everything. Tarren continued to take every meal with her. The food was well prepared. Every morning, a new dress lay on her bed, the old one gone.

One afternoon, the cabin boy brought Bethan a stack of books,, all hardback and brand new.

"Captain says these are yourn's." He spoke in the dialect of the river people of Kuvale.

She blinked.

The boy held them out to her as if they were coals. She took them, fingering the gold filigree. They were the nicest books she had ever held; *Hersales,* she had never read that one. *Morgoran* made her think of Papa, He had read it to her when she was younger. The thought made her swallow. The last book made her breath catch. *Wexler's War.* Quinn's favorite book. She put that one aside. She couldn't read it now, maybe not ever again.

The next evening, Tarren found her on deck, leaning against the railing, gazing out at the endless sea. She had come here for solitude, to clear her thoughts. But Tarren did not allow her peace.

"You're restless," he observed, stepping beside her.

Bethan stiffened but did not move away. "What does it matter to you?"

He smirked, resting his forearms against the railing. "Because it means you're thinking of me."

She tried to hide her face.

Tarren chuckled lowly, the sound like velvet against steel. "Lying to yourself doesn't suit you, Pet."

That name.

She sighed. "I am Bethan."

He shifted closer, his voice dropping to something quieter, something dangerously cold. "You are what I have named you."

She swallowed hard, gripping the rail. Finally, she dropped her gaze. "Yes, Captain."

His breath was warm against her ear. His tone was not. "Good."

A shiver ran through her.

"You fight it," he murmured, his fingers brushing her wrist, not holding, just a whisper of touch. "You fight me."

She stared at his fingers on her wrist. "I don't know the rules."

His lips twitched.

"You do," he asserted.

"Obedience, loyalty, submission," she repeated, the list he gave her every day.

Tarren exhaled sharply. "And yet, I am so good to you, and still you do not show your gratitude."

Bethan's heart slammed against her ribs. "Have I displeased you?"

Tarren's eyes darkened, his hand falling away.

"Only when you hesitate," he murmured.

Then he turned and walked away, leaving her standing there, trembling in the night air.

Two weeks had passed since the auction. A fortnight of mind games, of stolen glances, of velvet threats and maddening restraint. But this day was different. Tarren had said nothing of where they were going, only instructed her to wear the dress he laid out for her that morning.

Royal blue. Silk. The fabric shimmered like water in the sunlight as he fastened the final clasp at her back, his fingers steady, impersonal.

But there was something in the way he paused, just for a breath, before his hand dropped away.

He had done her hair himself. She had expected roughness, haste, but instead, he had been careful. His fingers threaded the blond strands with deliberate attention, weaving in tiny pearls until her reflection in the mirror made her breath catch.

Now, walking beside him in the bustle of an exotic seaside port, she felt eyes on her, because she looked like someone important. The streets were crowded, colorful, alive. Markets spilled into alleyways, woven rugs and fruit carts and trinkets gleaming under the sun. Music echoed from a plaza nearby, lilting, and strange. She turned her face toward it like a flower to light, and Tarren noticed.

"Do you like it, Little Bird?" he asked quietly.

She started at the new name, not Pet, this one was spoken with tenderness, or something like it.

She hesitated. "Yes, Captain."

He did not correct her tone this time. He did not reach for her chin or test her obedience. Instead, he offered his arm, a gesture so unexpected she blinked. Then she took it. That was when he began indulging her. Every vendor they passed, glass beads, hand-painted fans, delicate rings, carved combs, Tarren stopped when her eyes lingered too long. He bought them. Not just one. Not just a token. All of them.

"You'll have a chest full of useless trinkets," she murmured, her arms full of wrapped parcels.

He leaned close, just enough for her to feel the heat of him again. "That is not your concern, Little Bird."

His voice was not cold, It was almost amused, but it still fell like a warning.

She lowered her eyes immediately. But Tarren only watched her with that quiet, unreadable expression and said nothing.

The day slipped by like a dream. She tasted sweet tea from a stall, fed bright green birds in the garden behind a temple. And all the while, he watched her the way a man might watch the sky after a storm, curious to see if it would break open again. *Maybe... maybe he's more than what he seems. Maybe this is something real.* The thought crept in. It curled around her heart and sank its claws in deep.

Because when he handed her a delicate chain with a sapphire

drop, blue to match her dress, she did not feel like a prisoner. She felt like a woman. Like a chosen woman. He led her back to the ship at dusk, her arms filled with silk and silver and things she had not wanted but now could not imagine giving up. He said little. And she came to dinner flushed.

~

Bethan woke early the next morning, the blue silk still hanging on the peg, so she was already dressed when he came for her. The moment the door opened, she saw the shift in his eyes. It was subtle, but deadly. A flicker of disappointment, of warning, hidden behind the slow drag of his gaze as he took her in.

She had brushed her own hair. Slipped her feet into soft shoes, laced carefully. She had waited with her hands folded in her lap, her heart fluttering like the Little Bird he had named her, hoping, perhaps, to be pleasing.

But when he stepped inside, he said nothing. He just shut the door with a quiet click. The silence stretched.

"You're early," he said at last, his voice smooth as smoke.

"I thought…" She swallowed, trying to stay steady under his stare. "I thought I'd be ready."

Tarren did not move. Not for a breath. Then he crossed the room in three quiet strides and stopped just in front of her.

"And who told you to think, pet?" His tone was not raised.

Her spine locked straight, her eyes lowering instinctively. "No one," she whispered.

"No," he repeated, circling behind her now. "No one told you. And yet, you assumed."

He did not touch her. Not yet. But she felt him. That controlled, electric stillness. Like a storm waiting to break.

"I thought I was doing right," she said. "You were kind yesterday…"

His chuckle was quiet. Cold. "Kindness?"

His breath brushed her neck.

"Is that what you think this is? Me letting you dress like a lady, letting you wander the market like some merchant's spoiled daughter?" His voice was full of mockery.

Her chest rose and fell faster. "I... I just wanted to please you."

"And you think pleasing me means acting without instruction?" His voice went icy.

A sharp silence. Then, finally, his hand found her shoulder. Just a touch. But it pinned her there like a nail to wood.

"You don't get to decide when or how, pet," he murmured, bending close to her ear. "You don't lead here. You follow. And when you forget that, I will remind you."

She dared a glance up. "Forgive me, Captain."

Tarren's grip tightened, just for a breath. Then he let her go.

"Bold," he said, stepping back. "Stupid. But bold."

She did not know if it was praise or a warning. Maybe both. He turned toward the door.

"You won't dress yourself again unless I tell you to. And if you're waiting, you wait kneeling. Head down. Hands behind your back." He glanced over his shoulder. "If you want to please me, pet, first learn your place."

Then he was gone out the door. Leaving her to stand there in the wake of his disapproval.

~

The next port was filthy, buzzing with heat and sweat and danger. Bethan could taste it in the air, salt and smoke and something unspoken. Tarren did not take her in the day, he waited until night. Men shouted over dice, over cards, over women. Rough voices. Rougher hands. He did not offer his arm. He did not ask if she was afraid. He just walked, and she kept close, her skirt catching in alley grime, her pulse a wild thing in her throat.

They passed through the casino first if it could even be called that. Smoke and laughter and the heavy clink of coin filled the space. Drunken bodies. Bare flesh. Every table a temptation. Every corner a trap. But Tarren did not linger. He moved to the back, past a velvet curtain thick as blood, and down a set of stairs carved into stone. The air cooled with each step, and so did her courage.

Then came the hallway. Dark. Narrow. The walls pulsed with sound. Bethan flinched, every door they passed a window into some new depravity. She wanted to run. Tarren caught her wrist. And his grip was not gentle.

When he opened the last door, she gasped. The room was lit low, red as wine. Chains hung from the ceiling, restraining a woman. Bethan tried to turn away. Tarren was faster. He moved behind her, wrapped an arm tight around her waist, the other catching her chin, forcing her forward.

"Open your eyes, Pet," he whispered, his breath like ice against her skin. "Or you'll be next."

She trembled. "I don't want to see this."

"I don't care." His voice was low, intimate. "You don't get to want. You watch. You learn. You understand what it means to belong."

The whip cracked. Bethan flinched, and Tarren's grip tightened.

"You'll never be that woman," he murmured. "Not unless you force my hand. But you need to know where your defiance leads. Where your choices end."

She did not speak. She could not. So she watched. And the whole time, his arm stayed firm around her. His body a cage. And in that moment, she understood. She was not his guest. She was not his companion. She was his Pet.

~

When it was over, as if they had merely witnessed a play, Tarren turned to Bethan and extended his arm. She took it and walked. Back through the corridors they went, up the stairs, past the curtain, through the noise and filth of the casino. None of it touched her now.

The stars blinked overhead when they reached the docks, cold and sharp and far too distant. He helped her into the dinghy. Steadied her hands when she faltered. No commands. Not even a look of mockery. He just was. And that unsettled her.

They climbed aboard his vessel, the ship creaking beneath them like it knew her silence. She did not stop at her door. She walked forward, past the crew, past the masts and ropes, until she reached the prow. Staring down at the carved woman. The figurehead with breasts tangled in seaweed and hair swept back in stone wind. She wondered who had carved her. To whom she had belonged. If she had once been flesh and blood before she became wood and salt and story.

Behind her, she felt him come. Not with heavy steps. Not with warning. Just presence. He did not speak. He did not try to pull her away. He only stood there. Always watching. Always waiting.

She stood there for a long time. The wind tugged gently at her hair, the scent of brine sharp in the back of her throat. Somewhere below, waves slapped against the hull.

When she finally spoke, her voice was hoarse. She paused, as if the word itself resisted being said.

"Why didn't she cry?" She asked with confusion.

Tarren was still behind her. Unmoving. When he spoke, his voice was velvet and iron all at once. "

She did," he said simply. "But there are times when pain makes what hurts on the inside better."

Bethan turned then, slowly. Her arms were still wrapped tight around herself. "But why would someone want that?"

Tarren stepped closer, the moon catching on the edges of his dark eyes.

"There are those," he said softly, "who find freedom in giving up the fight, and knowing someone else commands the storm."

He stepped even closer. She flinched, but she did not retreat or speak. Tarren leaned down, his voice brushing against her cheek like sin.

"You watched her like you were afraid. He gave her a beat of silence. "You were afraid of why she seemed at peace."

Her lips parted in protest, but no words came out.

"I told you, Pet," he whispered, stepping away and leaving her in the cold. "You'll come to me. You just don't know it yet."

He turned and Bethan watched him go, worrying her lip as his figure melted into the shadows on the deck.

Chapter 10

Bethan rose early the next morning. She dressed herself in the soft gray dress he had left folded at the foot of her bed. Combed her hair smooth and neat, tied it back with one of the silk ribbons he seemed to favor. She even sat quietly by the porthole, hands folded in her lap, waiting for him to summon her.

Maybe, if she gave him nothing to correct, he would finally let her breathe. But when Tarren opened the door and saw her sitting like that, his face did not soften. It hardened. He stepped inside, shut the door with deliberate care, and leaned his weight against it. Studied her. A long, slow look that started at her head and ended at her folded hands.

"You're learning fast," he said at last.

She swallowed. "I thought it might please you."

Tarren's mouth curled. Not a smile. A warning. "Careful, Pet. There's a difference between obedience and performance. One comes from the soul. The other is a lie with lipstick."

Her stomach dropped. She had meant it. Or thought she had.

"Then what do you want from me?" she asked, her voice quiet.

Tarren pushed away from the door and stepped toward her.

"Oh, I want everything," he said, his voice dark and low. "But I want it real. And right now, you're just mimicking the sound of surrender. I'll wait. The song always comes."

She turned her face to the porthole, her throat tight, her heart cracking like sea ice. And worse, some part of her wanted to. Not to escape. Not even to survive. To feel chosen again.

~

Dinner was quiet. Too quiet. She kept her eyes on her plate, every movement measured. Knife. Fork. Bite. Chew. Swallow. Smile when he looked at her. Tarren sipped his wine and watched her like he had all the time in the world.

"Tell me about yourself, Little Bird." He coaxed.

There was the tender name again.

She blinked. "What do you want to know?"

His smile was slow, not kind. "Anything you're willing to give."

She paused. "There's not much to tell."

"Little Bird, there's always much to tell." He leaned forward, elbows on the table. "I want to know what made the girl in the tattered dress flinch every time someone raised their voice. I want to know what you dream about, what keeps you up at night. I want to know what makes you scream."

She gripped her fork a little tighter. "You bought me," she said, keeping her voice level. "Not my life story."

Tarren chuckled, dark and low. "That's where you're wrong. I didn't buy a doll to dress and display. I bought you. Every memory. Every scar. Every secret. You just haven't unwrapped yourself yet."

She set her fork down slowly. "Maybe I don't want to be unwrapped."

"And maybe," he said, rising from his chair and circling the table toward her, "that's what makes you most interesting."

She stood up as he approached, too fast, too sharp, like prey suddenly realizing the shadows held something far worse than silence. But Tarren only brushed her hair back from her cheek, his touch deceptively gentle.

"It's enticing," he murmured, "how hard you fight to stay unknown."

She turned her face away. She did not move. She did not breathe as his fingers skimmed her jaw. He was too close again, always too close.

"You flinch when I am disappointed," Tarren said quietly. "But not when I raise my hands. You've never been struck before, have you? Not screamed at. Not truly screamed at. You're used to being disciplined, not frightened." She looked away. Then he said, "It was your father, wasn't it?"

Her whole body stiffened. And Tarren stilled. She was not fooling him, even when she tried to relax her hands.

"You don't know what you're talking about," she said coldly.

"Oh, but I do," he murmured, circling her now, slow, like a wolf around wounded prey. "He didn't shout. He disappointed. He disapproved. And you, what did you do? Try harder? Shrink smaller? Did you think if you were just good enough, he'd love you?"

She flinched as if the words were slaps because they were not true, Papa had loved her, deeply. "

You don't know him, and you don't know me," she hissed.

Tarren stepped behind her again, his voice low against her ear.

"No. But I will. Because every time you try to hide, you tell me exactly where to dig." He whispered.

She swallowed hard, lips trembling, but said nothing. Not because she could not. But because she would not. Because it hurt too much. When Tarren finally stepped aside, she practically ran from the cabin to her own. She shut the door behind her and leaned against it, her breath shallow, her chest tight.

Her quarters were silent. She crossed to the cot and sat down hard, fingers digging into her skirts. She did not cry. That would have been a relief. Instead, she thought of her father. Cal Horsgaard.

He had never raised a hand in anger. He had never needed to. One disappointed glance from him had shattered her more deeply than any punishment ever could. She had wanted to please him. Desperately. Every time she failed, she carried the weight of it like a wound. Yet Tarren's voice echoed in her head like a bell. *"You flinch when men raise their voices… you're used to being punished, not frightened…"*

She covered her face with her hands. And when she realized it, she could not remember what her father had looked like, much less how his voice had ever sounded.

~

She lay on the cot and stared at the low ceiling, the oil lantern swaying faintly with the ship's motion. The wood creaked. Somewhere above, boots passed. Tarren's voice still lingered like smoke in her ears.

"You crave the approval of men who call it love when you obey."

She squeezed her eyes shut. "Yah-Roi..." she whispered, and the name caught in her throat. It had been so long since she had prayed. Longer since she had felt worthy to. But now, curled small in a stranger's ship, in a stranger's life.

"Father..." The word broke her. Her voice trembled, thin in the silence. "I sold you for a crust of bread and a lie. I didn't mean to. I just... I just wanted Quinn to live. I wanted us to live." She sat up, burying her face in her hands. "And now I'm here. In this place. With him." A sob worked its way loose. She pressed her fist to her mouth. "How could you want to listen to me?" she choked. "I betrayed you. I can't. I can't ask you for anything."

Silence. Heavy and vast.

She bowed her head.

"But if you're still listening," she whispered, "please... don't let me forget who I was. Who I am. Even if he tries to make me something else."

The words faded. She did not know if anyone heard. They felt like they bounced off the ceiling. But they had been said.

~

When he called her for dinner the next evening the table was set with too much care for a man who claimed not to care. Candles flickered in iron sconces, and the roast on the plate before her smelled faintly of cinnamon and clove, spices from a land she had never seen. She sat straight-backed, dressed in deep green tonight. Tarren had chosen it, of course. Her hair curled loosely down her back, pearls tucked in like bait.

He watched her across the table with that same lazy, wolfish smile, knife flashing softly in his hand as he cut a piece of meat, slow and precise.

"Tell me about yourself, Little Bird," he said.

His voice smooth as the wine in his glass, repeating the words from the night before.

She glanced down. "My life did not change from last evening. There is still nothing to tell."

"Oh, I doubt that," he said, leaning back in his chair. "You have the look of someone carved in layers. Paper-thin. Peeling. I'm curious what's underneath." She did not answer. He sipped his wine. "No? Still clinging to your secrets, then." He chuckled, low and dry. "Or perhaps you're still praying Yah-Roi might rescue you from me."

Her fork stilled.

"I heard you last night," he said lightly. "Begging your god not to forget who you were."

He leaned forward, elbows on the table now. "That was sweet."

She looked up sharply but said nothing.

"That's the thing about prayers whispered in the dark, Little Bird." He smiled. "Sometimes the wrong god answers."

Tarren's tone dripped with bemusement, as if his words were meant as comedy. She felt heat rise in her chest. Humiliation. Anger. Dread. He continued casually, as if discussing the weather.

"Try the bread, ." He held out the basket to her with a chuckle. "You sit at my table. No vows required."

She stared at him, her throat thick, her lips pressed tight.

Tarren continued softly, "You're not really looking for a way out anymore. Tell me, Little Bird, are you wondering what it would feel like to fall?"

He lifted his glass. "To surrender?" he asked, twisting the knife once more. She sat frozen, her chest heaving quietly. He did not press. He just drank and smiled again. The kind of smile a serpent might wear before it swallows.

~

She didn't run when he dismissed her. She walked, steady steps, head high, because she would not let him see how gutted she felt. Not again.

Her quarters were too quiet. She closed the door behind her and sank to the edge of the bed, hands curled in the fabric of the dress. Green. Like hope, and new things. She yanked it over her head with shaking fingers and let it fall to the floor.

He'd heard her. That soft, cracked whisper in the dark, *I can't talk to You. I betrayed You.* And he'd twisted it into a blade. The worst part was that she hadn't really expected an answer., and Tarren seemed to know that.

She sat curled in a blanket on the floor, forehead pressed to her knees. She remembered her father, He had spoken of Yah-Roi like a friend. Like someone who showed up. She had believed him. But faith was easy when nothing had yet been taken.

Where are You now? she wanted to scream. *Why didn't You stop it? Why didn't You stop him?* But she didn't scream. She didn't cry. She just sat there, letting the weight of shame settle over her. And somewhere in the back of her mind, a darker voice echoed with Tarren's: *You didn't really think He'd come for you, did you?*

She did not sleep. She lay curled on the floor until the lamps burned low and the ship rocked slow and steady beneath her. Her body ached in strange places. Under her ribs. In her bones. When morning came, she found her dress, a deep honey color, and walked to breakfast.

She knocked and heard Tarren call, "Come."

She pushed the door open, and there he stood, outlined in the window, all dark lines and quiet power. On the table sat tea and honeyed bread.

"Did you sleep well, Pet?" he asked, his voice roughened by the sea air, or something else.

He finally turned to look at her face, and his lips twitched. He did not wait for her reply.

He answered as if she had spoken. "That won't do."

She walked to her place and sat, her back straight, unfolding the cloth napkin over her dress. He walked over and poured them both tea, handing her the cup, then looked at her. Not with heat. Not even with victory. With something close to concern. It disarmed her.

"I heard you pacing," he said simply. "Figured you were up late."

"You heard everything," she said, not as accusation, just fact. Her voice was hollow.

He did not deny it. He buttered the bread. Then, quietly,

"You're not the first to curse heaven, Little Bird." He intoned the name gently. "Nor the first to think silence means you're alone."

Her hands balled in the napkin.

"You don't believe," she whispered.

"No," he agreed. "But you do. Or you did." He placed a slice on her plate. "And that matters."

She stared at him, waiting for the cruelty that usually followed. But he only held out the honey.

"Eat. "He commanded.

She reached for the bread, if only because her fingers were too numb to resist.

"I didn't always hate Yah-Roi," he said softly, like he was confessing something.

She looked up sharply. There. That flicker. That trace of something beneath his armor. Was it pain?

"I wonder…" he continued, then let the thought trail.

He stood. Not unkind. Not smug. Just Tarren. Deep and dangerous and dark.

"Eat. Drink. You must keep your strength," he said as he opened the door.

And then he left. Leaving her alone again, with tea and bread.

Chapter 11

Bethan was back on the farm. The air was warm, the kind of warmth that only came in spring, when everything smelled of new growth and lilacs. The hum of voices, a gentle murmuring of the faithful, filled the space as their gathering crowded around the hearth. She could hear their soft laughter, the familiar sound of her mother calling from the kitchen, a plate of bread in her hand.

She held her father's worn hymn book. The words they sang together filled her mind, a tune without words, mumbled like a forgotten song. Her heartbeat faster as the opening notes of the old hymn filled the room. Unease settled in her chest because she could remember the music, but not the words.

The fire in the hearth roared as the song rose in volume, until it spilled outward and began licking at the walls. The smoke. Blood, dark red, staining the floor. Her mother's melodious voice turned to soft cries torn from her lips. And there she stood, frozen in the middle of it all, watching as the farm she had known for years, her home, her family, was consumed by the flames, reduced to nothing but ash.

The hymn still played, but now it was distorted, almost mocking in its beauty. Then, as the fire roared louder, she heard him. Tarren's voice, smooth and cold, calling to her from the darkness. "You see what happens when you don't listen?"

The image shattered. The smoke faded, but not the ache. Tarren's face replaced the comforting warmth of her father's, his eyes cold, pinning her down. His smile was cruel and satisfied. And she was on her knees before him. But before she could scream, the sound of the hymn came again, louder now, sharp against the pain, and she shot upright, gasping for air.

Her heart raced in the darkness of her quarters, her breaths ragged as sweat clung to her skin. She felt the echoes of the dream still lodged in her chest, heavy, like a stone pressing down. The door creaked open, and without a word, Tarren entered. He stood still for a moment, observing her, the air between them thick with something neither of them acknowledged.

"Nightmares, Pet?" His voice was low, devoid of sympathy. But there was something else too, something almost too careful.

She did not answer, her pulse still thumping in her ears as she tried to shake the image of her family burning.

Then, in a voice that almost mocked her confusion, he said, "It's not your family you're mourning, is it?"

She froze, her blood running cold. Her mind raced, her heart clenching in the dark.

"Get out of my head," she snapped, but her voice wavered, betraying the terror she felt.

Tarren did not move, did not even seem bothered by her defiance.

"If I am there, it is because you want me there, Pet." He said simply.

She bit back the knot in her throat, but he was not done.

"The problem with you," he continued, stepping closer, "is that your mind is still attached to a life that no longer exists. That's why you feel torn. And you will keep feeling torn, no matter how many prayers you whisper to a God who doesn't listen."

His voice was almost consoling, as if he sympathized.

Her jaw clenched, her hands curling into fists. *How does he know?* She wanted to scream, to push him out of her room, but the fear of her own thoughts, and the fear of what he might say next, held her rooted to the spot.

Tarren watched her closely, his gaze not just predatory, but calculating.

"You're mine now," he said quietly, each word slicing through the silence. "And nothing can change that. Not anymore."

His footsteps retreated as he left her there, her chest heaving with a mix of anger and desperation. And as the door closed softly behind him, her hands trembling, she could still hear it. The hymn. Faintly. And it was still the sound of loss.

~

Two nights later she sat at the dinner table, her fingers wrapped tightly around her wine glass, trying to keep the tremor in her hand hidden. The lump in her throat felt like it had a life of its own, swelling with every breath she took. She swallowed hard, again and again, but it didn't help. The dry ache persisted, like the early stages of a cold, but this was something far worse.

The feeling wasn't just physical; it was the raw sensation of being vulnerable in front of him. And she could not afford that. She forced her attention back to the meal in front of her, picking at the food, her appetite non-existent. Each bite was agony. The heavy silence stretched between them, but his gaze never wavered. His eyes followed her every movement, as though he could smell her discomfort.

She could feel the weight of his scrutiny. Her stomach tightened in knots, and the wine in her glass felt heavier than it should have been. She reached for it, lifting it to her lips with a hand that had started to shake, but she wasn't sure if it was from the cold that had begun to creep up her spine, or the tension that twisted her insides like a vice.

She tried to act normal. But she was teetering on the edge. She could feel the fever, that creeping warmth crawling through her skin. Her head started to pound, and still, she tried to mask her discomfort behind the slow sip of wine. It wasn't enough.

He hadn't touched her yet, but she wasn't naive. Not anymore. She knew what he wanted. She wasn't stupid. He thrived on fear. And if he sensed that she was slipping, it might be the thing that broke her for good. She forced down a cough, her chest tightening in protest.

Another moment of silence passed, longer this time, as if he were considering something. It was deeply unsettling and made her try for another breath. Which made the tickle in her chest flare. And for the first time since she had been thrown into this nightmare, She thought that maybe she had done the best acting of her life. Because Tarren didn't say a word.

~

She did not get out of bed the next morning. She lay there, shivering beneath the thin sheets, her body burning with fever, her thoughts incoherent. The room spun in dizzying circles, her head heavy, her limbs like dead weight. Her throat was raw, each breath a struggle.

But what terrified her more than the fever racking her body was the silence. Tarren had not come. No knock at the door. No low voice telling her to rise, to dress, to move. Nothing. And that silence felt like the weight of an entire world pressing against her chest.

Her mind spiraled as the hours crawled by. He was not here. And in that absence, she realized something that turned her stomach in a way no touch ever had. His absence felt like abandonment. And worse, it felt like he was waiting for her to show him how fragile she was.

She could not stand it. She could not breathe. Her eyes fluttered closed, and as the fever consumed her, she drifted into delirium. It was in that half-conscious state, between reality and dream, that he appeared. Not in the shape of a man. Not this time. Instead, he came as a dragon.

The creature towered over her. Heat radiated from its body, unbearable, flames licking the air around her, searing her skin. The fire consumed her, but it did not burn her away. Not completely. She tried to scream, tried to push against the weight of its presence, but her voice was lost in the heat. She could not escape. The fire pressed in from every side, each lick of flame turning her skin to ash.

But then there were the eyes. The dragon's eyes burned through the flames like twin stars, cold and burning. And for some reason, those eyes grounded her, even as they threatened to consume her entirely. In them was a strange reassurance. Tarren's eyes, even in the form of the dragon.

"Don't fight it, Pet," a voice rumbled from deep within the creature. It was his voice, low, deep, commanding. It pulled at her like smoke from a fire. "You don't need to fear me. You just need to trust me. I know what is best."

She wanted to scream. She wanted to claw her way out of the

dream. But the fire and the creature's presence felt like gravity she could not resist. When she woke, drenched in sweat, she knew that part of her could never leave him. And that thought alone made her weep.

~

When she finally came around again, the room, dimly lit by the late afternoon sun, seemed to sway before her eyes.

She had tried to rest, to push through the fog of sickness, but it was impossible. The ache in her body was unbearable, and her mind was clouded, heavy, like the weight of an ocean pressing in on her chest.

Then the door opened.

She blinked slowly, trying to focus, but her vision was still a blur. Tarren stood in the doorway, his figure tall and imposing, but something in his stance made her breath catch. There was a softness to him that she hadn't seen before; something almost tender in the way he watched her.

He moved toward her, his footsteps quiet and deliberate. She swallowed hard, the lump in her throat worse than ever. Her heartbeat erratically, and she struggled to keep her mind from slipping further.

He was beside her in a moment, his hand reaching for her forehead, his fingers cool against the heat radiating from her skin.

"You're burning up," he said, his voice low and smooth, the same tone he used when he wanted her to listen, to fall into his words. "How long have you been like this?"

She tried to speak, the words trapped inside her. She barely managed a faint shake of her head. His touch was soothing, almost kind. He seemed to sense her hesitation, his gaze sharpening. But his hand remained on her forehead.

And that was when the warmth of his touch seemed to change. His fingers brushed her cheek, a slow, deliberate movement that seemed too intimate for the moment. He let his hand slide down to her neck, his thumb brushing along her pulse, sending a shiver through her body.

"You know, Pet," he murmured, his voice low, seductive even. "I've been thinking about you all day. My cabin boy said you did not rouse for breakfast, I had business ashore, but I am here now. Tell me where it hurts."

Her chest tightened at the way he spoke, the way his voice wrapped around her like a snake, squeezing out any rational thought. He was feeding her with his words, making her feel special, important even. As if he cared.

For Just a moment, she let herself believe that was true

"You're so strong," Tarren continued, his voice a soft caress. "You know that, don't you? Even when you're like this... weak... you're still so strong. I admire that. Most people would collapse under this, but not you."

Her breath hitched. She wanted to say something, but the fever made everything feel so wrong, so confusing. His words swirled in her head.

"I don't think you realize how much you're worth," he said, leaning down to whisper in her ear. "I think you forget that I see everything about you, every part of -you, Pet. Your beauty. Your strength. Your flaws. I can take care of all of that. All you need to do is trust me. Let me in, and I'll give you everything you've ever wanted."

Her heart raced. She wanted to believe him. She wanted to surrender to the idea of being loved, being cared for—just for once. She was so tired. So weak.

"You don't need to fight anymore," Tarren whispered, brushing a lock of hair from her face. His eyes were darker now, more intense, but there was still that softness in them, that promise. "You're not alone, Pet. I'll always be here for you. I'll make sure you're never alone again."

His lips brushed the side of her forehead, lingering just long enough for her to feel the warmth of his breath against her fevered skin. "Rest now," he murmured. "I'll take care of you."

And as he stood, leaving her in the dim light of the room, She felt something stir deep inside her, a flicker of hope. It was fragile, delicate, But she couldn't help herself. She closed her eyes, and the last thing she remembered before sleep claimed her was the feeling of his warmth against her skin, a warmth that felt much like safety.

~

For two days, Tarren had tended to her with careful attention. He kept a watchful eye over her, made sure she drank enough water, and kept the room dim and quiet. He even managed to coax a faint smile from her with small gestures of seeming kindness.

Night came again, and with it, the return of the dream. She closed her eyes, too tired to fight sleep, and in the quiet of the dark room, she slipped into a restless slumber. The dream struck immediately, more vivid this time. This time, Tarren was no longer a dragon. He was a wolf.

His eyes, the same eyes that had always been cold and calculating, were an abyss that swallowed all light. There was no warmth there. No tenderness. Only hunger. An emptiness stretching into the distance, consuming everything in its path. She was trapped in a clearing surrounded by trees, moonlight casting long, twisted shadows across the ground. The air was thick with tension.

"Pet," his voice growled, low and guttural, seeping into her bones like ice. It was not the soft, coaxing tone he used in her waking hours. This was a voice that carried a warning. There was no safety here. "You're mine now. You always were."

She tried to speak, tried to move, but her body was frozen, locked in place by an unseen force. Her throat constricted. No words came, only the rush of panic building in her chest. She could feel the weight of his gaze, the way it pinned her in place, stripping away her defenses.

Tarren's black eyes never wavered as he approached, his massive form towering over her. For a moment, she thought she saw the shadow of a smirk curl on his lips, though his face was now entirely that of the beast. He stopped just inches from her.

"No one will save you," he whispered, his voice dark, like the growl of a wild animal. "You don't get to run. You don't get to escape."

Her pulse quickened, her breath shallow as fear clawed at her throat. She had never seen him like this. Feral. Unrestrained. She turned her head, trying to push away the fear, trying to steady herself. But the forest around her seemed to close in. In that moment, it felt as though she were drowning in the suffocating weight of Tarren's presence.

"Look at me," he commanded, his voice a growl, the menace in it too real for comfort. Those eyes kept pulling her in.

Her heart pounded in her chest, her limbs trembling, but she could not look away.

"Why do you run from me?" he asked, his voice dark and mocking, as if it were a game to him. "Why do you try to hide from what you want?"

Her throat tightened, a lump forming there, but no words came. She wanted to scream, to tell him she did not want this, that she was not his to take. But it felt useless.

With a sudden, terrifying movement, he lunged forward, teeth bared. "You don't even know what you want, Pet," he murmured, his voice cold. "But I do."

Her breath caught. The vision of the wolf swam before her, and just as quickly as it had come, it vanished, leaving her gasping for breath, the taste of bile at the back of her throat.

She woke with a jolt, her heart hammering in her chest. Her skin was slick with sweat, her breath coming in ragged gasps. The room was pitch black. Only the rocking of the ship told her she was awake. Tarren's voice came then, the soothing one he used when she was awake. It was the only thing that grounded her.

"I am here, Little Bird," he said softly.

Her shoulders loosened before she could stop them.

Chapter 12

The fever broke on the third day. It didn't leave with a gasp or cry, just Like a tide pulling back from the shore, leaving behind nothing but raw sand and spent wreckage. Bethan blinked against the dim light spilling through the window, every part of her body heavy and sore. Her nightclothes clung to her skin, damp with sweat. Her lips were cracked, throat dry. She could barely lift her head from the pillow.

But she knew it was over. Whatever storm had torn through her body had passed. And he was still there. Tarren had not left her side. Not once. Always watching.

He said nothing. Not a single word of comfort or warning. Just the quiet, unwavering presence of a man who did not intend to be anywhere else. His hand only moved to steady her when she faltered or to place a cool cloth on her brow. There was no kindness in it. No cruelty either. Just certainty. And that certainty settled over her like a second blanket. He was not leaving. Maybe not ever. There would be no door flung open in mercy. No disappearing into shadow. He was the shadow now, and he had made his place beside her. She closed her eyes again, too weak to fight it. Too tired to feel the weight of what that truly meant.

Tarren stepped from the shadows near the window because he had never left. His arms were crossed, one foot braced against the wall, watching her like a man studying a snare, waiting for it to spring.

"You said a name," he said quietly.

She blinked slowly. Her voice was cracked from days of fever, but she still managed to whisper, "I don't remember."

"I do." He said.

He pushed off the wall and crossed the room with the same fluid, predatory grace he had mastered.

"You weren't calling for me. You weren't praying to your Yah-Roi." He challenged

He crouched beside her, and his hand brushed a damp curl from her face. "You were crying for Quinn."

She stiffened. Her lips parted, but no sound came.

Tarren's voice dropped lower, like distant thunder. "Who is he?"

She looked away, but his fingers caught her jaw, turning her face back to him. Not roughly. Almost tender. Almost.

"I want to hear you say it." He commanded.

She swallowed hard, her throat burning. She could still feel the ache of that dream. Quinn's smile. The hymns in the air. The blood. The fire. The way his voice had steadied her.

"It doesn't matter," she rasped.

Tarren's eyes darkened. "It does. Because he's the only one you begged for when you thought you were dying. So I'll ask again, Pet. Who is Quinn?"

She tried to shake her head, but she did not have the strength. Tears stung her eyes. "He's dead."

Tarren's hand tightened at her jaw. Not enough to bruise. Just enough to make her feel the weight of his patience thinning.

"Tell me what he meant to you." He demanded.

Her whole body trembled. "He was my brother, and I loved him."

Silence. Sharp. Sudden. Final. Tarren rose slowly to his feet, his gaze flat now, like he had gotten exactly what he came for. He did not say another word. He just left her there. Alone. And she did not know if she was relieved or destroyed.

The room swayed gently as the ship rocked and creaked beneath her. She lay still, watching the shadows shift across the ceiling beams. Her body still ached, as if her bones were hollow. The fever had broken, leaving her sweat-drenched and trembling. But it had also taken something with it. She was not sure yet what. She tried to count the days of her illness, but time had folded in on itself.

She knew he had been there. Through it all. Sitting. Watching. Tending to her like he cared. It felt like relief. Not the silence. Not the gentleness. The safety. The rest. She had let herself feel safe. And she had said his name. Quinn. Her mouth dried at the memory. Her chest twisted. She pushed herself upright slowly, wincing at the pull in her limbs. Bethan reached for the wash basin, dipped her hands into the cool water, and pressed them to her face.

A soft knock. Not a demand. Not yet. Just a warning. He was coming. The door opened like it belonged to him. Because it did. Tarren stepped inside, his eyes already locked on her. No pretense. No greeting. Just heat. He did not come close. He did not have to. His voice filled the room like smoke, thick and impossible to ignore.

"Quinn," he said, testing the shape of the name. "You said he was your brother. Tell me of him."

She flinched. Tarren saw it. He waited, then drew himself up and crossed his arms.

"You cried for him," he said, coming closer now, slow, and certain. "You must have loved him very much. Surely you would want me to know of him."

Her fingers curled around the edge of basin. There was no threat in his tone. Not really. But the weight of him settled over her like a damp blanket. She opened her mouth. Closed it. The ache in her chest was worse than the fever. Tarren had held her hair while she retched. Had whispered something like comfort when she could not stop shaking. Had stayed. He did not have to. He had been kind. Maybe if she gave him this, he would stay like that.

She forced her voice past the lump in her throat. "He was my brother."

Tarren's jaw twitched. "So you said," he replied, unimpressed. "Go on."

Her eyes flicked up, searching his face. She whispered, "He died. It's my fault."

Silence fell between them like a blade. And she saw him lean toward her and told herself that this would be enough.

Tarren stepped closer. She kept her gaze fixed on the edge of the wash bowl, tracing a chip in the porcelain with trembling fingers. "How did he die?"

She hesitated.

"Pet." The name came with a warning. Just her name.

No not my name. She thought, but spoken like a command, and with her head spinning it felt like one.

She swallowed hard. "We were starving. The winter was cruel. I left to find food. I told him not to steal. I begged him not to." Her voice broke. "I was going to trade myself for a week's worth of rations. That was my plan."

She still could not meet his gaze. A pause. A breath that was not quite a sob. Silence stretched.

Then Tarren moved. He crossed the room in two strides and sank onto the edge of the bed, dragging her, limp, and trembling, into his lap. One hand came to her jaw, firm, and possessive, guiding her face up. His thumb brushed her chin. Not soft. Intentional.

"Your brother is dead," he said, low and cold, close enough that she could feel it on her lips. "Whose fault was it, Pet?" he whispered.

She did not answer.

He leaned closer, his voice sharper now. "Tell me."

She shook her head once, desperate to look away, but his fingers held her fast.

"Say it." His voice brooked no argument.

Her whisper barely made it past her lips. "Mine." Tarren's gaze burned into her. And in the fractured corners of her heart, the smallest thread of hope frayed.

~

Tarren held her through the night, and when morning came, she found he had taken nothing more. Hope sparked anew. Perhaps she had misjudged his actions in having her tell him of Quinn. Still, the hope was fragile, so she stayed in her bed the next day, and the next, watching to see if Tarren would come for her.

He did not. Not in that way. He made sure she had food and drink, books to read, and a new dress laid out every morning. He was giving her choice and that felt… hopeful, and terrifying.

On the third day, she ventured from her bed and walked to the washstand, picking up the turtle shell comb Tarren had bought for her in port. She moved to the window and began brushing her hair in the reflection when she heard his footsteps outside her door.

She was not sure why, but she dashed back to her bed and scrambled under the blanket as he knocked, then entered before she could speak. He watched her for a moment, his face neutral.

Then he spoke. "You are doing better?"

She pulled her knees in, dipping her head. "Yes, Captain."

He nodded. "You will inform me when you are well enough to walk again. Sea air will do you well."

She swallowed. "Yes, Captain." He stood there another moment, then turned and walked back out the door as quickly as he had arrived. Leaving the rest up to her.

~

She hesitated the next morning before venturing from her bed. Tarren had left her alone, allowed her another day of rest. He wanted her to go topside, but he was not pushing. Which felt like kindness. This morning, they were docked in a port she had yet to see, and through her porthole, stringed music played. She was curious, and the sun seemed warm. So she donned the deep maroon dress he had left for her and a straw hat and left her cabin.

On deck, the crew moved with purpose, and she stayed out of their way. She walked to the starboard railing and looked out at the docks. The day was indeed lovely, and the crew knew better than to interfere with her. She stayed there, letting the warmth of the breeze and the sun do its magic.

It would be spring back home. That thought twisted in her chest. Spring. The time of planting. Her birthday had passed, and she had not noticed until now. And that thought brought the sadness of her memories flooding back. Papa. Mama. Quinn.

She was lost in her thoughts and did not hear Tarren's approach behind her until he cleared his throat. For one fleeting second, she thought of ignoring him. But ignoring him had never been an option. Tarren stepped up beside her. He wore dark trousers, his navy overcoat unbuttoned, the gold trim glinting under the sun. He was calm, composed, as if he had all the time in the world.

She swallowed hard. "Captain."

Tarren arched a brow at the formality. "Pet."

She turned her attention back to the docks, the men scurrying to bear their loads and sell their goods. Tarren let the silence stretch, watching her from the corner of his eye. Her hands on the rail were steady, but her breathing had changed.

Slowly, he stepped forward, placing a hand on the rail beside her. "You've been avoiding me."

She blinked. "I've been recovering."

He hummed, amused by the lie. "Is that so?"

She nodded. Tarren exhaled through his nose, then, with calculated ease, reached out and tucked a lock of hair behind her ear. She tensed. He plucked at the white ribbon dangling from her hat, fiddling it between his fingers, examining it as if it were of great interest. Then, just as lazily, he let it go.

"Look at me, Pet." He commanded.

She hesitated. Tarren waited. And when she finally lifted her eyes to meet his, his lips curled in satisfaction.

"There you are," he murmured.

She blinked, a foreign ache settling in her bones. She hated how easily he unraveled her, how a single look could make her stomach twist.

"I... I don't know what you mean," she said, but her voice was weaker than she intended.

Tarren leaned down, bringing his mouth close beside her ear. "You've been running," he said, his voice a silken thread winding around her throat. "But we both know you don't really want to escape."

Her breath hitched. He was not wrong. And that was the problem. She turned her gaze away, staring at the flickering lamp instead.

"I just needed space." She finally offered.

Tarren clicked his tongue and straightened. "And I gave it to you. But now, I think you've had enough."

She stiffened. He reached out, grasping her chin and forcing her to look at him. His grip was firm, unyielding, but not cruel.

"You are mine, Pet. Your people are gone. I am all you have left."

His thumb brushed over her lower lip, his gaze dark with something unreadable. "And you will not run from me again."

A tremor ran through her. Tarren watched it happen. Saw the way her body reacted despite her best efforts.

And then, softer, dangerously soft, he added, "Do you understand?"

She swallowed hard. She exhaled shakily, her lips parting, hesitating, before finally whispering, "…Yes, Captain."

Tarren smiled, for the first time.

~

She could not sleep. She had tried. She had willed herself to push his words from her mind, to pretend they did not burrow under her skin, did not wrap around her ribs like a vice.

You are mine.

You will not run again.

I am all you have left.

That line had hit hardest because it was true. She was not free. She was owned. The realization struck her like a jagged blade. And with it came the grief, hot, suffocating, unbearable. It clawed up her throat in gasping, broken sobs, her chest heaving, her hands clenching the thin blankets beneath her as if she could ground herself against the agony. But there was no stopping it. The truth had come crashing down, and she was drowning in it.

A moment later, the door to her cabin opened. She did not hear it at first, too consumed by her grief. She had curled in on herself, her body shaking as she wept into her hands. Then came warmth. Large hands slipping beneath her body. Lifting her. She gasped, instinctively tensing, but there was no fight left in her.

Tarren carried her as if she weighed nothing, his arms solid, unchallenged. She barely registered when they crossed the threshold into his quarters. He settled onto the edge of the bed, cradling her against him, one hand smoothing over her trembling back.

But when his voice came, low, coaxing, wrapped in the dark silk of the night, she heard every word.

"Hush, Little Bird." His lips brushed her temple. "I know you're in pain."

She choked on another sob, pressing her forehead against his chest.

"I... I can't. I can't stop it." She sobbed.

Tarren's grip tightened around her, just slightly.

His voice was steady. Unwavering. "Do you want my help?"

She gasped in a breath and nodded. But Tarren would not accept anything less than words.

"You must ask me," he murmured, his lips ghosting over the crown of her hair. "Use your words, Pet."

She squeezed her eyes shut, her heart was sick.

"Please," she whispered, so softly it was barely audible.

Tarren tilted her chin up, forcing her to meet his gaze. All she saw were his eyes. Deep. Waiting. His thumb traced along her jaw.

"Please what?" He pressed.

She swallowed, her voice breaking.= "Please... make it stop."

Tarren's smile was slow. Indulgent. Inevitable. He leaned in, his breath warming her lips.

"Of course." He replied. As his hand tightened on her arm.

Chapter 13

The ship rocked under her feet, as Bethan stood in front of her mirror, running her fingers over the soft fabric of the scarlet dress Tarren had commanded her to wear. It clung to her body, hugging her curves with a low neckline. There were bruises and marks on her arms and collarbone, and the dress rubbed raw welts on her back. She needed distance, she would have none. It was her birthday, nineteen. Tarren had said they would celebrate. She smoothed the dress over her still flat stomach. The nausea that had plagued her for a week had settled some tonight. Tarren did not know. That meant she was walking a razor's edge

He entered the room, the subtle smirk playing on his lips as he took his seat. His eyes inspected the dress, his gaze entirely proprietary and possessive. She did not look up. She kept her eyes on the brush wishing she were allowed her old cabin. Anyplace with walls.

"Come, Little Bird." Tarren called.

Gesturing to her chair. She moved woodenly, trying to hide her wince as she sat in her chair. The meal was served. The warmth of the food hit her senses, but she barely tasted it. The only thing she could focus on was the churning in her stomach. The physical manifestation of the secret she carried. Tarren didn't rush her, didn't hurry her along. He let her sit there in silence.

The tension between them was thick. She kept her face angled downward, avoiding the intensity of his gaze. Finally, as the last of the food was cleared away, Tarren leaned back in his chair, his eyes locking onto hers.

"Did you like it?" His voice was low, the words coming with a dangerous edge, a thread of something darker beneath the surface. "I had the cook prepare your favorite."

Her mouth was dry. She knew what he was doing. He was reeling her in, testing to see if she would play the game she had learned well. She didn't answer him immediately.   But the longer the silence stretched between them, the more she felt the pull to fill the void.

"It was a good meal Captain, Thank you," she finally said, her voice quieter than she intended

Tarren's smile deepened, as if he had been waiting for those exact words. His eyes glittered. "You're very welcome, Little Bird," he said softly, leaning forward slightly. "You enjoy being mine, don't you?" His voice was coaxing.

Her throat tightened. She pushed the food around on her plate, pretending she did not feel the way his words pulled at her. The way the nights always ended now with her in his bed, giving him exactly what he wished.

"I... I do not know," she said, trying to break the script gently.

"You can't lie to me, Pet," Tarren replied, his tone dark with warning,. "Unless, of course, you are asking to be punished tonight." He paused, letting the threat hang. "Are you?"

Her heart raced. Her hands gripped the edge of the table. "No, Captain. Forgive me. I very much enjoy being yours."

"I'm not a fool, Pet." His voice was a low growl now, the edge of danger sharpening. "I know you better than you know yourself. And I know you're fighting it. It has been a season since you resisted this hard. The question is why?"

The words twisted in her chest like a knife. Tarren leaned back in his chair again, watching her closely, his eyes narrowing.

She shifted in her chair, nausea surging hard and sudden in her throat. Before she could stop herself, she was on her feet, the movement violent enough to scrape the chair back. She pushed past him without a word, urgency driving her forward. Tarren did not stop her. He knew she could go nowhere. He simply let her go.

Her footsteps echoed as she reached the deck, the wintry night air striking her face like a slap. For a moment it steadied her, then reminded her of the truth. Surrounded by ocean. No escape. Not from him. Not from this.

She leaned over the railing, chest heaving as she fought the urge to retch into the black water below. *What am I doing?* The question rose unbidden, fragile as a prayer she could not speak. *This ship is no place for a child.*

Footsteps sounded behind her. She did not turn. She wanted to keep the secret. To hide it. To pretend just a little longer, that it might disappear if she waited. Tarren stopped a few paces back.

"You appear unwell," he said mildly. "I will allow you to rest tonight."

It sounded like mercy. It was permission.

She tasted blood where her teeth bit into her lip, staring out at the dark horizon as the wind cut across her skin.

He moved closer. "I can feel you resisting me," he continued, almost amused. "But it won't do you any good. You've been mine a long while now." A pause. "So I will ask again. Why?" The word burned.

"Thank you for the rest, Captain," she said quietly, and she meant it.

He lingered a moment longer, then turned away, calling to the crew in the language she was still learning. She stayed where she was. Alone at last. But not free.

~

True to his word, he did not touch her all night. The next morning, the eggs were overcooked. She focused on that. Not the smell. Not the cabin. Not the way he sat across from her, sipping his tea. Tarren cut into his meat with the ease of a man at peace. He did not look at her. He did not ask if she had come up with a reason for fighting him. Not yet. He never rushed these moments. He liked the anticipation more than the truth.

She swallowed around the dry lump in her throat and forced a bite down. It stuck halfway.

"You're quiet this morning," he said conversationally. He finally looked up. Smile lazy. Eyes sharp. Always sharp.

She nodded, barely. "Didn't sleep well."

"Mmm." He took another bite. "Strange. You were still all night."

Because she had stayed frozen, back to him, hands pressed beneath her to keep from shaking. He let the silence stretch. Drew it out like a blade being unsheathed. Then he folded his napkin and set it beside his plate.

"Anything you want to tell me, Little Bird?" He coaxed.

There it was.

Her stomach flipped.

He knew. Somehow. Maybe.

He wanted the words. Wanted them dragged out of her throat like a confession. He wanted her to tell him why. She reached for her tea, her hands trembling just enough to betray her. She swallowed again. Her voice was dust.

"I am not feeling well." She answered tightly. It was not entirely a lie.

His gaze sharpened. "Unwell." He repeated the word, flat and suspicious.

She forced herself to look up. "It is an issue with my stomach."

He raised an eyebrow, as if the question amused him. "Your stomach?"

She did not answer. Could not. She flushed. "Yes, Captain."

He reached across the table and placed a hand over hers. His palm was warm. Heavy. Binding.

"I'm going to take care of you," he said, his voice both coaxing and possessive.

She almost choked. He lifted her hand to his lips and kissed her knuckles. His grip was tight enough to grind her bones, a warning. She knew he knew she was not telling him the whole truth.

"You should lie down," he continued. "I will go ashore today, and then I will see how you are this evening."

~

She sat by the small porthole of her cabin, staring out at the dark sea. The steady rocking of the ship was barely enough to comfort her. It was late, the world outside quiet and empty. But her mind was a storm, and her stomach just as tossed.

Tendrils of thought about Yah-Roi echoed in the recesses of her mind. She did not know if she was being punished by Him or ignored. She did not know which was worse. Part of her wanted to call out to Him, to beg for forgiveness for everything she had done. But another part told her it was too late. She had betrayed Him.

She had chosen the Oath and Tarren, and now the baby was her consequence, she told herself. Her arms drew her legs in closer as a tear slipped down her cheek. The idea of a child being born in this place made her ache. She should try to run.

The door creaked open softly. Tarren.

"I thought I'd find you here, Little Bird," he said. His voice was low, dangerous in the way that still made her heart stutter.

She did not answer. She could not bring herself to look at him. She was afraid of what he might see.

"Such a thoughtful little thing," he murmured as he stepped closer.

She felt the weight of his gaze, felt him reading every shift in her body, every hesitation, every breath. He always did.

"Tell me," he continued softly, "are you ready to confess?"

She did not want to answer. But the words slipped out before she could stop them.

"I... I think there is a baby." She finally confessed.

His lips curved into a faint, knowing smile. He moved to stand beside her and watched her for a moment, sensing the fracture in her composure. Then he reached out and touched her shoulder, his hand warm against her chilled skin.

"You think?" he asked.

His tone was gentle, almost tender. But beneath it lay something sharp and predatory that sent a shiver down her spine.

"Or you know?"

She did not answer. She did not need to. The guilt sat heavy in her chest, impossible to hide.

Tarren stepped closer. His fingers traced the line of her jaw, guiding her face toward his.

"You think you can run," he said quietly. "But you chose me. And

I won't let you forget that."

She tensed. His grip was subtle. Practiced. Firm enough to prevent escape without ever seeming cruel.

"Let me remind you why you're here," he continued, his voice darkening. "Who do you belong to?"

He leaned closer.

After a year of the ritual, she knew the words that would come next by heart. Knew the role she would play.

"Who kept you safe?" He pressed. "Fed you? Cared for you when you were sick? What do you think would have happened to you without me? To someone like you?"

She flinched. The truth cut deep, sharp as a blade. She hated that he was right.

"I am yours, Captain," she answered by rote.

He purred his pleasure.

"I've given you everything," he whispered, his breath warm against her ear. "And now you've given me a legacy, as is only right."

Her pulse quickened. What had she been thinking? He had become a constant in her life.

"You're wrong," she whispered, more to herself than to him. "I don't want this. This is no place for a child."

His eyes gleamed, but it was not mischief. He leaned in, his lips brushing her ear.

"If you ever think about leaving me, I will hunt you down, Little Bird, and your cage will be smaller than you can imagine." He warned.

Her breath hitched.

He leaned back then, his hands resting on her shoulders, as if he had not just threatened her.

"I'm the one who can fix you, Pet," he said softly. "After all, what an honor to bear my son." His voice was velvet and poison.

She closed her eyes And a tear slipped down her cheek.

He watched her dress. Watched her braid her hair and slip on her sandals. Then he reached for the gold necklace, the one with the crescent moon charm, and fastened it around her neck.

"So they all know you shine because of me." He said possessively.

She did not speak. He took her up to the deck, where the crew stood gathered and silent. The table was spread, wine poured, a sweet cake already sliced. Tarren raised his glass.

"To my Little Bird," he announced, his voice bold and clear. "And the new life growing in her. A son. I am certain of it."

Cheers followed. Hollow. Forced.

She stood beside him, hands flat on the table, as if steadying herself. She waited until the clamor died, until the wine had reached lips, until he leaned close again, smug, and victorious.

Then she whispered, "It's early."

He did not flinch. Not at first.

"It's still very early," she said again, a little louder. "These things... they don't always last."

She did not mean it as a warning. But the second the words left her mouth, she saw the switch flip. His smile did not falter. But his eyes turned cold. Controlled. He took her hand, laced their fingers like lovers.

"Are you threatening me, Pet?" He voice was sharp and icy.

"No—" She tried to explain.

"Because it *sounds* like you are suggesting that the life I gave you, my heir, is somehow... fragile." He leaned closer, voice low enough for only her to hear. "Like you might lose it."

"I'm not—" her voice caught. "I would never—"

"I *know* you wouldn't," he cooed. He kissed her temple, too soft, too slow. "Because if you *did*, Pet, if you dared let my child slip from you, I would carve the failure into your skin."

She froze.

He chuckled. "Smile now," he said, lifting his goblet again. "This is a celebration."

~

She did not lose the baby. But there were mornings she wished she had. The sickness came like waves crashing on rock. Violent. Relentless. Leaving her bruised and shaking. She could not keep water down for days. Her knees buckled on deck more than once. Once she vomited into the sea and nearly went overboard with it, and Tarren did not stop her. He only stood behind her, one hand on the small of her back, the other in her hair.

She woke in his bed, fevered and dry-mouthed, and he was there with broth and cool rags and a look in his eyes that made her want to scream. Possessive. Triumphant. He was not angry. That was the worst part.

"You see?" he whispered against her forehead, stroking her sweat-soaked hair. "Your body wants to keep him. It's fighting for him, just like I knew it would."

She could not answer. Could not tell him she did not want a son. He fed her sips of broth, one spoonful at a time. Praised her when she kept it down, like she was some wounded little bird.

"Good girl," he said, again and again. "So strong for me. So loyal."

And every morning she did not die, he smiled like it was a gift she had given him.

Chapter 14

It was just a flutter. Barely there. A whisper beneath her skin. But it was him. His movement. Tarren's son.

She froze, one hand pressing low on her belly. Her breath caught, her heart slamming against her ribs. Not because she was afraid of the child, but because she wasn't. For one brief second, something in her dared to feel wonder. Then the fear swallowed it whole.

Tarren told me to come to him the moment it happened.

She was alone in the tiny galley, scraping the edge of a bowl she had not been able to finish. She dropped the spoon. Bolted upright so fast the bench scraped loudly against the wood. He was not aboard. He was in the port town, handling "business." And she had not been told she could leave the ship.

Her fingers trembled as she rushed up the narrow steps to the main deck. The crew barely looked at her now, whether well trained or well warned, it did not matter. She ran to the closest man she recognized.

"Please," she gasped. "I need to find him. I need the captain. Now."

The man blinked at her, his jaw twitching like he did not know if he was allowed to respond.

"He told me to come," she said quickly. "Told me I had to tell him."

She was shaking now, both hands gripping her stomach as if she could hold the baby in place if she had to. She did not even know why it mattered. Only that it did. That he said it did.

But the man did not move. He only looked past her to the first mate who had come up from below deck, and everything in her sank when she saw his face.

"You know you are not to leave the ship," he said. Calm. Cold.

Bethan's throat tightened. "But he told me. He told me to come when—"

"And he also told you not to leave." The sailor replied annoyed.

Her mouth snapped shut. Tears burned, but she refused to let them fall.

The mate gave a clipped nod to the sailor behind her. "Take her back below. He'll be informed."

He'll be informed.

Her stomach rolled. Not from sickness this time, but from dread. She had obeyed. She had obeyed one order and broken another. And now he would decide which one mattered more.

~

The air in the captain's quarters was thick with silence when Tarren returned, the creaking of the ship underfoot the only sound that filled the space. She had been waiting in the corner, standing stiffly by the small window. Her fingers twitched at her sides, but she did not move. She knew what was coming. The walls had already begun to close in on her.

Tarren stood in the doorway, tall and imposing, his dark eyes scanning her. There was something in the way his gaze settled on her now. Calculating. As if weighing her like cargo, measuring her worth by how she had performed.

"You have something to tell me," he said, his voice low and controlled.

She swallowed. "The child moved."

His eyes narrowed, and he took a slow breath. "When," he demanded.

She flinched. "This afternoon, while you were ashore."

He did not react. Not at first. He only tapped his thumb against the ruby ring on his left hand. Her stomach pitched with dread.

~

She stared at the plate like it was mocking her. Just one piece. One stupid, cold, rubbery piece of potato. Her fifth turning of the moon. Over halfway now. Her body was showing it, the soft swell of her stomach betraying her to anyone who looked long enough. Her skin was pale, her hands trembling slightly as she pushed the last bit of food across the plate with her fork.

She could not do it. Her throat locked as she tried to swallow, the nausea curling hot and sharp in her chest. Her stomach turned. She took a sip of water, forced the glass down, then quietly set her utensils aside. It was just one piece.

She felt him before she saw him. Tarren's boots on the wood floor behind her. The scrape of the chair as he pulled it out and sat across from her. Slow. Intentional. She did not look up. She could not. The silence was the worst part. That long, drawn-out stretch of nothing, filled only with the sound of the ship creaking and her own heartbeat hammering in her ears.

Then his voice. Calm. Too calm. "You didn't finish."

She stared down, her voice barely a whisper. "I can't."

Tarren's hand reached across the table. Not to touch her, only to pick up the lone potato. He turned it between his fingers as if it were something sacred. Or something shameful.

"One piece," he said, his tone still deceptively gentle. "That's all you left."

"I tried." She pleaded.

"You didn't." He insisted.

Her breath hitched, her eyes flickering to the floor.

"You chose not to finish. You chose disobedience. And you're carrying my son." There was steel in his voice now. He stood slowly and walked around the table.

She sat perfectly still, stiff as stone, barely breathing. Tarren crouched beside her, his fingers curling around the arm of her chair as he leaned in.

"This is not about you anymore, Pet," he said, low and sharp against her ear. "You are not allowed to be weak. You do not get to refuse food and claim sickness. If he does not thrive, if my son suffers, you will answer for it."

She blinked fast, swallowing against the tight knot in her throat. "I'm trying," she whispered.

"Try harder." He snarled softly.

He stood, took the piece of potato from the table, and dropped it back onto her plate with a soft clink.

"You will sit here until you finish. And if I come back and it is still there, we will find a different way to feed you. Understand?" He said with disdain.

Her whole body flushed with shame. But she nodded because it was all she could do. He did not wait for her response. He was already walking away. Already done with the conversation. So she picked up the fork with shaking hands. She chewed the last piece, fighting the texture, the nausea, the potato itself.

She kept it down. That last bite of potato Because she had to. When the door opened again, Tarren stepped in, eyes scanning the empty plate. His silence stretched as he approached. He touched her cheek, thumb dragging across her jaw, inspecting her like livestock. She didn't flinch. She knew better than to speak first.

"You did well," he murmured finally. "That's how you protect what's mine."

She nodded, barely.

That night, he was gentle, more lover than tyrant. It wasn't rough. Not like usual. His movements were slow, careful, almost reverent. She felt it more than she wanted to. The tenderness. The intimacy. The illusion of love.

"You *earned* this," he whispered into her skin, lips brushing her throat. "My good girl."

Tears slid silently from the corners of her eyes. She didn't speak. Didn't push him away. Just let him have her. Again. Because if this was tenderness, it was only ever conditional. And she knew exactly what it would cost if she failed again.

She stared at herself in the mirror. The fabric of her dress, stretched over her swell. The ship dipped in the sea beneath her, and she steadied herself on the edge of the vanity. She was nearing her time.

She waddled now when she walked. She felt the need to use the chamber pot a shameful number of times each day and night. Sleep was becoming more difficult. So was breathing. But none of those things compared to the thought that she would give birth alone on Tarren's ship.

A fortnight into her ninth moon, she approached him with her request.

"My time is near," she said quietly, "and I fear giving birth to your heir without the aid of a midwife. It is my first time."

Tarren tipped his wine glass with the edge of one finger, considering. It took him only a moment to decide.

"No." He said flatly.

She blinked, biting back a rush of fear. She could not ask why. That would be treachery. So she dipped her head and murmured her ritualized thanks.

"Yes, Captain." She had answered obediently.

He returned to his meal. And she began, in her heart, to prepare to give birth alone. And to accept the consequences if she failed to deliver safely.

~

The storm raged like something summoned. Wind howled through the beams, water lashed the deck, and every timber of the ship groaned as if warning her. The contractions had started at dawn, steady and slow. By midafternoon, they were unbearable. And Tarren never left her side. Not even once.

He had sent for no midwife. No healer. No woman who might speak softly or ease her fear. He said nothing when she asked in a whisper if someone, anyone, was coming, even though she knew he had already denied her.

His reply had been a hand on her thigh, his voice like steel. "You'll do as I say. You will bring my son into this world. For me."

And now, keening on their bed, soaked with sweat, her body tearing itself apart, there was only him. She screamed, and he pressed a rag between her teeth.

"Quiet," he snapped, crouched behind her. "Breathe through it. You were made for this."

Every part of her body burned. She shook with the effort not to collapse, not to disobey. And he watched her like a hawk. He praised her when she bore it well. He scolded her when she faltered.

"Focus," he barked as another contraction tore through her. "You do not dare lose control now."

There were no soft words. No gentleness. Only command. Only control. And through it all, the storm raged louder.

By the time the final scream ripped from her, she had no voice left. Only raw breath and the faint, furious cry of a newborn. Tarren cradled the child like a trophy, blood still on his hands, pride gleaming in his eyes.

"My son," he said, lifting the baby for her to see. "You did it. For me."

Tarren lifted the boy, as the swaying lantern light caught the sheen of his wet skin.

"Colton. My legacy." He spoke the name as if it had been waiting in the stars, just out of reach, until the moment he'd claimed his son with blood still on his hands.

She collapsed onto the soaked sheets, too weak to speak. Too numb to feel joy. Too broken to cry. Even this had been obedience. And in her exhaustion, in the blur between pain and emptiness, one thought echoed in her hollow chest: *He took everything. Even this.*

Chapter 15

She sat on the bunk watching Colton play with a spoon.

"Mama, we going to port today?" The toddler asked in his tiny three-year-old voice.

She reached forward to brush the dark hair from his green eyes. Eyes that reminded her of Quinn. She shut the thought down like she did every time.

"Not today, sweet one." She answered.

The boy nodded and went back to his play.

She sat back, and let herself, wonder once again at the only beautiful thing in her life. When he had been born, she hadn't wanted to hate the boy, but she didn't want to love him either. Loving him would make her vulnerable again, open a door she had sealed shut with iron and grief. But babies don't know the rules. They don't understand walls, chains, or silence. They just *are*.

The night he had been born she had wished for labor to take her, until the baby began to nurse, the instant the child had sighed against her and fallen asleep, she had felt something other than pain for the first time in years. Love. Real honest, and warm. Love was dangerous, and she had carried out her duties as a new mother.

Joy though had come the day the baby had looked up at her.

Colton's eyes had met hers and his mouth had opened wide into a gummy smile. She blinked once then twice. Her heart had physically squeezed in her chest. She gathered him close and kissed his cheek.

"This is mine." She had whispered. "It is our secret."

Tarren had seen her love though, leveraging it as only he could. Threatening just once to get a wet nurse for the boy if she failed to obey.

Colton toddled to the door, "Da?" He asked.

She pressed her lips together. "We will go outside." She finally answered.

She donned a straw bonnet, and made sure the boy had his coat. The wind off the water was cold this time of year.

They arrived topside and the sun shone down on his raven curls, immediately he toddled toward the railing.

"To see fishes," He told her.

She gripped his hand tighter but allowed him to peer between the banisters to the sea below. A pod of dolphins broke the surface and Colton giggled with glee. That sound made her breathe just a little easier. She smiled down at him, mindful that Tarren could see and would use that.

The captain's voice came over the deck and Colton's head came up.

"Da!" The boy squealed. Tarren actually laughed, scooping the boy up into his arms. "Fishes."

The little hands grabbed at Tarren's coat.

The captain grinned. "Indeed? Show your papa?"

He stepped toward the railing and let Colton point.

She watched closely, *Be mindful.* She wanted to press but it was not her say, and she would not bring attention to herself. To do so was to invoke cruelty or wrath. For now Tarren was ignoring her, and that was just fine.

~

The following morning, they docked in Caerdis, the capital city of Gershan, a country of considerable history and culture. It sat on a peninsula that opened to the wider ocean beyond. Of all the harbors, this one was her favorite. Here, Tarren was known as a merchant, not a pirate. It was nothing like Ingerside or Sasfriska, and there were times when Tarren would allow her to accompany him ashore. They had not been here since she had given birth to Colton.

At dinner the night before Tarren had sat across from her tipping his wine goblet.

"You and Colton will accompany me ashore tomorrow." He had ordered.

She had dipped her head, "Yes Captain."

The next morning he dressed her. Not like a trophy. Not like a captive to parade. Like a wife. The dress he laid out was not one that clung or shimmered. Nor was it the color of dirt or ash that he made her wear when he wished her to remember her station. It was simple. Modest. Soft at the sleeves and hem, with a sash the color of sunrise. She blinked at it when she saw it.

"You are the mother of my son. The court will respect this," he said, fingering the linen.

He carried Colton. She trailed half a step behind Tarren. The captain smiled as he walked, speaking to the boy about small, idle things. The shape of the city. The fruit stalls lining the dockside road. He pointed out a carved figurine in a window, and when Colton reached for it, Tarren immediately ducked into the shop to make the purchase. Men and women in the marketplace eyed her strangely, her blond hair stood out among these people. She did not speak. Not because she feared reprisal, but because she did not know how. The mask of submission had grown so tight she was no longer sure she could peel it off.

Around the corner came a man in a red tunic and cream britches. A man, ordinary by every measure, calling out in the street. His clothes were worn but well mended. His voice was not loud, but it pierced the air, cutting through the noise of the market like an arrow straight to the soul.

"Come hear of Yah-Roi," The man called.

Her head came up, that Name.

"He is a God of mercy and Justice." The man went on. "Mercy because He withholds that which we deserve. Justice because His holiness must be satisfied."

She shivered. Mercy was a concept long since forgotten. Justice she knew.

"He paid for justice Himself," the man continued. "To offer it freely to all."

Her mouth went dry, as her heart started to pound.

"He loves you, no matter what you've done." The man's eyes met hers and for a second she could not breathe.

She looked away.

"He has paid so that you do not have to remain in chains.." The man said, still looking at her.

She swallowed as panic started to rise in her chest. She had been seen. She wanted to hide, but her feet were rooted to the spot. Her hands started to shake, and for the first time in years she offered a prayer. *See my son,* she begged. *Set him free. But do not waste Your time with me.*

~

When they returned to the ship, Colton reached for her, and Tarren let him down. The boy toddled over, sleepy eyed.

"Tired, mama." He said rubbing his eyes.

She smiled softly and lifted him into her arms. Carrying him below deck she bathed him with a warm cloth and rocked him on her bed. Singing softly under her breath. It was only after the boy snuggled into her chest, his breath moist on her skin that she realized she had been humming a hymn her mother used to sing to her.

She set the boy in his bed and a covered him with a blanket, pressing his stuffed horse under his arm, only then did she allow herself a moment to reflect on the strange longing still buried in her chest. What would Yah-Roi want to have to do with her, after the life she had lived, after the woman she had become? She shuddered to think it.

She did not let the fear show on her face, not around the boy. But when she reached the privacy of their quarters, she closed the door with trembling hands and leaned her forehead against the cool wood, just breathing.

I am fallen.

It was the only truth she allowed herself. A reminder to keep hope at bay. But the sickness that knotted her belly carried hope of a different kind. *See my son,* she asked again. *Take compassion, not for my sake, for the boy, let us escape.* The word stopped her, that was dangerous. Deadly, *if Tarren discovered* . . . She ran a hand down her skirt. *He would beat me to death.* She allowed herself to finish the thought. Closing her eyes, against the harshness of that reality.

, Colton would be raised by her. Another woman with no memory of pain. Or worse, raised by his father alone. She stared into the mirror now, hands white-knuckled on the vanity. So lost in her thoughts that she suddenly realized she could not even remember which earrings he had told her to wear. Crimson dress. Yes. That had been clear. He always laid it out when he wanted to remind the crew she was his. When he wanted blood and beauty in the same breath. That was the dinner gown. But had he said diamonds? Or rubies? Rubies matched. Diamonds pleased him more.

She touched the rubies first, then hesitated. Tarren would know. He always noticed. The wrong choice would earn her that quiet, seething disappointment. The kind that did not explode in front of the crew, but behind closed doors, leaving bruises she could not cover. She swallowed and reached for the diamonds. She would wear what pleased him. She had to. She needed him in a calm mood tonight.

~

She should have picked the rubies. The moment Tarren's boots hit the deck outside their quarters, she knew. The diamonds caught the candlelight too sharply, his candlelight, and when his eyes locked on them, she felt the weight of it. The wrongness.

She sat at the table in the crimson gown, napkin in her lap, awaiting dinner as she did every evening aboard Tarren's vessel. A tiny pulse in Tarren's temple told her she would pay for the error. Her heart stuttered. Her breath hitched. Tarren caught it. He had barely shut the door behind him, and already the storm was rolling in. Not the one outside the hull, but the one behind his narrowed eyes. "The rubies," he said, low. "I laid out the rubies."

She straightened, shifting her fork. "I... I forgot. I thought you..."

"You thought?" he cut in, his voice quiet enough to chill. "You thought when I already gave instruction?" He stepped closer. "You cannot follow the simplest order. And now you think I should trust you to watch my son?"

Her breath caught. "Captain…"

He bent and whispered in her ear. "Tomorrow you will watch me tend to the boy. You will be silent, and you will learn. I do not tolerate incompetence in any form."

She flinched. "Please. There is a storm rolling in. What if it is not abated before morning?"

Tarren's eyes narrowed. "You dare question my judgment?"

She lowered her gaze. "I am sorry, Captain. I meant no disrespect. Only that he is curious. He gets near the railing, and I fear one day…" Her words died as Tarren's hand wrapped around her throat.

"Do not even dare speak it," he hissed. "Do you think me so trivial I would ever let the boy come to harm?"

She struggled for air, desperate to shake her head. Her toes scrabbled for purchase on the floor. Her vision dimmed.

Then he threw her down onto the table. Food went everywhere. Soiling the dress. Her hair. Dinner.

"You would do well to keep your fears to yourself," he sneered. "You will remember your place, Pet." His hand reached for his belt. "Or it will be the last thing you ever learn."

~

The sun was shining the next morning, but the wind was troublesome. The ship creaked despite being anchored just off Gershan's coast. She pulled herself from Tarren's bed, the pain of the beating she had endured the night before, and the chill of the day, settling deep into her bones. When she checked Colton's crib, the boy was already gone. Her heart thudded. Tarren had made good on his promise. She stifled a sob and sank against the wall.

She finally returned to Tarren's cabin, fingers shaking as she dressed. She could hear Colton above her on the bridge, chattering to his father, pushing blocks across the deck. She chose a knitting project she had begun for Colton's birthday. A stuffed horse. She sat wearily and began to work, aching for the boy with every stitch.

The wind was fickle as the day wore on. Twice she was thrown against the bulkhead, in other moments the sea as calm. The sound of toys had ceased, and she wondered if Tarren would come put the boy to bed for a mid-day sleep. Then she heard Tarren's boots pounding above her. A door slammed as another wave pitched the vessel hard to port.

Shouts followed. Then Tarren's voice rose above them all. Panicked. She froze. Dread surged in her chest. Tarren never panicked. Boots thundered. Rope scraped. Her chest constricted until she could hardly breathe. Then silence far too long. Footsteps returned. Tarren's.

The door opened. He stood in the frame, seawater streaming from his hair and cloak, chest heaving. And in his arms was Colton. She made a sound that did not belong to her. A scream or a sob. She could not tell. Soaked. Limp. Much too small. Much too still.

She stumbled forward, hands reaching. "No."

Tarren did not move. His face was not angry. Not cruel. Not triumphant. It was disbelief. Fear.

Before she could think what this would mean for her, she tore the boy from his arms. She sank to the floor, cradling Colton's body, rocking him as if she could will warmth back into him.

"No. No. No, no, no." It took her a moment to realize she was speaking.

She did not look at Tarren. She did not have to. He dropped to his knees beside them, breath still ragged. She looked up then. Her fury was quiet. Cold.

"You took him from me," she whispered. "You told me I was not fit to protect him. You. And yet look at what has happened. On your watch." Her voice ended in a hiss.

Tarren opened his mouth. Nothing came out.

She curled tighter around her son, rocking slowly. "You did not deserve his love."

~

Bethan did not cry. There was no space for it. No time. She stripped off her wet shift, dragged the blanket from the cot, and pulled Colton to her chest, skin to skin, her own body trembling from the cold. She did not care. She wrapped them both in the blanket and curled around him in her bed. Lending warmth where there was none.

She whispered his name. Over and over. "Colton. My love. My brave boy."

Nothing.

She held him tighter. Because you do not call something dead until it is warm and dead. So she waited. She prayed. She begged. But he did not stir.

He did not twitch, or hiccup, or cry. His small body remained still. Too still. And slowly, warmth crept back into him. Not the warmth of life, but the hollow warmth of something that would never open its eyes again.

Bethan's breath caught in her throat. Her hand shook against his weight. And she knew. He was gone.

The world narrowed. Sound dulled. Even her sob came out soundless and dry. She cradled him anyway. Rocked him anyway. Kissed his curls and held his fingers in hers, willing the miracle that did not come.

Chapter 16

She wrapped him in the black wool herself. The finest on the ship. The one she had been saving to line his winter coat. The one he would never wear now. She tucked it around his small frame carefully, making sure his feet were covered, as if the cold might still reach him under the waves.

Then came the horse. The lopsided stuffed one she had stitched from old sailcloth and yarn, back when he was barely crawling. He had chewed the ear nearly clean off. The eye was gone. But it had never left his side. She placed it in his hands and pressed his fingers around it, firm, like she was telling him to hold tight. She stared down at the face that looked like him and now did not. Her breath caught in a shudder.

She stood and walked. Not fast. Not dramatic. Just steady steps away from the table, away from the small, silent form she had carried and fed and rocked for so long. She did not look back. She could not. She willed one foot in front of the other. If she stopped, she would never make it out the door.

Behind her, Tarren said nothing for a long time. Then she heard him move. The rustle of fabric. The shift of his boots. The faint clink of a belt buckle.

And then his voice. Low. Unsteady. "If you had just…" A pause. "It is not…" Another pause. "The earrings."

Bethan kept walking. She did not care what excuses he made, whether they were for her or for himself. He could mumble and justify and rot in the madness of it. It did not matter. None of it mattered anymore. He had taken her son. Her only reason to keep living.

She tried. Yah-Roi help her, she tried. As Colton's body slid beneath the waves, wrapped in a shroud weighted with stones. The black wool showing through the wet cloth. She did not think. She ran. Nothing else existed, just the sea and the cold and the pull in her chest that said *follow him.*

She made it to the rail. Almost. But then his hand was in her hair. Not rough, not yanking, no, worse than that. Firm. Controlled. He knew exactly how much pressure to use to keep her from slipping away. Her body slammed against his chest, her feet still kicking, hands clawing for purchase; on the railing, on his face, on anything.

She bit him. He did not flinch. She screamed, the sound ragged and wild, but he did not let go. Instead, his other arm wrapped around her waist, crushing her against him. Her face was pressed to his shoulder, and she could not see the ocean anymore, could not see *him.*

"You do not get to leave me too, Pet." He whispered in her ear. His voice was not cruel, just sure.

She tried to fight it. To see where Colton had disappeared beneath the waves. Tarren just crushed her harder to him.

~

He took her back to his quarters, refusing to leave her. She moved to the window while he kept watch. She stared at the distant shoreline of Gershan. They had pulled farther out to sea because of rumors of a skirmish between Gershan and Talsia, but they remained close enough that she could still make out the golden-hued land.

The sky was much too blue. The sun too bright. The breeze too warm. Her son was dead. Because her master had been careless. She had never hated him more. Not when he silenced her. Not when he ravished her. Not when he struck her.

He had stopped her then. He was stopping her now. And she hated him. So the day was too bright, and Tarren too close. She shifted on the seat and thought of her prayers. The ones she had whispered on Colton's behalf.

The child was well beyond Tarren's reach. And hers too. *Is this punishment?* she wondered. Only the cries of the gulls answered.

~

Tarren drank steadily when their dinner arrived. He said nothing. She ate less. She waited for him to dismiss her. Instead, he let her sit. He kept pouring whiskey older than himself into his glass as if it were water. When the bottle ran dry, he set it aside and fixed his gaze on her.

"You will bear me another," he said. "And he will be stronger."

She felt it then. The surge. White hot and visceral. Her vision blurred. Before she could think, she grabbed the knife from the table and lunged.

"How dare you!" she screamed. The blade missed his eye by the width of a finger. "You just laid him to rest. You just threw his body to the sea, and you are already ready to replace him. You vile, vicious man."

Tarren's eyes widened in shock. Had she been trained, he would have been dead. He was drunk and his movement was slow. But not slow enough. His hand caught her wrist in an iron grip. Pain shot up her arm, sharp enough she thought the bones might splinter. His other hand came up, open. The ring on his finger struck the bridge of her nose with a sickening crack.

He said nothing as she dropped to the floor. He simply loomed over her, breathing hard. She tried to clear her head, but her ears rang and her vision pulsed in and out of focus.

"I know what you are doing, Pet," he said at last.

Blood slid warm over her lip.

"You are baiting me. Trying to make me kill you. It will not work." He finished.

He crouched slightly, forcing her to look up at him.

"You are mine. Say it." She clenched her jaw against the trained answer rising in her throat.

Tarren regarded her darkly. "Very well," he said. "It seems a reminder is in order."

~

Tarren did not speak when he lifted her from the floor. His hands were steady. His jaw was locked. There was no gentleness, only purpose. His grip did not bruise, but it held no comfort either. It was not care. It was control. She stared past his shoulder.

He laid her on his bed like something to be used and returned, and she felt the old panic rise. But she tightened her jaw and looked away. Her defiance only seemed to make him bolder. He undid her dress with detached efficiency, the silence stretching thin and taut between them. His eyes never left her face, watching for some flinch of resistance, some flicker of rebellion. She gave him nothing. Not anymore. Not ever again.

"You belong to me," he said, voice low and empty of emotion.

A statement. A verdict. She turned her face to the wall.

He took what he wanted. No kisses. No tenderness. Just possession. Final. Absolute. She went limp, a shell dressed in skin. He was a storm, cold and unstoppable, uninvited. She did not cry.

Not even when it ended and he collapsed beside her, dragging her close as if they belonged together. His arm draped over her waist. His breath burned against her neck. She lay still beneath him.

"Good girl," he murmured, more to himself than to her.

It was not praise. It was confirmation. Ownership.

She closed her eyes. Her mouth held the bitter taste of surrender. A silent scream lodged in her throat, echoing in the place where her soul used to be. Tarren fell into a stupor afterward. The ship rocked in the wind of a spring storm.

She left the bed. Not furtive. Done. She climbed the steps to the deck and walked with purpose to the prow. The wailing woman carved there looked ghastly in a flash of lightning. She would join Colton. She stepped onto the railing.

Heard someone call, "My lady."

The ship pitched. Lightning split the sky. And water closed over her head.

Act 3

Chapter 17

It was quieter under water. Not peaceful. Just muted. She sank. Closed her eyes. The sea pressed in. Her lungs burned. Instinct surged, violent, and unwelcome. Her body convulsed and she kicked, her body screaming for air.

Her head broke the surface. Rain slashed her face. Tarren's ship loomed behind her. Beyond it, faint through the storm, the scattered lights of Gershan. She dragged in air, choking on salt. A wave struck and rolled her under again.

This time something scraped across her palm, rough, fibrous, taut. Her fingers closed around it. The rope jerked hard in her grip, but she managed to hang on.

Shouting cut through the storm. Her head surfaced. Voices from a fishing trawler in front of her. Hands seized her tunic. Her arms. Her hair. She did not fight. She was hauled over the side of another vessel and struck wood hard enough to rattle her teeth. More rain hit her face.

Gershani words washed over her. Urgent. Not cruel. An older man bent over her, water streaming from his beard. He stared as if she were something hauled from legend.

"Dohita," he said. "Daughter of the sea."

Darkness folded in.

~

She woke in a bed that did not move. No pitch. No groan of timber. No salt in the air. An older woman sat nearby, fingers sliding over wooden beads, whispering in Gershani. When she saw open eyes, her face broke into light.

"Grazi, Deo." She whispered.

The woman pressed a hand to her forehead. "Dohita Alana." Then she said something in Gershani before she touched her own chest. "Abbya."

She blinked. *Alana?* The name settled over her like borrowed cloth. It was not the right name, but she scarcely remembered any name other than Pet.

Bells rang somewhere inland. Hooves struck cobbled stone below the window. The air carried citrus blossom and roasting meat. She glanced at the door. Abbya reached toward her and stopped when she flinched.

The woman's voice softened, low and steady. She did not look away. Abbya withdrew her hand. A phrase slipped free.

The woman whispered. In a tone full of sympathy.

Alana turned her face to the wall

~

Alana waited until the woman left. She swung her legs over the bed and tried to stand. She shifted, steadying herself on the bedpost. The nightgown she wore slipped off one shoulder.

A clay jar dropped.

"Deo me!" a young girl in a servant's dress exclaimed.

Alana immediately sat and pulled the nightgown back up over the scars that covered her shoulder, letting her hair fall forward to hide her face.

Abbya must have heard the commotion because she came in next, holding a pitcher and towel. She scolded the servant in Gershani. The maid crossed herself, then scurried off. Abbya clicked her tongue.

The woman called Abbya, peered at Alana and she whispered soothing words in her tongue. Then gesturing to Alana, she asked a question.

Alana glanced up at the woman. Who made a motion of scrubbing with her hands. *Wash?* She thought about it, then slowly nodded. She supposed she would like a bath. Abbya handed her the towel and offered her arm to steady Alana down the tiled hall to the washroom. Copper pipes ran up and down the walls, and warm water steamed from the ceramic tub.

Alana nearly stopped. *I have not seen such luxury since. . .* she did not allow herself to finish that thought.

Abbya left her, and Alana shed her gown and stepped into the water, gasping. It was scented with something citrus, and the warmth soothed her aching muscles. A bath. The steam rising from the pipes caught her eye, and she let herself reach for it, running her fingers through it where it met the sunlight. She closed her eyes and let herself soak for just a minute. Then she scrubbed, dried, and dressed.

When she appeared in the hall, Abbya was returning from her room with fresh sheets.

The older woman asked another question, her voice full of curiosity. Alana blinked and hesitated, taking a half step back, wondering if she had offended in some way. Then she nodded slowly. Abbya frowned, then smoothed her expression. Then she waved a hand and laughed softly as if it was no matter.

Alana tilted her head, then nodded again before slipping into her room.

~

Alana watched the road beneath her window. Carts moved through the fading light. Ships cut dark shapes against the sea. She did not look at them long. A shuffle at the doorway.

A bearded man stood there with two steaming cups. It took her a moment to place him. Then she remembered, this man had pulled her from the sea.

"Wesaly." He said offering a cup.

She took it and sipped. Orange and spice burned her tongue.

She nodded. "Graci."

His beard bobbed as he inclined his chin pointing to himself, speaking in Gershani. She caught the words, 'Babba,' and 'courtyard.' He offered his arm.

She blinked, slowly taking it, her fear of offending was greater than her desire to remain untouched.   He did not tighten his grip. That surprised her.

The courtyard walls were high and white, palms cresting their edges. The last of the sun slid behind them. They sat. Fireworks cracked from the direction of the palace. Babba spoke, animated. She caught only fragments. Prince. Victory.

The meal was warm and plentiful. They piled her plate and she ate until she thought she would burst. Finally, they ceased giving her food.   They asked questions. She nodded. Listened. She tried Q'inosian, Tarren's language.   Blank stares. She tried Kuvalian. The words felt rusted.

Babba's eyes lit. "Ah, Kuvale. Se?"

She nodded. Babba, nodded once, short and firm. Using a string of words in Gershani, and she hardly caught any of them, but the older man seemed pleased with himself.

She watched the brazier flames. Listened to bells beyond the wall. A six-stringed gita hummed somewhere nearby. Abbya reached forward and pointed at her,

"Dohita" she said again, Babba smiled and repeated the word. She studied the kind faces of this couple who had taken her in. *I will learn their tongue.* She decided. *It is the least I can do.*

~

The next morning, Alana was sitting in the window seat of the front room, watching the sun cast shadows as it moved across the sky. The sound of Abbya's slippers on the tile had her tensing.

"Ah, Dohita." The woman continued speaking in rapid Gershani, and Alana lost the thread. The intent was clear, though. Abbya pressed a trowel into her hand and beckoned her to follow to the courtyard.

Alana came willingly enough. Abbya dropped to her knees, pointing to plants and speaking their names. Alana worked beside her, letting the pungent aroma of herbs, some familiar and some not, fill her nostrils. A plant she recognized as Vasi, Abbya called Baselle. Another, with green woody vines and red fruit, Alana called Domdo, and Abbya called Doma.

They exchanged words with halting effort later into the afternoon.

Babba did not return until very late, but he knocked on Alana's door well after dark. She peeked out, and he held out a book. She blinked, her breath hitching, because the title was not Gershani. It was Kuvalian. She reached for it with suddenly trembling hands, hesitating only once before nearly snatching it from him.

"Graci," she gasped.

He smiled, wide and bright, almost reaching for her hair before she stiffened. His smile faltered, but then he looked into her eyes and his own softened.

"Enjoy, Dohita." He said gently.

She dipped her head and tucked the book against her bosom.

"Goodnight, Babba." She said politely.

He nodded and walked back down the hall.

She closed the door behind her and sat on the edge of the bed. Opened the book. The script curved in shapes she had not seen in years. Her breath left her slowly. She traced one word with her finger. A drop struck her knuckles. She blinked at it. Another followed. She turned the page. Losing herself in a book her papa used to read to her late into the night.

~

Alana blinked as the sound of Babba preparing to leave for work reached her ears. She finally closed the book. The candle had burned down to a nub, and her vision blurred for a moment. She went in search of Babba to return it and found him in the courtyard. Babba took the book from her hands.

"Another?" He asked

She ducked her head, but her shy smile gave her away.

Babba chuckled. "Come, Dohita. You will like what I have to show you."

Alana donned a blue scarf over her blond curls and followed closely behind him. The street was just beginning to stir as the sky lightened toward dawn. Donkeys and oxen passed, pulling narrow carts, their owners calling to one another. She glanced furtively around her, feeling out of place among the red-roofed homes.

The closer they drew to the palace, the more traffic met them, until they stepped onto a wide avenue leading to the gate. Guards stood watch but did not stop them as Babba waved and made his way into the palace courtyard. Alana heard the shouts of hawkers. The smell of spiced beef filled the air. Bright fabrics and exotic goods caught her eye.

She moved closer to Babba, weaving through the throng, her heart beating rapidly. They stepped into a white building with an arched roof, and the cool air of the sanctuary enveloped her. Her eyes adjusted to the dim light, and she stopped in the aisle. Shelves lined the walls from floor to ceiling, filled with books of every shape, size, and color.

"Bibliotory," Babba explained.

Alana reached out to trace the gold filigree on a spine, jerking her finger back at the last second. Babba gently removed the book from its place and held it out to her. She searched his eyes, and he nodded permission. She reached again. This time, she did not hesitate.

~

Alana opened the book. Thin pages. Dense script. Her finger caught on a familiar shape. The name. She froze. For a breath, she nearly closed the cover.

"Yah-Roi."

The word left her quietly.

Babba's face brightened. "Yah-Roi. Deo."

She echoed the Gershani word. He motioned toward a table, then pointed upward and held up seven fingers. She lowered her head and sat.

When she opened the book again, a shadow fell across the page. A man in a red tunic placed a second volume beside her, the same text in Kuvalian. She glanced at him; it was not the man preaching in the street. She looked around. All the helpers in the bibliotory wore the same tunic.

"Graci," she said softly.

He nodded once. He inclined his head and stepped away. Babba squeezed her hand lightly before leaving her alone with both volumes

Chapter 18

Alana used the book to compare languages, much was different, but much was the same. She did not see the shadows of morning slide into golden afternoon. Until the man in red returned to light a lamp over her head.

She startled and he spoke gently in Gershani. She swallowed and let her eyes return to the text. The sound of the bells in the tower rang seven and moments later Babba appeared.

"Dohita, much reading, yes?" He asked gently.

"Se." She answered.

Babba seemed pleased she used his tongue. She left the books on the table and the man in red collected them while she followed Babba out. Pulling her scarf tighter. They were quietly walking the streets, windows shuttering. The sounds of families gathering, laughing, playing gitas and hand organs filled the air.

When they entered the house Abbya was waiting. She reached her hands for Alana and guided her to a settee.

"Tell me." Abbya said warmly.

Alana stumbled over the words but used as many Gershani ones as she could remember. Neither of them corrected her pronunciation, just used it back to her in conversation. Delighted she was trying.

They ate a simple meal and after, Alana yawned wide enough her jaw popped. Abbya smiled gently and shooed her to bed. Alana slipped between the covers; The sea sounded beyond the walls. She shut her eyes. Colton's small fingers curled in her memory. The preacher's voice echoed faintly in the back of her mind.

Yah-Roi. Her throat tightened. She had asked for freedom, *I am free*, she pressed her face deeper into the pillow. *The cost was my son.*

~

Alana returned to the bibliotory at dawn. A different man in red placed the books before her. She turned to the marked page.

Moshe. *"If you turn from Me..."*

Her finger traced the line that followed.

"...cursed shall you be."

She read until midday. Babba appeared sooner than she expected.

"Come, Dohita. Abbya waits." He said.

She closed the book carefully and followed him into the sun. White stone terraces held the garden in careful tiers. Abbya waved from below.

"We eat. Rest. Wait for shade," Abbya said, pressing her hand.

Alana worked beside her, repeating plant names under her breath. But the word lingered. Cursed. *It fits.* She thought patting the dirt around the roots. *I turned away.*

The guards grew used to seeing Alana arrive with Abbya or Babba. The bookkeepers smiled when she appeared, setting the scriptures out for her. The palace became familiar, and days folded into weeks. Then a moon cycle, and then three. Gershani came easier. She understood more than she could speak.

One night they sat at the evening meal after returning from the palace. Babba leaned back and belched, patting his rotund stomach before turning to Alana.

"There is a need for a new maid in the scullery. It is good, strong work. Would you like that?" He asked.

She glanced at Abbya, but the woman only watched her face and tilted her head.

Alana swallowed.

"I am a burden on you," she said, her voice barely above a

whisper.

Babba's brow furrowed, and he immediately raised his hands, palms out.

"No, Dohita. I am only thinking of a job. A place." He admonished.

Alana studied him. Thinking.

"I like the gardens," she admitted.

Babba nodded. "The gardens would not give you position."

Alana frowned. "You want me to have position."

Babba opened his mouth to answer, and Abbya cleared her throat.

"No, Dohita. We want you to be happy." The older woman reassured her.

Alana's eyebrow twitched.

"I am content," she finally said, raising her chin.

Abbya exchanged a glance with Babba and nodded, placing a hand over Alana's.

"Then we are happy for you." Abbya said.

Babba nodded, and nothing more was said.

~

Alana settled into a routine. Mornings with Abbya in the gardens. After the midday meal, Alana would retire to the bibliotory until Babba came to collect her after the court had taken their meals. Her evenings stretched late. Her mornings came early. Callouses developed on her hands, and the swirl of Gershani became more and more familiar. Her dreams settled. But she still cried at night for her son. She never went anywhere without Babba or Abbya.

Until one morning, Abbya had her working in the garden on a row of bushy purple herbs. Alana looked up, startled, when she realized she was alone. Her heart jumped. Her eyes scanned the yard. She set the trowel down slowly, ignoring the sudden trembling in her hands.

"Abbya," she called. Her voice scraped the back of her throat.

The older woman appeared around the corner, carrying a flat tray full of pepper sprouts. Alana felt her shoulders ease. Abbya did not seem to notice. Instead, she handed her the first clay pot holding a seedling, and Alana resumed her work. Abbya worked alongside her in silence, then finally peered at her.

"You can go to the market. Se?" Abbya said off handedly.

Alana blinked. "For what?"

Abbya smiled. "I want goat cheese with our meal."

Alana dipped her head. "You think I can go alone?"

Abbya searched her eyes. "I think you need to know you can."

~

Alana gathered her scarf and a basket. Abbya wanted cheese. She would choose cheese. Alana stepped out of the building that kept the royal gardens separated from the main palace bazaar. Smoke rose from a grill where cuts of lamb were roasting. The scent of nuts and fruit, spices and cooking meat mingled with the shouts of hawkers and the squawk of parrots.

Alana kept to the shadows, pulling her scarf tighter, letting her face get lost in the folds of fabric. She made her way to the stand where Babba purchased their dairy. A slight young woman with a hawk nose stood weighing a heavy white cheese while her daughter, Suara, collected coins from a young man in a striped tunic and green-gray breeches.

The man turned abruptly, running into Alana. He reached out, snagging her scarf, and the entire length of fabric pulled back, revealing the blond hair beneath. He blinked. Suara audibly gasped.

"Yellow hair. White like the sun." The little girl's voice was filled with awe.

Alana immediately tried to rearrange the garment.

The man smiled down at her, not leering, but politely interested.

"You are new to Caerdis." He observed.

Alana felt her cheeks flush. "I am new," she confirmed. Her voice was tight.

The man's grin faded some. "You work here? In the palace?"

Alana pulled her scarf back over her hair. "I do."

He laughed, as if this delighted him. "Tell me, lovely maiden, where in the palace do you work?"

Alana found his manners forward and unsettling. He was not leering, but the questions made her want to run back to the safety of Abbya.

"The gardens," she finally managed.

He nodded as if the answer pleased him. "That is wonderful. I should have known, with the dirt under your nails."

Alana stared. The comment had not been spoken rudely, but somehow it felt that way. She sniffed. Perhaps he had not meant it to sound derogatory.

"Yes, gardening is not a chore for those who wish to have perfect skin." She said with a touch of edge to her tone.

He laughed again. "I meant nothing by it. It suits you."

Alana frowned. "Excuse me. I must see to Suara about some cheese."

He stepped aside amiably enough. "Certainly. I am Phillipe, by the way."

Alana looked up at him, taking in the young, sincere face, the flippant attitude, the merchant's clothing.

"I am called Alana," she said.

He nodded. "Alana it is. I do so hope to see you again, Alana."

She dipped her head as he stepped into the crowd, and she hoped he would forget all about her.

She had turned to Suara when Phillipe turned back.

"Perhaps I should tell you, rumors around the docks are swirling about a green-eyed ship captain seeking a maid with blond hair." He said, his voice lowered conspiratorially.

She looked up at him startled, *Tarren's eyes were brown.*

She frowned. "I am sure it is not me, I do not know any ship captain with green eyes. If you'll excuse me."

She turned back to Suara, and Phillipe bowed slightly. "As I said, it is only a rumor. It was nice to meet you Alana. Until we meet again."

And then he was gone and Alana smiled at Suara. Only glancing back once to see that Phillipe had already disappeared into the crowd.

Chapter 19

Alana swung her basket in a short arc, walking from the gardens to the kitchens. The palace teemed with servants and soldiers. Victory banners snapped from the towers. Word of the battle at Gilbrath had reached Caerdis at dawn. Tonight the court would honor the return of their warriors and the Crown Prince, whose actions were reported to have turned the tide.

Alana paid the crowd no mind. She would retire to the bibliotory as always. Her scarf slipped. A soldier stared. She rushed past him and pulled it tighter. After two solar cycles of living near the palace most of the servants and merchants were used to her hair. She was also used to being singled out for her looks, from those who were not so familiar.

The wafting scent of baking bread and fish filled her nostrils as she entered the warm kitchen. Babba was in a corner, waving a knife and shouting orders, his apron already stained from labor despite the early hour. He beamed when he caught sight of her.

"Ah, Dohita, my Alana. You bring only the best produce for my kitchen, se?" The older man beamed.

She smiled softly and blushed. "Se. Domas for gorru, and Abbya sent musker and chevya for the soup."

Babba clutched his belly and laughed. "You see what wonderful fortune Yah-Roi gave me in such a fine dohita."

Alana dipped her head and blushed, but his praise did not stop the smile from forming on her lips.

Suzanna, a young baker, punched the yeasty, salted dough and kept kneading. Her eyes twinkled.

"Phillipe was in here. He wanted to know if you are ready to answer his proposal." Suzanna teased.

Alana flushed. "He knows the answer."

Suzanna laughed. "Perhaps. But I think he is hoping you will change your mind."

Alana wrinkled her nose. "He should know that if I said yes, his fortunes would change. Too many would judge him for taking a foreign wife."

Suzanna shrugged. "Perhaps. Or perhaps your Babba keeps filling your head with ideas that—"

"Par." Babba clapped his hands. "We do not have time to speculate. The first course is served in five hours, and I will not have this kitchen lose its reputation while you discuss my Alana's choices." His voice was firm.

Suzanna shot a glance at Alana, who ignored her. Alana mouthed a thank you to the man who loved her like his own and turned to walk back out the heavy oak door to the gardens beyond.

Alana returned to the garden beside Abbya when the trumpets on the ramparts began to sound. Both women paused in their discussion of rose hips for the night's tea and turned to watch the road leading to the palace. A cohort of men on horseback rode in formation across the causeway. The leader sat astride a raven stallion with a white blaze down its forelock. The sun glinted off silver armor and helmets and caught the lead horses' coat turning it nearly blue in sheen.

The man on the dark horse lifted his arm in greeting to a group of citizens who shouted well wishes.

"That is him," Abbya said softly. "He used to walk in these gardens as a boy." Her voice was wistful.

Alana blinked. "You know him?"

Abbya shrugged. "Only as a servant. The queen insisted he treat us kindly."

"And did he?" Alana asked, curious.

Abbya smiled. "He did. He asked me about grapes once. Paid

close attention. Even pruned correctly."

Alana lifted an eyebrow. "You must have been impressed if you let him near your vines."

Abbya huffed. "He is the Crown Prince. I could not tell him no."

Alana smiled but let her eyes drift back to the man who looked more warrior than prince. He removed his helmet. Brown eyes. Steady. Assessing. Alana's breath hitched before she could stop it. She looked away before he could catch her watching, ignoring the flush of heat rising in her neck.

~

At the end of the day Alana slipped into the cool air of the bibliotory, as the door closed, shutting out the noise of revelry from the main hall. The smell of books and parchment met her nose, and she let herself breathe deeply. She found her favorite corner and lowered herself into the chair by the lamp with a grateful sigh. She reached for the book in the drawer where she had placed it last, with Pedro Carmine's permission.

"You read here often enough, Alana. It might as well stay." The keeper had told her.

She had thanked him and now she opened the book, pulling a pad of parchment and a charcoal pencil from her skirt pocket. Letting her scarf slip down her hair. She opened the book and began to read.

"Yah-Roi commanded the earth and the sea to give up its dead, and he judged them both great," she hesitated then read the last line, "great and small." She whispered the words.

Her charcoal moved without her willing it. She printed a single name beneath the verse. *Colton.* The lamp burned down beside her, and the bells in the tower tolled, late, then early.

She had just leaned in closer for a look at a word she did not quite recognize when she heard the scrape of a boot on tile. She stilled. Her heart thudding, then her hands moved for the scarf without thought.

"Please, forgive me, I did not mean to startle you." Alana turned, her breath catching in her throat, no helmet or armor, but the same brown eyes now held hers. Her heart lurched.

"Your highness, I-" Alana started to stand, to leave.

He held up a hand. "Please, stay, it is I who interrupted you, I had seen a light and came to check."

Alana stared down at the book and then pressed her hand against the parchment. . Not sure at all what to say.

She did not have to wait long.

"You read prophecy?" He asked softly.

She tilted her head. "I read justice."

He raised an eyebrow. "A heavy topic." He was quiet for a moment. "You speak the language of my people well."

She raised her chin. "I have lived here two sun cycles."

The prince regarded her. "Not many stay, my people are not always welcoming of outsiders."

She flushed at her boldness. "I have found kindness among your people."

He got quiet at that, thinking, before finally nodding. "That makes my heart glad."

She shifted, suddenly and painfully aware they were alone.

"I must be going," she said nearly breathlessly.

Gathering her pencil and parchment, before placing the book back in in the drawer. He did not stop her; he shifted but the passage was narrow. She brushed by him before attempting a curtsy.

"Good evening, Highness." She bade him before pulling up her scarf and turning to slip out of the door.

~

The scent of oranges mingled with smoke from the fireworks mingled in the air as Alana stepped into the night. Her heart continued to rush in her ears. The prince had spoken to her. Her steps hastened as she made her way through the narrow streets to Babba and Abbya's house.

He had smelled of cedar and the sea. *Par*, she would not let herself dwell on that. She slowed at the top of the hill looking down on the sea. Ships anchored in the deeper harbor. The Gershani navy proudly returned from war. The breeze coming off the bay was cool, and salty. Her life here in Caerdis had settled, small and routine, until tonight. He had been kind, apologized in his own bibliotory for intruding on her. Alana shivered, being seen scraped against something old, and something that she had long ago buried.

He did not pry, nor did he shrink.

That one thought now sent her mind racing. The crown prince had seen her, and he had not turned away.

Chapter 20

The hour was late when Alana entered the bibliotory. She settled into the chair facing the door and tightened her scarf this time. She had just settled into the Book when she heard the scrape of a boot on tile. She looked up and met the prince's brown eyes. They sparkled in the lamplight.

"Back at it, I see." His voice was warm, not mocking.

She dipped her head. "Your Highness," she answered in acknowledgment, unsure what else to say.

His lips twitched. "Tristan, please."

She started. "Highness, I am but a maid. That would be highly irregular."

He studied her. "May I sit?"

She blinked. "It is your bibliotory."

He chuckled. "Not mine. It belongs to Caerdis."

She gestured to the empty chair across from her, watching him beneath her lashes. Her heart thudded against her ribs as she tried to return to her reading.

"Last night you said you were reading of justice. Do you seek it?" He leaned forward, hands loose in his lap as if this were dinner conversation.

She thought for a moment, then decided to answer honestly. "Only for myself."

His eyebrows rose. "You have been wronged."

She lowered her head, suddenly interested in a loose thread on her scarf. He waited and did not press.

"I have been wrong," she finally clarified.

His eyes never left her face. "You sound very certain in passing judgment. But how do you know?"

She frowned, searching for the words. "Because Yah-Roi is holy, and I am not."

Tristan shifted. "That is true for us all. You are a follower of Yah, then?"

She swallowed. "I used to be."

Tristan did not take offense. "And now?"

Alana pulled the book closer. "I am but a maid who reads."

"And passes sentence," he added softly.

She stiffened. "That is my business," she snapped.

Tristan's gaze never left her as he stood. "I am sorry to have bothered you, miss—?" He waited.

She turned her shoulder away. "Alana, Highness. I am called Alana."

"Alana." The name rolled off his tongue. Not seductive. Simply spoken. "It is a good name."

She said nothing. When she finally looked up, the only sign of his presence was the lingering scent of cedar. She set the Book aside. She would not finish the passage. His words were louder than the page.

~

"Alana!"

She looked up from where she had been planting Yar-how, its fernlike leaves sharp and green in the heat. Abbya's voice carried an edge of concern.

"Were you calling me?" Alana asked contritely.

Abbya frowned. "Is something troubling you, Dohita? You are slapping the dirt as if it had offended you."

Alana glanced down. Her palm print marked the soil, bold and accusing.

"I am sorry." Her voice thinned.

"You need not apologize to me." Abbya moved closer. "Something troubles you, Se?"

"I am well." Alana insisted. Abbya did not look convinced. "You were late returning last night."

"I read." She answered curtly.

She felt badly for being so short with Abbya. The older woman waited. Alana offered nothing more.

"Then perhaps you should rest early." Abbya suggested.

"Perhaps." Alana shrugged.

"I am here," Abbya said, resting a hand on her arm.

Alana swallowed the heat rising behind her eyes. "I am sorry."

"You are forgiven." The older woman squeezed her arm gently.

Alana nodded and turned away, tightening her scarf as she walked the narrow road toward the house. She had not slept. At the overlook she paused. The docks were alive with sound, the sea restless beneath the morning light. The prince had questioned the sentence she had passed on herself. He did not know. No one in Caerdis knew what she had done, who she had been. And she meant to keep it that way.

~

Alana had finally slept in the heat of the afternoon. She returned to the bibliotory that night and stopped short when she heard Tristan, conversing with Pedro Carmine. Neither man seemed to pay her any heed as she set out her parchment and pencil. She pushed her chair deeper into the shadow and opened to her passage to read.

She was halfway through the 82nd Song when the conversation quieted. She hoped that Tristan would take his leave. He did not. "I am pleased you returned tonight. I wanted to offer an apology if my words have caused offense." He spoke softly. "My mother says curiosity will be my undoing." He began.

Her eyes glanced up, and she sniffed. "The queen is a wise woman."

His lips twitched. "She is however, I hope I have not earned your displeasure."

She shifted in her chair. Not angry, just wary. "And why do you care, Highness?"

"Tristan, "He corrected again gently. She did not repeat the name. "I care because I recognize it." He offered with a slight tilt of his head.

Her back straightened. "Who says I am suffering." His brown eyes searched hers, "No one condemns themselves without cost." His voice was gentle. No pity, just fact. Alana frowned. "My suffering is my own." He nodded. "It need not be."

Alana took a deep breath, willing her heartbeat to slow. "I am content that it is." Tristan tilted his head. "Are you?" Then he amended, "I am sorry then. For a burden shared is a burden lifted." Alana lowered her eyes to the text. "It is my burden to bear," she insisted. "Your burden is your judgment," he clarified.

Her eyes found his. "And if it is?" The edge in her voice carried the challenge. "Then that is tragedy," he answered simply. "It is what it is, Highness." Her tone was wry, and she immediately flushed, aware she had shared more than she meant. His gaze softened. "Can I be of help?" His question was genuine enough.

She frowned. "Not unless you can raise the dead." He nodded sorrowfully. "Oh, that I could." He pointed to the book. "You read of the One who does." Alana huffed. "Yah does raise the dead, but not for me."

Tristan seemed not to take offense at her bitterness. "Why do you think that?" She laughed, sharp and brittle. "When you have buried as many as I have, there is no doubt."

Tristan sat. "It was family?" Her breath was sharp and broken. "Please do not." Her voice was pleading. Tristan raised his hands. "Very well. I am sorry to have tread there."

Alana shook her head. "You apologize much." His lips twisted into a grin. "I told you, my curiosity will be my undoing." She gripped the Book tighter. "Then why ask?" He shook his head. "Because you say your life is tragedy and act like you deserve it, and that bothers me." She blinked. "Why?" "Because you are too young to walk old and alone." He said like the answer was obvious. The answer was simple. The implication was not. She stared at him as if he had grown wings. "Highness, this is—" She swallowed. "Uncomfortable."

"Uncomfortable or irregular?" He stood, as if recognizing her need for distance. "Both," she answered honestly, looking up at him. He nodded. "It is not against the law." She sighed. "It is against custom."

"Custom bends," he said simply. Alana pondered that. "For what purpose?" He did not hasten to answer. Instead, he thought about it.

Finally, he spoke. "Because no one should have to live without one friend." She stiffened. "I have friends, Highness. In the kitchens and gardens, where I belong. Pedro Carmine here in the bibliotory."

"I meant myself, Alana," he said softly. She blinked. The defensive words on her tongue suddenly dying. "You would lower yourself so far?" He shook his head. "I am not lowering myself."

She stared at the flame in the lamp. "I do not know how." He nodded, apparently satisfied. "Then that is a good place to begin." Then he turned. "Goodnight, Alana." He walked out of the bibliotory, leaving her to think, she did not reopen the Book.

~

A day later Alana worked in the garden, the breeze tugging at her shawl. She sank her fingers into the rich, dark earth and breathed in loam and damp. Suzanna cleared her throat behind her. Alana turned. "Babba sent me for the limes. The Queen requested lemet."

Alana nodded and rose, brushing soil from her palms before walking the terraced path toward the trees. Suzanna studied her. "You are thinking loudly today, se?" Alana cast her a look. "I am thinking," she admitted slowly, well aware Suzanna did not always keep what was entrusted to her. Suzanna pouted. "About what?"

"Perhaps I am not yet ready to share." Alana shrugged. Suzanna spun toward her. "Is it Phillipe? Did he ask again for your hand? Will you accept him at last?" Alana reached for a lime, unconcerned with her friend's enthusiasm. "It is not Phillipe. And it is not an offer of marriage." Her tone made it clear the matter was closed. Suzanna caught the limes in a basket. "Oh, come now. You have been so quiet this past week."

Alana looked at her blandly. "I am always quiet."

"Yes. But not like this." Suzanna urged. Alana climbed another rung. "Not like what?"

"Introspective." Suzanna shifted the basket on her hip. "You are quiet and watchful. Today I had to make noise to gain an audience." Alana huffed. "Audience. Such a word. I am not a queen." Suzanna laughed. "I only meant you always hear me coming. Yesterday and today, you did not. You are distracted." Alana glanced down at her, reaching for another lime. "Is it a crime to think?"

"Only when you refuse to tell me what has you so intent." Suzanna stomped a foot. Alana stretched for the last lime. The ladder wobbled. She seized a branch to steady herself. The gate creaked open. She did not need to look. but she did. Tristan stepped into the garden and turned down the orchard path. Heat rose to her face. Of all days. Of all places. She was halfway up a tree. If he chose this path, there would be no hiding. She tightened her grip on the bark. *Do not come this way.*

Chapter 21

Alana held her breath, as the sound of Tristan's boots crunched on gravel. He was whistling. Alana watched from her perch, her heart thudding and her mouth went dry. She gripped the ladder harder. And then he stopped, and so did the song. Heat flooded her face and she closed her eyes.

Suzanna turned and gasped. Bobbing a curtsy. "Your Highness."

Tristan's voice came, baritone and polite. "Miss." He looked up and Alana looked down biting her lip. His own lips twitched. "An industrious day." He commented.

Suzanna raised an eyebrow. "The queen requested lemet."

He nodded. "She does love it. I will not keep you. Good day ladies."

He glanced up into the tree and Alana's breath hitched. He nodded at her but said nothing and continued on down the path. When he had walked out of sight she realized her knuckles ached from gripping the ladder, reaching for the last lime, and carefully climbing back down the ladder.

Suzanna raised an eyebrow. "He stopped to talk; he never used to do that before he went to the academy."

Alana blinked. "He hasn't always been friendly?"

Suzanna frowned. "Not unfriendly just never used to see the common folk. Normally he would have walked by and nodded at me, or you. But he stopped."

Alana forced her face to neutral. "Perhaps war taught him to be more open?"

Suzanna peered at her. "Perhaps, or perhaps he saw a maid up a tree, and it caught his fancy." Alana shifted her basket, "Suzanna!" She exclaimed nearly appalled.

Suzanna laughed. "Admit it, you felt the ladder wobble, the prince catching you, like a verse from a ballad."

Alana rolled her eyes. "More like a discordant tune, how mortifying."

Suzanna huffed. "I declare, you are the most difficult to please. Phillipe would woo you with song and flower, and the prince may stop to catch you before you fall to your death, and you call it embarrassing."

Alana peered at her friend as they neared the kitchen door. "Not all attention is kindness."

Her voice was so serious Suzanna was taken aback.

"You are too stodgy Alana, and I say that truly in kindness. Men find you attractive and you shun them, is there no one out there suitable?"

Alana handed her friend the basket of limes. "We were discussing the prince, not me." Her face was closed, clearly finished with the conversation.

Suzanna opened her mouth and then let her shoulders drop. "He stopped Alana, a prince does not stop unless something catches his eyes."

Alana stiffened. "Perhaps it was you."

Suzanna laughed. "Me, he never took his eyes off the tree. Even when I dared speak."

Alana felt her heart jolt, she opened her mouth to deny it, but Suzanna was right.

Suzanna shrugged, "Think what you may, but I do believe he will not forget."

~

Tristan did not appear in the bibliotory that night. Alana opened The Book, read her passage, marked her notes, and when the bell struck the twenty-second hour, slipped it into its bag and back into the drawer. She dimmed the lamp and pushed in her chair. Pedro Carmine nodded to her from his seat at the front table, taking notes with a quill.

She stepped into the dark courtyard glancing up once at the living quarters in the palace. Warm yellow beckoned from the windows and she pulled her shawl around her. To ward off the evening chill. Fog had rolled in off the strait and the moon hung like a pale sliver in the sky. She turned to leave and nearly bumped into a figure coming down the alcove.

"Alana?" Tristan's voice was steady and kind.

Her eyes darted up. "I was just leaving, Highness."

"Tristan," He gently corrected. He studied her face. "It is well after dark; may I escort you home?"

Alana hesitated. "I have walked the streets after dark many nights."

He blinked, "I am sure you have. However, the sailors are quartered near the docks just now and they can get rough."

Alana considered. The fog, the dark, his offer. "Babba would not want me to walk alone."

Tristan smiled gently. "Then allow me to make sure you arrive safely."

He offered his arm and Alana felt her stomach twist.

"If it is the same to you, I would prefer we walk side by side." She said softly.

He lowered his arm at once. If he was disappointed, he did not show it. "As you wish, lady."

Alana started at the title. But said nothing just stepped out of the alcove and began to walk across the courtyard.

"You live with Babba and Abbya, the Chef and Garden keeper?" He asked.

She nodded, forgetting it was too dark to see for a moment. "Se, I am their Dohita."

He glanced at her as they stepped under the portcullis, and out on to the main road. "You came after I left for the navy," he said quietly.

Alana bit her lip, thinking of how much she wished to reveal. "Indeed, I arrived after the battle at Moroko."

Tristan calculated. "Two sun cycles."

She inclined her head. "Se."

He was quiet as they navigated the narrow street down to the house. As they neared her door, she pointed.

"This is it. Graci, for the escort."

He walked her to the stoop. "They are fortunate to have you for a dohita, Alana."

She looked at him sharply. She wanted to ask why but bit her tongue at the last moment.

"Graci," she offered instead, she did not know what else to say.

"Goodnight, Alana," He called.

He turned to walk up the cobbles back to the palace and she lingered for a moment on the doorstep, watching the fog swallow his shadow before entering the house.

~

Alana slept well through the night, that alone was unusual. As the sun rose over Caerdis, she sat in her window seat running a comb through her hair and watching the sea. Ships docked at the wharf. Others farther out in the bay stood in silhouetted contrast against the warmth of the winter sun.

She did not think about the sun or the sea or the ships. She thought about Tristan. The way he had offered escort. The way she had felt conflicted. Not because he had shown attention, but because he had asked nothing of her. She sighed. *Why does he want my friendship? He is a prince; he could have me if he wanted and yet he does not take. Tarren was that way.* She reminded herself. But Tristan had something Tarren did not. Sincere kindness and that was her dilemma, *why show it to me?*

There was no easy answer. She dressed and made her way downstairs. Abbya placed a plate of cheese, bread, and fruit in front of her.

"You came home late," the older woman mentioned. Not scolding, but with a thread of curiosity.

Alana picked up a piece of cheese and chewed slowly before answering. "I was safe."

Abbya smirked. "I am aware.

Alana looked up, heat rushing to her face. "You saw him."

Abbya studied her. "Dohita, I have known that man since he was an infant. He is very loyal."

Alana dipped her head. "I do not understand why. He is a prince and I am a maid. A foreigner."

She stopped herself before adding another silent accusation.

Abbya nodded slowly. "He walks a knife's edge, Dohita. But friendship is not forbidden."

Alana stared at her plate, because she was not sure such a thing could ever be simple.

~

A week passed and Alana did not see Tristan, but she caught herself listening for his boot fall or whistle. Looking toward the alcove when she departed at night. He was a prince, and she felt foolish for looking, especially when she was unsure how she felt about him and his offer of friendship. On the eighth day after he had escorted her home, she entered the bibliotory and there he was, seated at her table, the Book opened in front of him.

She stilled.

He seemed to sense her presence because he looked up and smiled gently. "There you are."

She blinked. He looked genuinely pleased. She moved then, stiffly, toward the table.

"You have been busy." She filled in the question of his absence with the statement.

He tipped his head. "My duties do not leave me free to spend afternoons in libraries with friends."

She raised an eyebrow.

He amended quickly. "I do not mock your pastime, Lady. I would visit every day if I were able."

She frowned. "Why?"

He returned her look with a grin. "Because we are friends, are we not?"

She sat and folded her hands in her lap. "So you say."

He lifted his hands in surrender. "Humor me."

She pursed her lips, not angry, only wary. "I still do not understand why you desire to stay in my company."

He tilted his head. "Because you are thoughtful. And honest. And far more perceptive than you allow yourself to be." She startled at that. Her gaze flicked to the Book. *He read it? She wondered.*

Her glance and the look on her face must have given it away. He glanced down, then back up at her.

He nodded toward the Book. "I should not have read your markings. However, I could not help but notice you seem to read only the passages regarding judgment and justice and holiness. Do you not?"

She reached for the Book, tentative. "That is indeed taking liberties, even if you are a prince. What I read does not concern you." Her voice was tight and protective.

He lowered his gaze. "Truly, I am sorry that I took your book."

She frowned. "Anyone can read it."

He offered a palm outward. "Yes, but you have marked this one, and I should not have treated it like public property. I was curious, and I let that get the better of me. I do apologize."

She clutched the Book to her chest, his previous words still itching in her mind. "You believe the passages I read affect the way I see myself?"

He studied the wood grain of the table. He took a breath before answering. "I think that you have judged yourself worthy of a life sentence."

Her heart thudded once in her chest.

"If you knew," she began, then stopped.

His head came up. "If I knew what, Alana?"

She swallowed. "If you knew what I was, you would not find me so companionable."

He frowned. "Perhaps. Or perhaps if you knew what I am, you would not judge yourself so harshly."

She studied his face in the lamplight. "I am not pure."

He sat back. "I will not pretend to understand the weight of that. But I will not pretend to stop seeing what I see in you."

Her frown deepened. Curiosity tugged at her.

He answered the question she had not voiced.

"I see a woman who learned the language of a people not her own.

Beloved by two who never had children. And who still follows Yah, even if she believes His grace does not follow her." He explained plainly.

Alana's jaw tightened. Her eyes burned, and she turned away. "This is dangerous territory, Highness."

He studied her face carefully, then said quietly, "Then let me stand with you in it."

She rubbed her thumb over the rough cover of the Book, anchoring herself before answering. "That is the second time you have offered friendship."

He nodded. "And I will continue to offer it until you say yes. Or tell me to leave you alone."

She straightened. "And if I tell you to leave now?" He stood with the fluid grace of a man accustomed to unsteady decks. "Then I will take my leave and never bother you again."

"You are not a bother." The words escaped before she could stop them. She flushed. "I mean, I do not mind your company."

He smiled gently. "Then we are agreed?"

She swallowed, suddenly aware of the boldness of such a choice. "I will be your friend, Highness," she said before she could over think it.

He nodded. "Then I must insist you call me Tristan. Friends do not use titles."

She paused. He waited. And in that waiting, she found the safety to speak. "Very well." She drew a steady breath. "Tristan."

Chapter 22

Alana entered the bibliotory, relishing the cool air of the underground sanctum. The heat of summer had come on in full, and days spent working in the gardens left her wilted by late afternoon. Her eyes searched the rows. Tristan was not here yet. She would check the Book.

In the three moon cycles since she had agreed to be his friend, they had developed a quiet courier system. A blue ribbon meant he would be tied up in court or at the docks. A green one meant later. Pedro Carmine nodded to her. She waved and sat, letting her scarf fall as she pulled the Book from its drawer. Blue.

The navy ribbon lay stark against the white page. Alana sighed, picking up her pen and opening to the passage she had been reading on her own. Ancient prophecies cursing a people for wickedness. She bent over her work, reading and marking. Then she heard Pedro Carmine greet a newcomer. "Good evening, Highness. I did not expect you."

Tristan's answer came deep and warm. "I did not expect myself to be able to come tonight either." Alana's heart fluttered. Her mouth betrayed her before her thoughts caught up. Tristan came around the row of shelves, and she laid a hand protectively on the Book.

"You left the blue ribbon." She accused softly.

Tristan grinned. "Indeed. I was scheduled to take the Constance out for a patrol run. However, Father had me tending courtiers, and the navy sent another vessel."

Alana blinked. "The King is unwell today?"

Tristan's face lost its usual lightness. "He is in chambers."

Alana lowered her head. "I am sorry to hear that."

The illness of the king was a tender subject, both for Tristan and for palace politics. Lately, more of Tristan's deployments had been deferred as the crown adjusted to the king's increasing days locked away.

Tristan sat slowly, his face serious. "As am I. I cannot stay long this evening, but I wanted to try."

She gestured toward the Book. "I am glad you did, but the blue ribbon would have sufficed."

He studied her. "I had hoped it would not inconvenience you."

She sat back, thinking, then nodded. "It is no inconvenience. Although I am sorry for the reason you stay from sea."

Tristan nodded. "Thank you."

He turned his attention to the Book. "What are you reading?"

"Ezek," she answered. Her fingers tightened on the page as she said it.

He tapped a finger lightly on the table. "We were in the Songs."

She flushed. "I wanted to wait for you to continue."

He hummed softly. "I see."

She tilted her head. "Why do we not read one together?" she offered quickly.

"I am not angry if you wish to read Ezek," he said gently.

Her eyes found his. "Okay."

He nodded once. "Okay."

She handed him the Book. He drew the blue ribbon free and folded it once before slipping it into his pocket. Then he began to read. She leaned forward and her scarf fell the rest of the way.

Tristan's voice caught, he cleared his throat and continued. "The Lord is my strength and my song."

Alana closed her eyes. The words settled into the places she kept guarded. Tristan read as though the words had first been written to him. And somehow that soothed her. He fell quiet after the last verse and she opened her eyes. He was watching her as though she had given him something.

She flushed, feeling the heat crawl up her neck. "Thank you for coming to read tonight."

Tristan nodded. "There was nowhere I would rather have been."

And for the second time that night Alana felt an involuntary smile as she dipped her head.

Tristan rose. "I must be going, goodnight, Alana."

She nodded and placed the book in the drawer. Watching him walk to the door and into the night.

~

Tristan finally deployed, a three-week journey rendezvous up the coast to determine garrison readiness. Alana listened to palace gossip in his absence, usually from Suzanna.

"The King wants him to marry," Suzanna said offhandedly one afternoon.

Alana glanced up from the beans she had been weeding. "Marry?"

Suzanna hummed. "Se. The physicians are not pleased with the King's health. There is much pressure from the nobles and court for the prince to decide on a mate."

Alana tucked her hands into her apron. "He must wed before coronation?"

Suzanna shushed her. "Do not speak of the prince's ascension so lightly. It is bad luck."

Alana bit back a retort, finally trusting her fingers to reach for another bean.

"Forgive me. I still do not know all the customs."

Suzanna waved her off. "Listen. We do not speak of a ruler's imminent demise. That is custom. But there are laws that govern the suitability of an heir before being coronated."

Alana frowned. "Such as?"

Suzanna rolled her eyes. "A prince must be betrothed before ascendancy, and she must be a lady of Gershan, in noble standing."

The bean in Alana's hand snapped.

Suzanna reached for another and dropped it into her basket. "No one much cares for the noble standing part, or they did not used to. But the Gershani part, that is important."

Alana continued to harvest beans. "Why?"

Suzanna looked at her, exasperated. "Because he is the prince."

Alana frowned. "He is Gershani, therefore he must marry a Gershani?"

Suzanna's face lit up. "Yes."

"Is the law so fragile it cannot survive a foreign bride?" Alana asked, hoping her voice sounded casual.

The maid frowned. Alana could see she would get nowhere with her friend. She would ask Tristan when the green ribbon returned to the Book.

~

The ribbon was green, Tristan had returned. Alana smiled as her fingers smoothed the page. She pushed a lock of hair behind her ear and chose to focus on the words. It didn't stop her from keeping one ear on the door. Tristan entered as the bells chimed the sixteenth hour. This time her heart did skip a little.

"Good evening, Alana." He greeted as he slipped into his seat.

She smiled, "Good evening, was your mission well?"

His lips twitched. "I carried out my duties if that is what you ask."

She flushed. "I do not mean to press on state secrets."

He studied her face, "How are you?" He asked gently.

She sat back. Her hands gripping the table edge. "I am well."

He grinned. "There is a hesitation there."

She nodded. "There are rumors, you are being pressured to take a wife."

Tristan studied her. "The palace rarely keeps secrets."

She flushed, "Forgive me, it is not my place I simply wanted to hear it from you."

Tristan leaned forward. "Alana, that is what friends do, they check rumors at the source. It is your place."

Alana finally looked up from the table. "So is it true?"

Tristan looked at her, pausing before answering. "It is true, my father is ill and that means-" he paused again..

Alana nodded, "That means the court wants the matter of your ascendancy settled, with room for an heir."

Tristan looked down at his hands then back up at her. "It is the way of my people."

She leaned forward then, "But do you want a wife."

"Yes," he said and this time there was no pause.

"Is there a law prohibiting you from marrying who you will?" she asked.

His jaw tightened. "Yes."

She waited.

"There is a law forbidding my marriage to any foreigner." He admitted.

Her brow furrowed.

He sighed, "It is not a just law."

"Then why does it exist?" She pressed gently.

He sighed. "It was there from a time when bloodlines mattered deeply."

She laid her hand on the Book, "But does not the Book remind us that worship matters more than blood? As a follower of Yah and a man, you should not be bound by alliance or bloodline."

He frowned. "You would bid me marry?"

"As your friend, I would bid you marry whom you chose, not a woman for political gain." She answered carefully. "A law that dictates a covenantal partner seems archaic and cruel."

He leaned in. "A law that protects the realm is not cruel it just is inconvenient."

"A law that protects the realm at the expense of your covenant should be scrutinized." She argued back leaning forward now. "Is the realm so fragile it cannot tolerate a queen from another realm?"

"It is to protect from conflict with another realm." He answered with a rough voice.

She looked at him, "And are you fine with abiding by it?"

He blinked. Swallowed, choosing his answer carefully. "I want to try to change it."

Now it was her turn to still. She dropped her hands to the table. "Why?"

He stared into her eyes, looked away, then answered carefully, "Because you have no realm other than mine."

She felt the air leave her lungs, and her eyes burned.

"You want a wife?" She repeated.

"Yes." He said again with certainty.

"And you would choose—" She could not finish that thought, the idea was absurd.

"Yes." He answered simply.

She shook her head. "Tristan, I am a maid."

"You are Alana. And you are my friend." He answered surety in his voice.

She felt heat rush to her face. But could think of no quick reply.

"You have learned the words of my people, you have learned our laws and customs, you worship my God. I do not care you are not noble; you are Gershani by choice and that is important to me."

He reached then for the book, when his hand brushed hers, he stilled, and she did not pull away. For a moment they simply looked at each other.

The sound of Pedro Carmine clearing his throat filled the sudden silence. "Highness."

Alana jerked her hand back. As the red robed clerk peered at her. "The palace does not keep secrets well." He said echoing her earlier observation.

Tristan pulled away his hand slowly and rose, pushing in his chair.

"I bid you good evening, Lady." He said with a courtly bow. Returning to a princely posture.

Alana did not look up, the heat flooding her face felt hot enough to light a lamp.

"Good night," she whispered through stiff lips.

"Pedro" Tristan said, nodding to the clerk. Who bowed in return, eyed Alana once more and moved back into the shadows.

Tristan walked out of the door. Alana closed her eyes, hearing nothing but the sound of her own pulse in her ears and the circling thought that told her she had forgotten her place.

Alana turned the moment the door closed. She pulled her scarf over her hair, wrapping it tighter than necessary. Her fingers trembled as she gathered her pencil and parchment, thrust them into her satchel, slid the Book into its drawer, and stood. Her hands would not stop shaking. She pushed in her chair and turned.

She nearly collided with Pedro Carmine. She gasped.

"Forgive me," she whispered.

His brow lifted slightly, but there was no anger in his expression. He raised a hand, not harshly, but enough to halt her flight.

"I do not speak lightly, Alana," he said quietly. "You have been faithful to the Book these two sun cycles. You have walked carefully in your friendship with His Highness."

Her throat tightened.

"You must know," he continued, "that if this comes to light, it will cost him."

She swallowed hard and lowered her head. "I never meant to cause him pain."

"I know," Pedro said. "I do not question your intent. I question the court."

That made her look up.

"The prince walks a narrow line," he added. "There are those who wait for him to stumble."

The words settled heavily. She drew in a slow breath.

"I will not forget my place again." She whispered, shame tangling with sorrow in her throat.

Pedro studied her for a long moment. Something flickered in his eyes, not approval, not condemnation. Concern.

"See that you do not," he said at last, stepping aside. "Good night, Alana."

She tugged her scarf tighter and moved past him.

"Good night," she managed, though her voice cracked.

The evening air struck her face, cool and sharp. She did not slow. The narrow streets blurred as she hurried home.

Inside, she bolted the door. Up the stairs. Into her room. She sat heavily on the edge of her bed, fingers fumbling at the scarf. When it fell into her lap, the restraint fell with it. The tears came hard and sudden. Not because Pedro had rebuked her. But because he had confirmed her deepest fear. She was dangerous to the man she loved.

Chapter 23

Alana clipped the rose ends, pressing the bushes toward a second bloom. The breeze tugged at her scarf. She pulled it tighter. Snip. Another branch. She hissed as a thorn bit her finger. A bead of blood welled bright and accusing. She pressed the offended finger into her mouth.

"You are distracted today, Dohita." Abbya's voice drifted from the other side of the hedge. "That is the third time you have pricked yourself."

Alana exhaled through her nose but said nothing.

"I am here to listen," Abbya added softly.

Alana stared at the rosebush. Her grip tightened on the shears until her knuckles ached.

"I have been a fool, Abbya," she said at last, her voice small and edged with bitterness.

Abbya paused her pruning and peered through the hedge, waiting.

Alana swallowed. The words felt heavier than they should. "I have loved someone I cannot have."

Abbya's eyes gentled. "Oh, my sweet Dohita. It is not foolish to love."

"It is for me," Alana insisted.

Abbya resumed clipping, though Alana could tell she had not released the thread of it. Instead, the older woman reached toward a nearby stem and bent a tight bud toward the light.

"Come here," she said. "I want to try something."

Alana blinked, confused but obedient.

Abbya held the bud toward her. Green still. The faintest blush of pink tucked inside. "Make it bloom."

Alana stared at her. "Abbya?"

"Go on." The older woman urged.

Alana looked down at the bud. "If I force it, I will ruin it."

Abbya's eyes sparkled. "Why?"

"Because it is not ready to be seen," Alana said quietly. "If I pry it open, I will damage it. Only Yah-Roi can bring it out in its time."

Abbya tilted her head, studying her.

"Perhaps that is true of love," she said gently. "And perhaps of you as well."

Alana's fingers loosened around the shears. They fell silent at her side.

Abbya reached up and brushed her cheek with soil-roughened fingers. "Trust Yah-Roi to know when it is time, Dohita."

Abbya returned to her pruning, humming under her breath as though nothing weighty had just been said. But Alana stood very still. As if the ground beneath her had shifted.

~

Alana made her way to the bibliotory in the late afternoon. She had nearly stayed away. But a break in routine would stir more whispers than her presence ever could. The air inside was cool as always.

Her heart betrayed her when she saw Tristan already seated at her table She pulled her scarf tighter before taking the seat opposite him.

"Alana." He spoke as if last night had not happened.

"Highness," she replied carefully. Her own voice cooler than usual.

Abbya had been right about the bloom. Carmine had been right about the warning. A flicker crossed Tristan's face, pain quickly mastered. Alana withdrew the Book from its drawer and bent over it as though the page required her full devotion.

"Will you keep the words to yourself?" he asked gently.

She lifted her eyes slowly. His expression held no accusation. Only openness.

"Do you think it wise?" she asked.

He looked away. His jaw tightened, then eased.

"No," he admitted at last. "It is likely not wise."

The words settled between them like a verdict.

She lowered her gaze again. "I am sorry for it," she said quietly. "For I have enjoyed your companionship these months."

He did not answer immediately. Then he rose. "Happy reading, Lady."

The formality struck harder than any reprimand.

She closed her eyes briefly, willing her hands not to tremble against the page. "Goodnight, Highness."

"Goodnight, Alana."

The door closed. The bells chimed the seventeenth hour. A single hot tear fell, darkening the page beside her thumb.

~

Tristan did not return to the bibliotory. Alana grew accustomed once more to the scratch of her pencil on parchment and the steady quiet of the underground room. She did not allow herself to dwell on the absence of ribbon.

Ten days later, Suzanna found her in the garden raking beneath the fika trees. The girl balanced a basket on her hip and delivered palace rumor as faithfully as a town herald. The baker's wife had delivered another son. The Prime Minister of Franka had gifted ten stallions to the royal stables. Alana listened with half an ear, letting the rhythm of the rake steady her thoughts.

"And His Highness is out to sea again," Suzanna finished.

The rake paused. Alana looked up "What did you say?"

Suzanna rolled her eyes. "Honestly, Alana. I said Vizier Morlach sent His Highness on another voyage."

Alana forced the rake forward again. "Do they say why?" she asked, aiming for mild curiosity.

"We have been skirmishing with Morocan for years. Perhaps something has changed."

Suzanna was a reliable source for gossip. Not for policy. It was another reason she missed Tristan.

"Do they know when he will return?" Alana asked hoping it sounded like idle curiosity.

Suzanna stilled and studied her. "Why does that matter?"

Heat crept up Alana's neck. "I am curious."

Suzanna sniffed. "Is that the same curiosity that has you sitting in the bibliotory with him?"

The rake froze entirely this time. Alana stared at the fallen leaves.

"How do you know about that?" she managed, though her voice thinned.

"How could I not?" Suzanna said. "I hear everything in the kitchens. Pedro Norraine was speaking to Bissa. They are courting. He mentioned you had been seen discussing the Book with His Highness."

Alana's stomach tightened.

"Was that all?" she asked carefully.

Suzanna narrowed her eyes. "It was odd. But not unheard of. You have been seen speaking with him before."

The rake slipped in Alana's grip.

"What do they say?" she pressed.

"Only that he seems fond of your company. And that Phillipe has stopped hovering."

Her mouth went dry. "Do you think he has heard something?" she asked breathlessly.

Suzanna shrugged. "He chased you for two years. You told him no each time. Perhaps he has simply tired."

Suzanna resumed talking about something else. Alana did not hear it. The kitchens knew. Which meant the court was not far behind.

~

Alana picked at her food that night. Babba cleared his throat, and she finally looked up across the scarred table lit by candlelight.

"Are you unwell, Dohita?" he asked kindly.

Abbya laid a hand over his. "She is heartsick," she explained gently.

Babba looked at her with concern. "Dohita, is it the rumors?"

Alana looked up then, speaking more sharply than she had intended. "You have heard something?"

Babba hesitated. "I know about your friendship with His Highness, Se."

Alana clenched her fork. "It is not safe for him," she blurted out.

Abbya shared a look with Babba. "You mean the law.

"Yes," she gushed, "I mean the law."

Babba sat back, chewing slowly, thinking before answering. "You would not worry about the law unless you had reason to believe that he desired to marry a foreign woman," he said finally.

Alana turned away, staring at the milk pitcher. "He said he wants me for his wife."

The only sound to be heard was the guttering of the candle for a breath.

"You are worthy of a prince," Babba finally declared.

Alana flushed. "Babba—"

"No, Dohita, let me say it. You are an excellent daughter, a kind friend, a good worker, and a loyal follower of Yah. The prince would be a fool not to see it."

Abbya warned, "Babba."

He held up a hand. "The only thing that matters to me, Dohita, is this: Do you wish to be his wife?"

Alana held her breath, staring into the small flame; a tear streaked her cheek before dripping from her chin. "I do."

Abbya reached for her hand. "Oh, Dohita."

Babba nodded, "He will find a way," he said confidently.

Alana finally looked back at this man who was so like her father. "I do not see it."

He shrugged, "I do not see how a chair may hold me, but I still sit."

Alana frowned. Abbya waved Babba back. "Tristan is a good man; if he says he will find a way, he will not stop until he does."

Alana picked up her fork again. "I have not seen him since—"

The couple exchanged another look.

"He cannot forget someone like you," Babba said, "and if he does he is a—"

"Babba!" Abbya cut him off. "It is ill to speak such."

Babba waved her away. "Not treason, simply truth."

Abbya gave him a warning look coupled with exasperation.

Alana allowed herself a small smile but soon grew serious once more.

"What of his reputation?" she said forcefully.

Babba studied her face. "Do you think he has not counted the cost?"

Alana frowned, unsure of how to answer.

Abbya squeezed her hand. "He has been navigating politics and court a long time. Trust him, Dohita."

Alana finally allowed herself a deep breath, "Trust the bloom."

Abbya smiled. "Se, trust the Gardener."

~

The next morning, Alana was thinning carrot seedlings when the shadow of a woman fell across her hands. She assumed Abbya had circled back from the orchard, but when she looked up, the face was not Abbya's.

Queen Cerwyn stood on the flagstone path, her blue robes trailing. The faint musky scent of rosewater clung to her skin. She watched Alana as if she were observing the slow unfurling of a new species.

Alana rocked back on her heels and bowed her head. Her hands, caked with soil, hovered uselessly above the row. She tried to remember the formal greeting, but the words tangled in her mind.

"You are diligent," the queen said, her voice low and almost kind. "You have a skill for the garden."

"Graci, Majesty," Alana managed. She wiped her palms and then buried them in her apron to hide the trembling.

"Can I help you, Majesty?"

The queen smiled. "Let me work with you for a moment."

Alana blinked but scooted over. The queen sank beside her, seeming unconcerned for her fine robes.

"You are thinning them," she observed about the seedlings.

Alana nodded. "I am making sure the strongest survive."

The queen eyed her, then returned to the soil. She was quiet for several minutes as her own pile of seedlings grew.

"You are not from Gershan," the queen said wryly.

Alana did not flinch. "No, Majesty, I was born in Kuvale."

The queen raised an eyebrow. "An ocean away, yet you speak the language of my people beautifully."

Alana flushed. "Graci."

The queen pulled another carrot. "I am also told you keep our ways and serve our God."

Alana hesitated. "I enjoy reading the scriptures," she said mildly.

The queen's hand stilled for a moment. "You keep His commands; I am told you show kindness to those beneath and above your station."

Alana held her breath for a moment as her movements slowed.

"All are made in His image, Majesty," she finally answered.

The queen hummed. "And your friendship with the Crown Prince, is it just because he is a person?"

Alana swallowed, staring down at her fingernails.

"He has been a good friend; I only wish his best interest," she answered softly.

The queen shifted to look at her. "Do you have opinions on what that best interest would be?"

Alana finally met her gaze. "Majesty, the prince is a dear friend, and I urge him to do what is right for his people."

The queen's mouth twitched. She studied Alana's face for another moment.

"I will relay your message," she said finally.

Alana flinched. "He has spoken to you?" Her words were breathless.
The queen stood slowly, wiping her hands on a rag Alana had been using.
"He has spoken to me, yes," she said carefully. "I urge time and caution."
Alana could scarcely believe her ears; it was not a no—the queen was not forbidding their courtship.
"I would never act in a manner that would cost him," she assured.
The queen paused. "I believe you," she said finally.
The woman turned to go, drawing her train behind her. She had barely reached the garden gate when she turned back.
"Not all Gershani were born here, Alana. Good day."
The gate closed, leaving Alana to the birdsong and the pounding of her heart against her ribs.

Chapter 24

Alana sat in the kitchen scullery, scrubbing the potatoes Babba had requested for dinner. *Tristan will eat these*, she mused to herself, then splashed water harder than she intended, chiding herself for such whimsy.

Someone behind her cleared their throat. Alana turned to find the Queen's lady's maid, Kefira.

Alana straightened, drying her hands on her apron. "Se?"

Kefira raised her chin. "Her Majesty has summoned you to her chambers for tea this afternoon."

Alana swallowed. "What will I wear?"

Kefira perused her tunic. "Perhaps a clean apron. Your dress is acceptable. The Queen does not stand on such formality for tea."

Alana nodded, offering a quick curtsy. "I am honored. I will be there."

Kefira nodded and swept out of the kitchen. Alana tightened her grip on her brush as Suzanna appeared in Kefira's wake.

"What did she want?" Suzanna asked as she picked up a potato.

Alana bit her lip, unsure if she should say. "She was delivering a message."
Suzanna raised an eyebrow. "From whom?"
Alana sighed. "I've been summoned to tea."
Suzanna dropped her brush in the water with a plunk. "With the Queen?"
"Hush," Alana hissed.
Suzanna barely lowered her voice. "Tea? With the Queen?"
Alana sighed. "Se."
Suzanna squealed, and Alana shot her a look.
"I'm sorry," Suzanna said, her excitement not contained at all. "I will fix your hair," she offered as an apology.
Alana eyed her for a moment, then sighed again. "Very well, but you must not tell anyone," she said seriously.
Suzanna raised her wet hand over her heart. "I will not tell a soul."
Alana raised an eyebrow.
"I swear it," Suzanna added vehemently.
Finally, Alana nodded, loosening the scarf as Suzanna began to squeal again before Alana's look cut her off.

~

As the shadows of day lengthened in the palace windows, Kefira came for Alana. Despite the escort, she expected to be stopped; she had never been this deep inside the halls of the Royal Family's home.

Kefira reached a solid blue door inlaid with gold and opened it. "The maid Alana, Majesty."
Queen Cerwyn looked up from her place on a settee in front of a small hearth and smiled kindly, gesturing to Alana.
"Do come in, my dear."

Alana moved into the room and sat, her back ramrod straight.
The Queen leaned forward to pour tea. "Do you take it with sugar?"
Alana shook her head. "No, Majesty."
The Queen smiled. "How very Gershani of you."
Alana took the offered cup and sipped. The Queen added sugar to hers and stirred; the only sounds in the room were the crackling fire and

the clink of her silver spoon in the delicate cup.

"I have been thinking," the Queen said finally.

Alana held her cup and waited.

"In Gershan, many unfortunate souls have found themselves washed up on our shores through the centuries. When such individuals have been taken in by families of the realm, they are legally adopted."

Alana swallowed, unsure what the Queen was alluding to.

"Adoption grants citizenship rights in this country."

The Queen went quiet, and Alana gripped her cup tighter. "Forgive me, Majesty, but I do not understand."

The Queen smiled softly. "Adoption would mean you are recognized as Gershani."

Alana's heart began to pound as implications settled in. "I would no longer be a foreigner?"

The Queen tilted her head, pouring more tea. "Not according to the law."

Alana felt her breath come a little faster as her mind raced. "Tristan would be free to—" She stopped herself, realizing she had referred to him both informally and with hope for what this could mean for her future. "Forgive me; His Highness would have a way to honor the law," she amended.

The Queen studied her for a long moment. "You said you would never act in a way that would bring him harm."

Alana nodded so hard that her cup rattled in its saucer. "Se, Majesty, that is true."

The Queen sipped her tea before setting her cup aside. "You will speak of this to no one, not even the prince. You will return to the garden and practice patience. Can I trust you to do so?"

Alana blinked, eyes wide. "Se, Majesty. I will not tell a soul."

The Queen picked up her cup again. "Tristan tells me you are a woman of discretion. I trust his judgment and what I see with my own eyes."

Alana blushed. "Graci."

The Queen nodded. "Finish your tea; we will speak on this more another time."

Alana tipped her cup, looking at this kindly woman who seemed interested in her case if only for her son's sake. "Graci," Alana said again.

The Queen rose, and Alana did the same, offering a curtsy. "Good day, Majesty."

The Queen nodded, and Alana took her leave, wandering back through the halls to the kitchen. Hope and tension meeting in her mind.

~

Alana was closing the book in the bibliotory when the note fell from the Book.

She watched it spin to the floor then bent to retrieve it.

Her heart thudded as she opened the torn parchment to reveal Tristan's sloping masculine script.

Alana,

By now you will have spoken with my mother. And it is my hope that her plan will come to success. I have been away these weeks at sea and have been unable to attend you in the bibliotory.

I know that you fear for me. But I ask that you allow me the freedom to take my own risk concerning matters of our relationship. I have not been absent lightly, nor has the memory of your lovely face left my mind. The court is most unmoved on the matter of the law, but we do have more allies than you know.

Stay strong, take courage from the Book, and read for me.

Yours,
Tristan.

Alana felt her eyes burn as she glanced around the bibliotory. Only Pedro Carmine and Pedro Alejo were near, bent over a tome from centuries past.

She tucked the letter into her pocket and drew her scarf over her hair.

~

The walk to her home was cool and brisk and Alana looked out at the sea. She let herself stop and turn to look at the palace. Dinner would be finishing. Babba would come home soon, and beyond those warm yellow windows was the man who held both fear and hope for her. She thought of the queen's proposal and the implications. Her hand clutched the letter. She was not noble. She was a maid, she was-. She cut off the thought and stepped firm and sure toward the house.

She turned to finish the walk, entering through the back door. Abbya looked up, stirring a steaming pot on the stove. Her face lit. "Ah Dohita. Come, I have prepared corda."

Alana's mouth watered at the scent of the thick creamy stew made from fish and vegetables.

She hung her scarf on the wall and had just sat down when the door came open and Babba walked in.

He walked to Abbya and pulled her into his arms, kissing her soundly. The woman laughed, getting stew on the back of Babba's tunic from the spoon she still held.

Alana watched them together, smiling, Would Tristan and I-? She cut that thought off too.

She set out the bowls and Babba turned to her, his arm still around Abbya's waist.

"Have you told her?"

Abbya glanced at Alana and shook her head. "She just arrived."

Babba smiled, "It is well. We will sit and eat first."

The stew was warm and filling, and conversation moved easily as they broke bread.

Finally Babba wiped his mouth and pushed back his bowl.

"Dohita, Abbya and I have received a letter from the magistrate of Caerdis,"

Alana's hand gripped her spoon.

"It is an offer of adoption." Abbya spoke up.

Alana said nothing, her throat was too tight. Babba took her silence as permission to continue.

"We have never been able to afford the levies and fees that would come with such, which is why Abbya and I have never officially made you our own. But it appears that a generous patron has paid the way, and we can now move forward if we wish."

Babba seemed to run out of steam then as Abbya laid a cautious hand on his arm.

"What Babba means to say, Dohita, is if you wish, we would very much like to start the process of making you our legal daughter."

Alana stared at the table, her eyes burning.

"You have wanted me that long?"

Babba looked slightly offended. "Dohita, you have been wanted since the moment I pulled you from the sea."

Alana blinked several times, her vision fuzzy.

"Someone paid?"

Abbya smiled. "Se, but you must agree, Dohita. We will not make you ours if that is not your wish."

Alana studied them, this childless couple who had taken her in and made her their own in all but legality.

"Yes." She said, and she meant it. She wanted to be theirs. Even if it never worked with Tristan. She wanted to belong once more to a family in name and title, and she was looking at them.

"Yes," She repeated.

Abbya smiled, Babba clapped and laughed. Both had tears in their eyes. "Oh Dohita, you have made us the happiest parents in the world.

Alana felt her chest tighten and now she could not hold back the tears as they came to hug her. She was loved, she was wanted, she was home.

~

Kefira announced her as she stepped inside the warm room.

Queen Cerwyn sat in a chair near the window where the bright afternoon light fell across her lap. She was working quietly at a piece of needlework. When she saw Alana enter, she looked up and smiled.

"Alana. Do come in."

Alana stepped forward and stopped near the hearth. She clasped her hands in front of her and bowed her head, offering the queen a small curtsy. Then she waited.

Cerwyn watched her for a moment.

"You do not feel you belong here," the queen remarked.

Alana hesitated before lifting her eyes.

"Do look at me, child," Cerwyn said gently.

Alana raised her gaze to meet the queen's.

"You do not feel you belong here," the queen repeated, not unkindly.

Alana paused before answering, searching carefully for the words in the queen's language.

"Majesty… I do not know court well enough to navigate its intricacies," she admitted slowly.

The queen smiled and tilted her head.

"That is actually something I wished to speak with you about this afternoon."

Alana studied her face.

"One of my lady's maids is to be married in a fortnight," Cerwyn continued. "I therefore find myself in need of another to assist Kefira directly. And I believe you are uniquely suited for the position."

Alana did not answer at once. She turned slightly, looking into the fire.

"It is your choice, my dear," the queen said quietly. "I know there have been a great many changes in the last month."

Alana swallowed. She glanced down at her hands, studying her fingernails before lifting her gaze again.

"I am deeply grateful, Majesty, for the opportunity you are giving me." She hesitated. "If I say no—"

The queen raised a hand.

"You are allowed to say no, Alana."

Alana bit her lip, clearly unaccustomed to the idea.

"I… I would need to think on it. Pray over it. I am not yet sure."

The queen nodded.

"I would expect no less. Pray on it. And do let me know. As I said, I will need a new lady's maid in a fortnight."

Alana nodded, but another question lingered.

"What would the position entail?" she asked softly.

Cerwyn smiled.

"Domestic duties. Research. And it would give you a unique opportunity to learn the ins and outs of the court."

Alana understood immediately.

The garden had taught her patience and work.

This would teach her something else entirely.

How to speak to noblemen and women.

How to carry herself among the royal household.

Who in the court might be an ally.

And who must be handled with care.

"It is a diplomatic position?" she asked carefully.

The queen's smile deepened.

"You could say that. It is also a position that would give you experience." She returned to her needlework. "As I said, pray on it. Do not answer me now. Simply think on it."

Alana inclined her head.

"I will, Majesty."

Cerwyn stitched another careful thread into the cloth in her lap.

"I look forward to your answer, Alana."

Alana turned to leave. At the door she paused and looked back.

"Yes, Majesty," she said quietly.

"So do I."

~

Alana set her scarf on the peg.

Abbya was in the sitting room and called out as soon as she heard the door.

"Dohita, you are home early."

Alana glanced at the late afternoon shadows stretching across the floor.

"I did not go to the bibliotory tonight, Abbya."

Abbya appeared in the doorway, wiping her hands on her apron.

"Then something must be happening. The only time you miss the bibliotory is when you are sick." Her voice sharpened with concern. "You are well, are you not?"

Alana nodded.

"I am well in my body, Abbya."

Abbya's eyes narrowed. "Then this is a matter of the heart."

Alana paused and reached for the large copper pot hanging from the ceiling hook.

"I am thinking." She finally admitted.

Abbya folded her arms. "You usually go to the bibliotory when you are thinking. So out with it, Dohita."

Alana smiled faintly. Between Abbya and Babba, Abbya was the one who never tolerated emotional hesitation.

Alana sighed. "The Queen has made me an offer."

"What kind of offer?" Abbya asked, curious rather than suspicious.

"An offer to become one of her lady's maids."

Abbya's eyebrows shot up. "A lady's maid? In the Queen's service?"

Alana nodded. "One of her ladies is to be married in a fortnight. The Queen wishes me to take the position."

Abbya tilted her head thoughtfully. "And how do you feel about that?"

"I am not opposed," Alana admitted. "But I told Her Majesty I would have to think on it."

Abbya nodded approvingly. "That is wise. And Babba? Have you spoken with him?"

Alana shook her head. "He was busy in the kitchens when I left."

Abbya clapped her hands once. "Then we will make dinner, and when Babba comes home we will speak with him."

Alana nodded and began chopping vegetables.

It was several hours before Babba returned, but when he did he greeted them both with a kiss before settling heavily into his chair.

Abbya placed his bowl in front of him. "Alana has news."

Babba looked up at her. "Is this true, Dohita?"

Alana nodded. "It is as Abbya says. The Queen has asked me to enter her service."

Babba leaned forward, elbows on the table, studying her carefully. "And what would this service entail?"

Alana repeated what the Queen had told her earlier. Babba leaned back slowly, crossing his arms over his broad stomach while stroking his beard.

"This is an interesting opportunity," he said thoughtfully. "You would not be free to garden as before. Or even visit me in the kitchens."

Alana met his eyes. "But," he continued slowly, "that is not always meant to remain the same."

Abbya pointed her spoon toward him. "It would be good for her experience."

Babba gave her a sidelong look. "Yes. But she will also see a side of Gershan that is not always kind."

Alana swallowed. "The Queen said it would be… diplomatic."

Babba snorted softly. "Of sorts. Anything near the court always is."

He leaned forward again. "Is it what you want, Dohita?"

His gaze sharpened. "And if it is… are you doing it for the Queen? Or for Tristan?"

Alana stirred her soup slowly. "I want what is best for Tristan," she admitted. "But the Queen is kind. Serving her would not be terrible."

Babba nodded. "Then we will pray with you, daughter. May Yah-Roi's will be known."

He had just lifted his spoon when a knock sounded at the door. Alana glanced up. Babba rose.

From the kitchen she heard him greet the visitor. "Your Highness."

Alana froze.

Tristan's voice answered quietly. "Good evening, Señor Travino."

Alana exchanged a startled look with Abbya. The prince was here. They could hear Babba taking Tristan's gloves and cloak.

"To what do I owe the honor of your visit in my humble home?" Babba asked politely, though his tone carried a firmness beneath it.

"I wish to seek your permission to speak with your daughter," Tristan replied.

Babba was silent for a moment.

"Alana," he said finally.

"Yes," Tristan answered. "She is my friend. And with your leave, I wish to make her more than that."

Another pause followed.

"It will cost you," Babba said.

"I have counted it," Tristan replied.

Babba chuckled softly. "You have counted what you can see. And does my daughter share your affections?"

Tristan's voice lowered. "I believe she does."

The two men spoke quietly for a moment longer before Babba

stepped into the kitchen doorway.

"Alana."

She looked up to see Tristan standing just behind him, tall enough that his head nearly brushed the lintel. Her face flushed as she rose quickly and curtsied.

"Your Highness." She murmured.

"In your home I am simply Tristan," he said gently.

She nodded and gestured toward the table. "Will you join us?"

"I have taken my supper," he said. "I came because there is urgent news from the palace. My father has taken a turn for the worse."

Abbya gasped and grasped Babba's hand. The older couple quietly withdrew from the room.

Alana's chest tightened. "I am sorry to hear it."

Tristan ran a hand through his hair. "As am I. The nobles will press even harder for me to take a wife now."

Alana nodded slowly. "I understand if you cannot wait for the adoption to be formalized."

Tristan frowned. "That is not why I have come, Alana. I will wait. You are already in process. You have lived faithfully among my people for three years and are beloved by many in the palace."

He took a step closer. "I came to ask your parents' leave to seal our betrothal. If you will have me."

Alana could hardly breathe.

"You play a dangerous game, Tristan."

"I am not playing," he said quietly. "I am calculating the risk of a mission I intend to see through."

She snorted softly. "I am not a military campaign."

"No," he said. "You are the woman I wish to make my queen."

Alana sank into her chair as her knees weakened. "Tristan... are you certain? Absolutely certain?"

"You doubt me?" He asked and this time the pain in his voice was evident.

"No," she said quickly. "I doubt the nobles. I doubt the adoption process. But I do not doubt you."

"I want no other wife," he said steadily. "Alana... will you have me?"

Her fingers trembled against the table.

"I want to," she whispered.

"Then let that be your answer." He placed his hand over hers and held her gaze.

"We will survive this," he said softly. "We will navigate it together."

She turned her hand and laced her fingers through his.

"Together," she whispered.

Because tonight, hope outweighed fear.

Chapter 25

Alana took the position the Queen had offered. The transition from garden maid to queen's lady was stark. Kefira was a good teacher, if a bit formal and Alana learned quickly what the woman found satisfactory and what she did not. The king did not worsen, nor did he recover, which left Tristan running much of the government and restraining the far more progressively minded vizier Morlach.

His occupation left little time for Alana, and the biblotory was empty most nights. Her position kept her busy. Mending, needlework, charity, for the queen was heavily involved in many community projects. Alana was either accompanying her or doing research on the projects the many patrons who came to her seeking her aid.

Overall Alana was grateful. The Adoption was moving forward in the slow boring process of legal proceedings and for a short season all seemed to be going to plan.

It was early in the afternoon on a summer day when Alana entered the kitchen to find Babba absent and the two cooks preparing for the nightly meal, as she reached to grab the tray of the tea service from the counter.

"I heard, he's already asked Babba, taken her hand, and betrothed her. Said to hades what the court thinks."

"I heard more than that."

The conversation droned on Alana picked up the tray and

breathed to make her limbs stop shaking. The servants were talking again. Someone had stirred the rumor.

She turned and nearly ran right into Suzanna.

"Oh, Alana, there you are." The girl said loudly.

Alana winced and the conversation beyond the half wall abruptly ended.

"Were you looking for me?" Alana asked softly, heat flooding her face.

"No, I mean yes." Suzanna added hastily, her own face matching Alana's.

"How is it working in the Queen's service, I'll bet you've forgotten all about us scullery maids."

Alana blinked, never had Suzanna's tone been on of such contempt. She frowned. "Of course not. Babba works here in the kitchens."

Suzanna studied her, her arms were still crossed but her shoulders had dropped a fraction. "How come I never see you.?

Alana peered at her. "Honestly, I am always off on one errand or another. The queen is fair, but I cannot afford to come to the kitchens for conversation."

Suzanna glanced into the other room where the cooks were still slicing lamb for the night's dinner. "There are rumors." She whispered softly. "Rumors that the prince has betrothed you. Are they true?"

Alana bit her lip, she and Tristan had not openly spoken of the arrangement lest his enemies use it as leverage.

Suzanna's eyes narrowed. "You used to tell me everything." Her voice was full of genuine hurt.

"There are things I cannot say lest they implicate you."

Suzanna looked at her in alarm. "Alana, what have you gotten into?"

Alana shook her head trying to move past with the tray. "Please Suzanna, I am not at liberty to say, just now, but if you can wait and believe that I am still your friend and have not forgotten my place, I would be most grateful."

Suzanna narrowed her eyes. Studying her for a long moment. Finally she nodded. "Very well, but if you disappear with the prince, I will tell everyone I knew it."

Alana shot her an exasperated look. Grateful the girl's anger had not lasted long. "I am in your debt." She said finally moving to the door.

Alana stepped into the hallway thinking about the rumors and counting the shift this now made at court.

The fire crackled in the queen's suite, casting flickering golden light over Alana's hands. She bent close to her needlework, checking the point on the fine silver thread. The queen sat reading while Kefira played a gita. The sound of the door opening lifted the women's heads.

Bethan's heart leapt. Tristan's arrival sharpened the angles of his face in the firelight.

The queen stood and smiled, offering her hands. "Tristan, what brings you here tonight?"

Tristan took his mother's hands and smiled down at her.

His rich baritone filled the room. "Good evening, Mother," he said, leaning in to kiss her cheek. "I cannot stay long, but I wished to visit you."

His eyes traveled to Alana, but he was disciplined enough not to let them linger.

Cerwyn gestured to a settee, then turned to Kefira. "Thank you, dear. You may take the rest of the evening off."

Kefira stood, placed the gita in its stand, and curtsied to Tristan and the queen before making her way out.

Tristan released a breath, letting his gaze find Alana's.

She flushed. "Good evening, Tris—Tristan."

He leaned forward, taking her hand. "How are you?"

She smiled. "Happy you have come," she said honestly.

Now he smiled. "As am I." He paused a moment, just staring into her eyes before the smile faded. "I do not, however, bear good news tonight." She

held her breath. "The adoption is progressing, but the nobles are not inclined to support a match, even if you are legally Gershani." Tristan continued.

Cerwyn sat forward. "You know this for certain?"

Tristan turned to look at his mother but did not let go of Alana's hand. "As much as I can be. I spoke to Lord Sora and Lord Michalo.

They are my closest allies, and while they are willing to concede the legality of the adoption, the court is not suited to an heir taking a common bride."

His eyes met hers.

"You are anything but common," he added, as if needing to reassure her.

She dropped her eyes to her needlepoint.

"I am not noble either, not in the way they mean," she replied.

It was not self-loathing, just fact. He squeezed her hand. The queen sat quietly for a few moments, the pop of the fire the only sound in the room once more.

"You were trained in the High Keep," Cerwyn finally said, breaking the stillness. "As was your father, and his father, and his father. I was trained there as well, as were the queens before me."

Tristan shifted, rubbing his thumb on Alana's knuckles. "Indeed, it was traditional for all noble children to be trained in the High Keep."

Cerwyn stared into the fire. "Many nobles no longer send their children, but if Alana were to go, the nobles would be at a disadvantage when presenting their own daughters who were not educated there."

Tristan's hand squeezed tighter. "Do you think the nobles might accept?"

Cerwyn tilted her head. "Perhaps." She looked at Alana. "It is your life. What do you think, my dear?"

Alana looked between them, knowing she was not ready to leave the palace—not Babba and Abbya, not the queen and her new position. Her heart ached at the thought of leaving Tristan's friendship, even if she had not reconciled his notion of making her his queen.

"I am not sure, Majesty," she answered thoughtfully. "I understand what you both are trying to do for me, and I am grateful." She paused, searching for the words. "I have just started learning to be in your service. I still know so little of this world."

Tristan looked at his mother. "Then we will think on it. We will seek Yah-Roi, and I will continue to quietly seek out the nobles who might vote in our favor."

He offered a brief prayer and rose. He looked at his mother, then took the liberty of cupping Alana's face in his palm. He leaned down and brushed his forehead with hers.

"I will not stop until I have found a way," he vowed.

Her stomach tightened at the words. She nodded slowly, and he straightened.

"I bid you both goodnight," he said, then turned to leave.

Alana watched the door close and turned to the queen. "You still are not sure?"

The woman was perceptive.

Alana swallowed. "Majesty, I am a maid."

"And he is a man, prince though he may be titled." His mother assured her.

Alana turned her gaze to the fire. "A man who does not deserve the fight they will give him over me."

Cerwyn studied her features. "He chose you."

Alana's eyes burned. "I know, and I still do not understand why."

Cerwyn sat at her dressing table and handed Alana her hairbrush.

"I did not understand when His Majesty chose me, not at first. But we were well suited, and you are much more in love with my son than I was with the king."

Alana kept her strokes even and steady. "I love him enough that I wish him no harm," she finally admitted.

Cerwyn turned in her chair. "You love him enough to give him up, and that, my dear, is the deepest love of all."

~

The air in the hall was stifling as music wafted through the latticework of the palace. The king had rebounded to health, hale enough to sit for a court gathering. Alana stood behind the queen's throne, ready to serve her majesty. Ladies-in-waiting were traditionally called upon to dance with noblemen, which meant Kefira was on the floor as Alana watched. She had learned the common steps of the marketplace and city, but the decorum here was still unfamiliar.

Girls in bright hues of silk and lace made their way to the center of the room as the traditional Halva step was called. Tristan stood at the center of so much attention that Alana fancied he looked rather like a parrot with plumage. He was gracious and kind, but she could see he was uncomfortable with the attention. She lowered her gaze and checked the queen's goblet before refilling it. Stepping back into the shadows, her taffeta gown rustled enough to draw nearby eyes. A young noblewoman leaned over to her friend, tittering behind her fan, cutting eyes her way. Alana lifted her chin and ignored the girls. Their gossip was harmless enough, she told herself. Still, her fingers tightened on the pitcher handle.

As she stepped back into the shadows, someone bumped into her. She turned, but there were only more couples pressing closer to the edges of the room. Alana set the pitcher down and reached into her pocket for her kerchief. Something sharp shifted against her fingers. She jerked her hand back as pain sliced across her skin. Carefully, she pulled out a piece of paper wrapped around a shard of glass. Her hand shook as she leaned forward.

"Forgive me, your majesty, I have injured myself and must step away for a moment," she whispered softly.

Cerwyn looked up at her with concern. "Are you well, child? You've gone quite pale."

Alana inclined her head. "I am fine. It is but a small cut."

Cerwyn stood and took Alana's hand in hers. "That is not small. Come, I will tend to you myself."

Alana's face flamed. "Oh, it is no trouble, Majesty."

The queen shook her head. "That is right, it is no trouble for me."

"Majesty, I will return." The queen curtsied to the king, who nodded and returned his bloodshot gaze to the dancers. Cerwyn pulled Alana into the anteroom. "Let me see," she said, taking Alana's hand. Alana held out the bleeding finger, and Cerwyn hissed.

"It will need a good bandage, and perhaps even sewing." The Queen said gently.

Alana winced. "I would rather avoid being a human pincushion if I may."

Cerwyn laughed softly. "Bleeding like a pig and still able to crack a joke. Whatever did you slice it on?" she asked.

Alana swallowed and then held out the paper and glass. "This was in my pocket. I refilled your goblet, and someone bumped me. I cut myself right after."

Cerwyn's gaze turned instantly serious as she carefully took the message.

"Foreign girls do not become queens in Gershan. Leave the court while you still have the chance."

Cerwyn frowned. "You did not see who bumped you?" she asked slowly.

Alana shook her head. "No, Majesty."

Cerwyn inspected the glass. "I will call for the physician. We must be sure the glass is not laced with poison."

Alana's heart raced at the words. "Poison? Why would anyone want to poison me?"

The queen simply sighed as if the answer was too heavy to speak. She wrapped the glass in the paper. "Stay here. I will speak with the captain of the guard and Tristan."

Alana reached for her. "He will be angry."

Cerwyn stopped at the door. "Yes, I imagine he will, but not at you. You have done nothing wrong."

Alana watched the door close behind the queen and wished she could believe that was true.

Alana heard Tristan's boot fall just before he opened the door, and she stiffened. He entered the room, his gaze sweeping over her, assessing. "Are you hurt?" he asked urgently.

"It's just a small cut," she replied.

He took her hand, turning it over and unwrapping the kerchief. A slash of red split her skin from lengthwise on her index finger.

"That's not small," he declared. His calm tone allowed no argument.

The captain of Tristan's guard, Pater, entered the room, his short blue cape swinging as he tucked his helmet under his arm.

"Do you have the note?" Tristan asked, his voice commanding.

"Yes, Highness, the Queen gave it to me herself." Pater nodded formally.

"Did you see who did this?" Tristan asked, looking at her while still holding her hand with gentle pressure on the kerchief.

"No, Highness," she answered, her eyes darting to Pater.

"He knows," Tristan assured her.

She swallowed but said nothing as Cerwyn entered with the court physician, a gruff man with thin gray hair and a large nose that showed signs of past tavern fights.

Cerwyn handed his assistant the glass. "We need this tested immediately."

Alana wanted to melt into the floor as the doctor took her hand. "Let's see what we have, young lady."

Tristan shifted but continued to hover. "I'm fine," she said firmly.

He did not move. Instead, he turned to Pater. "Lock it down."

Cerwyn looked at him, startled. "Tristan, you can't lock down a court gathering for a glass cut. The nobles are already stirred."

He stared hard at his mother, and Alana felt her shoulders tense, wincing as the doctor pressed on the wound.

"It's a clean cut," the man finally pronounced. "I'll wash it and give you a poultice. Avoid using it for the next few days."

"What about poison?" Tristan asked.

"I see no sign the cut is anything but a cut," the doctor murmured as he began to wrap her finger. "However, if it swells or you feel unwell, summon me at once," he advised. She nodded.

When the doctor left, Tristan turned to Alana. "Are you sure you didn't see who did this?"

She shook her head. "The room was crowded. Many people were pressing against me."

Tristan ran a hand down his short beard, his eyes filled with concern.

"Perhaps the High Keep is the better choice," Cerwyn spoke softly.

Tristan looked at his mother. "She would be away from court."

"Yes." The Queen acknowledged.

"And she would still be in Gershan awaiting the outcome of the adoption." Tristan continued.

"Yes." His mother affirmed.

"Not to mention training and skill." Tristan's tone had taken on that of a man thinking.

Cerwyn clasped her hands. "Yes."

Tristan took a breath, then blew it through his lips, a mannerism Alana found endearing.

He turned to her. "It would only be for a time. I will bring you home, I swear it."

Alana searched his gaze, seeing the worry and pain. "I'll go if it means they can't use me to cause you pain."

He took her hand. "My heart will ache regardless, but the High Keep is safer now, and my mother's point stands. It's where generations of Gershani nobles have trained."

She looked at their hands. "Then I'll go if it will help your cause."

He pulled her uninjured hand to his chest. "Our cause."

She nodded.

He turned to Pater. "Have a carriage ready for tomorrow. You will attend her in Doreth."

If Pater disagreed with the command, he didn't show it. "As you wish, Your Highness," the guard bowed and left the room.

Tristan looked at her with sorrow. "I will come for you," he promised.

"I know," she answered. Even if it caused problems.

~

Alana stood at the edge of the palace courtyard, watching as the final preparations for her departure were made. A carriage waited, the royal sigil of Gershan emblazoned on its door. A retinue of guards had been handpicked to escort her safely to the High Keep. The sky remained gray with the early morning light.

She stood beside Queen Cerwyn, her hands clasped tightly before her. Her face remained neutral despite the slight tremor in her fingers. She inhaled deeply to steady herself and turned to Babba and Abbya, who stood to the side. Abbya had tears streaming down her face, while Babba kept blinking and sniffing.

"I will write," she promised around the sudden catch in her throat.

Abbya wrapped her in her arms. "Oh, Dohita, Yah go with you."

Alana tightened her hold on the woman as Babba threw his burly arms around them both. They stood there for a long moment, her family, her home.

"You will always be our Dohita, do not forget it." His voice came gruff.

"Perhaps you can visit after the rains and the adoption," she offered.

Abbya stepped back, nodding, aware the Queen and Prince were standing kindly to the side but still present.

She turned to Tristan and, for one brief moment, nearly rushed into his arms to beg him not to send her away. Instead, she stepped toward him, and he took her hand, kissing it politely in the company of so many. He pressed a paper into her uninjured palm. She squeezed his hand before letting go and curtsying to the Queen.

"I should go," she said softly.

"Are you afraid?" the older woman asked.

Alana hesitated, then nodded once. "Yes."

Cerwyn reached out and took her hand. "Good," she said. "That means you will lean on Yah-Roi, and He will not fail you."

Her lips parted slightly, as if prepared to finally bare her soul, but there was a crowd, and a rooster crowed in the yard.

Tristan stepped close enough that she could feel his warmth.

"I will come for you," he continued, his voice steady despite the sorrow in his eyes.

A breath shuddered through her, but she did not look away. "I will hold you to that, Your Highness."

His lips curved faintly. "Tristan," he corrected. "Always, for you, just Tristan."

Alana swallowed, then stepped back. She surveyed them all. "Yah be with you." Her voice caught on the last word.

She turned, stepping toward the waiting carriage. Pater handed her up, and she sat on the brocade cushions, pulling back the curtain to see out the window.

The door shut, and the driver called to the horses. The carriage jerked into motion.

Alana sat stiff on the seat for only a moment before the facade came crashing down, first with a quiet sob, and then another. She tried to read the paper Tristan had given her, but her eyes were too blurred with tears.

Once again exiled from home and leaving behind those who loved her, Alana felt something shift in her soul. *Yah-Roi, must every home I find be taken from me?"*

The only answer was the creaking of the wheels and the sound of her own sobs.

Chapter 26

The journey to Doreth allowed Alana to see the country of Gershan as she never had. The flat of the coast had given way to high prairie and then river, the Aligre River that meandered from the mountains of Doreth down to the Great Gray Sea.

They had sailed up the river as far as Venora and then taken a team of mules into the high country. The foothills rose before them, and Alana had been reminded of Home.

On the eleventh day of travel, they arrived at the High Keep. The Ancient fortress seemed carved from the mountain itself. As it came into view Alana gasped. The setting sun cast the stone in a golden rosy blush and the walls themselves seemed to sparkle. Far below the southern edge of the keep was the vast blue of the Meridian Sea beyond. It was a lovely, cold, intimidating place.

Alana slid down from the mule with stiff legs. The mountain air struck her face sharper than the coast winds ever had. It smelled of pine, stone, and cold water somewhere far below the cliffs.

The gates of the High Keep stood open. Not welcoming. Not hostile. Simply waiting.] The escort that had brought her this far spoke quietly with the guards. Their armor was dark and unadorned. One of them glanced at Alana once, assessing, then turned and disappeared through the inner gate.

Moments later an old man emerged. He was tall though age had bowed his shoulders slightly. His white hair hung long and was tied simply at the nape of his neck. His robes were the color of winter wheat. His eyes found Alana immediately. Not searching. It was as though he had expected her.

He descended the steps slowly, leaning on a staff polished smooth with years.

"You have traveled far," he said.

Alana dipped her head. "I am Alana."

"I know." He said with a twinkle in his eye.

The answer made her pause.

The old man smiled faintly. "I am Elranth. Elder of the Keep. Servant of Yah-Roi."

He studied her for a quiet moment. Not rudely. Simply observing. Then he stepped aside. "Come inside. The mountain grows colder after sunset."

Her escort seemed satisfied. Their captain saluted Elranth briefly before turning his men back down the road. Alana watched them disappear into the fading light. For a moment the Keep felt very large. Then Elranth turned and began walking inside, and she hurried to follow.

The interior of the Keep was quieter than she expected. The halls were wide and carved directly from the mountain. Torches burned in iron brackets, their light warm against the gray stone. Their footsteps echoed softly as they walked.

A few acolytes passed them. Each bowed slightly to Elranth. Each glanced at Alana with mild curiosity and continued on their way. No whispers. No lingering stares. It unsettled her more than either would have.

They reached a long hall where tables had been laid for supper. The smell of roasted lamb and fresh bread made her stomach tighten with sudden hunger. Elranth gestured for her to sit.

"Travelers should eat before they speak too much." He said with a grin.

A young acolyte placed a bowl of stew before her along with bread still warm from the oven. Another filled their cups with watered wine.

For a while they ate in silence. The warmth of the food spread slowly through her cold limbs. Elranth broke a piece of bread and dipped it into his bowl.

After some time he looked up at her. "I am sorry for your sorrow."

The words were simple. Alana's spoon stopped halfway to her

mouth.

"How do you know I have sorrow?" she asked suspiciously.

Elranth tore another piece of bread. "It is written in your face."

Her fingers tightened around the spoon. Her gaze dropped to the table. "You cannot know that."

The old priest smiled slightly. "A good shepherd knows when a storm is coming."

He let the thought rest there.

Alana set the spoon down carefully. "You do not know me."

"No," Elranth agreed easily. He studied her a moment longer." "But sorrow leaves a mark that time does not hide well."

Her shoulders drew in just slightly. She picked at the edge of the bread instead of looking at him. Elranth noticed. His voice softened.

"There is a reason the acolytes of this place worship Yah-Roi." He began again as if changing the subject.

At the name her grip on the bread tightened. She did not look up.

Elranth continued gently. "Because Yah-Roi is the God who sees."

Alana's eyes dropped further.A faint line formed between her brows. The hall had grown very quiet.

Elranth watched her a moment, then took another sip of wine. "Most people find that unsettling at first."

He did not press the matter further. Instead he pushed the breadbasket slightly closer to her.

"You should rest." He rose slowly, leaning again on his staff. "A room has been prepared."

An acolyte appeared to guide her. Alana stood. Before leaving she glanced once over her shoulder.

Elranth had returned to his meal. But when he noticed her looking, he gave a small knowing smile. Not intrusive. Just patient. As if he had all the time in the world.

Alana turned quickly and followed the acolyte down the corridor.

Her room was simple. A narrow bed. A wooden chest. A basin of clean water beside folded linens. Nothing more. But it was warm and safe.

When the door closed behind her the silence settled over the room. Alana sat on the edge of the bed. Her hands rested in her lap, still curled slightly around the memory of the bread.

The God who sees.

She lay down slowly and pulled the blanket around herself. Sleep came slowly. But eventually…

It came.

~

Morning in the High Keep came quietly. Alana woke to pale light spilling through the narrow window carved into the stone wall. The air was colder than the coast, clean and sharp in her lungs. For a moment she lay still, listening. No shouting. No chains. No waves slapping against hull planks. Only the distant sound of wind moving across the mountain.

She rose, washed quickly, and followed the corridors back toward the main hall. She found Elranth in the chapel. It was a large chamber carved from the heart of the mountain. Tall narrow windows opened toward the sea far below, and morning light spilled across the stone floor in pale gold bands.

The room was empty except for the old priest. He stood near the front, leaning lightly on his staff. When he saw her, he nodded once and handed her a broom.

"Sweep the chapel." He said.

Nothing more. No explanation.

Alana took the broom.

"Yes, sir." She answered.

She began at the far wall and worked across the stone floor. Dust had gathered in the corners where the wind carried it in through the high windows. The work was simple. Familiar. Her hands moved automatically. An hour later she returned the broom to Elranth.

"It is finished." She told him.

He looked at her. "Did you sweep to please me?"

Alana hesitated. "No."

"Did you sweep because you desired to worship Yah-Roi?" He pressed.

Her fingers tightened slightly where they rested at her sides. "No."

Elranth waited. She lifted her chin just slightly.

"I swept because you told me to." Her voice bore her confusion.

The old priest nodded as though that answer satisfied him. "Come."

He turned and walked from the chapel. Alana followed.

They passed through a narrow passage that opened onto the southern edge of the Keep. The ground dropped away sharply there, and beyond the cliffs the Meridian Sea stretched vast and blue beneath the morning sky. Wind tugged gently at her hair. Far below waves rolled endlessly toward the shore. Elranth stepped to the edge of the stone overlook and rested both hands on his staff.

"Do you see Yah in it?" He asked her.

Alana followed his gaze across the water. The sea shimmered in the morning light.

"I see that Yah made it." She replied honestly.

Elranth nodded slowly. "Are you grateful He made the sea?"

The question caught her off guard. Her brow furrowed slightly.

"I... do not know." She answered.

She had never considered whether she should be grateful for the sea. The sea had taken. The sea had carried. The sea had simply been.

Elranth smiled. "That is honest." He gestured toward the endless water. "Worship comes when we see both the beauty and the power." His staff tapped lightly against the stone. "And recognize that Yah-Roi can do both."

Alana looked out across the water again. The wind carried the scent of salt even this high above the cliffs. he sea rolled on, vast and unbothered. For the first time she found herself studying it. Not as a road. Not as a threat. Just... the sea.

Elranth watched her quietly. Then, satisfied, he turned back toward the Keep.

"Come," he said. "There is more sweeping to be done."

Elranth did not hurry. He walked the halls of the High Keep as though the mountain itself had all the time in the world. Alana followed a step behind him, her eyes moving constantly. The corridors twisted through the stone in ways that felt older than the Keep itself. Some passages were broad and lit with torches. Others were narrow and quiet, their walls worn smooth by generations of hands.

Students moved through the halls. Young men. Young women. Most dressed simply, but Alana noticed a few with signet rings. The embroidered hems. The careful way they watched Elranth pass.

"Nobility," she said quietly.

Elranth glanced back at her. "Some."

They passed a wide courtyard where several young men were practicing with wooden swords.

"The High Keep has long been a place of learning," Elranth said. "Kings once sent their sons here."

He paused. "And their daughters."

Alana watched a young woman loose an arrow across the training field. It struck the target cleanly.

"You train them to fight?" she asked.

"We train them to live." He answered.

He continued walking. Alana followed.

"Tristan sent me here," she said after a moment.

Elranth's mouth curved in a faint smile. "Yes."

He did not elaborate.

They passed through an archway that opened into a training yard carved into the mountainside. Racks of weapons lined one wall. A stable stood beyond it where several horses shifted and stamped. Elranth stopped.

"Your mornings will be spent here." He pointed with his staff.

Alana looked around.

"You will train your body," he said. "Archery. Riding. Movement. Balance."

He gestured toward a group of students practicing footwork across wooden beams raised above the ground.

"The mind is bound by the body's capability."

Alana studied the weapons rack. Swords. Spears. Axes. Her eyes lingered on the long wooden staff resting across two hooks.

Elranth followed her gaze. "You may choose a weapon to study."

Alana stepped closer to the rack. Her fingers brushed the smooth length of the staff. It was longer than she was tall. Balanced and Simple.

"Bow staff," she said.

Elranth nodded. "A wise choice."

He turned and continued walking. "In the afternoons you will join the scholars."

They entered another wing of the Keep where the walls were lined with shelves of scrolls and books. "Diplomacy."

He gestured toward a room where several students sat around a table in quiet debate.

"Gershani case law." Another room held a group studying a large parchment spread across the table. "History."

They passed a classroom where a woman demonstrated a formal bow while several young girls mirrored the motion carefully. "And the finer etiquettes of court."

Alana felt a faint tightening in her chest. Court. The word carried weight she did not yet know how to hold. They continued through the hall.

"And in the evenings," Elranth said, "after supper has ended, you will study the Book with the acolytes."

They reached the chapel again. Morning light now filled the high windows. Students sat quietly in rows while an older acolyte read aloud from a worn manuscript. Alana stood in the doorway.

"You expect much." She observed.

Elranth rested both hands on his staff.

"The world expects much of those it places in high places." His eyes shifted toward her. "And sometimes Yah-Roi calls them to meet those expectations as well."

Alana did not answer. After a moment Elranth smiled again, that quiet patient smile she was beginning to recognize.

"And besides," he added lightly. "Your betrothed survived it."

Alana blinked. "Tristan studied under you?"

"Oh yes." Elranth's eyes glinted with amusement. "For three years."

He began walking again. Alana followed quickly.

"What was he like?" she asked.

Elranth chuckled softly. "Tall."

She frowned slightly. "I know that."

"And stubborn." He continued.

That sounded correct.

"And very certain he was right about most things." He added with a chuckle.

Alana felt the corner of her mouth twitch before she could stop it. Elranth noticed.

"One winter," he continued, "he decided the archery master's targets were placed incorrectly."

Alana looked at him.

"He argued this for two days."

"What happened?" She pressed.

Elranth's smile widened. "The master told him to prove it."

They reached the training yard again. Elranth gestured toward the far target line.

"Your betrothed moved every target on the field himself."

Alana raised an eyebrow. "And?"

Elranth tapped his staff lightly on the stone. "The archery master then beat him in every round."

Alana blinked. Elranth's eyes sparkled.

"Tristan spent the next week putting the targets back where they belonged." Elranth finished with a huff of amusement.

For a moment Alana said nothing. Then, quietly— "He did not quit?"

Elranth looked at her. "No."

The answer was simple. Certain.

They stood there a moment in the mountain wind. Finally Elranth gestured toward the staff rack again.

"Tomorrow morning," he said. "We begin."

~

A hand knocked once against Alana's door. Not loud. But firm. She woke instantly. The window was still dark. For a moment she lay there, confused, the blanket pulled tight around her shoulders. Then the knock came again. Alana swung her feet to the floor. Cold stone bit into her skin.

By the time she stepped into the corridor the acolyte who had knocked was already walking away, carrying a lantern. "Training yard," he said over his shoulder. They stepped out into the mountain air. The sky was still black, though the faintest gray line had begun to gather along the horizon.

Elranth stood waiting in the yard. He leaned on his staff as always, though Alana had begun to suspect he leaned on it less than he appeared to.

"Good," he said when she approached. "You are awake."

Alana dipped her head. He gestured toward the far end of the yard.

"Run."

She hesitated. "Where?"

Elranth pointed. "Until I tell you to stop."

So she ran.

The air burned cold in her lungs. Gravel shifted under her boots as she crossed the yard and circled the stone boundary wall. When she returned Elranth was standing beside a row of low wooden beams set across the ground.

"Again."

She ran again. And again.

Then he pointed to the beams. "Jump."

They were not high. But they were placed close together.

Run. Jump. Land. Run again. Her breath grew ragged. Her legs burned. The mountain air felt thinner with every pass.

Elranth watched silently. When she stumbled over the fourth beam he did not comment.

He only said, "Again."

By the time the sun began to creep over the distant mountains Alana's arms trembled when she pushed herself upright. Sweat clung to her neck despite the cold. Elranth finally raised a hand.

"Enough." He said pounding his staff for emphasis.

Alana bent forward, hands braced on her knees, trying to steady her breathing. When she straightened he was holding something. The bow staff. He offered it to her.

The wood was smooth beneath her palms when she took it. Long. Balanced.

He stepped back. "Show me what you think it is for."

Alana shifted her grip. She had watched one presentation of the bow staff in Caerdis. She tried to imitate the movements she remembered.

The staff wobbled in her hands. She swung it. Too wide. Too slow. Her foot slipped on the gravel and the staff dipped. The staff caught awkwardly against the ground and jarred her arms. She reset and tried again. Clumsy and crude.

Elranth watched quietly through the entire attempt. Finally he lifted his staff and tapped lightly against the ground.

"Stop." He commanded.

Alana lowered the bow staff, breathing hard.

"I know it was not good." She said with embarrassment

Elranth smiled faintly. "It was not."

She expected criticism. Correction.

Instead he stepped closer and gently pushed the end of the staff upward until it rested level between her hands.

"The staff is only a tool." He lectured gently. He stepped back again. "The power is not in the wood." His eyes moved to hers. "The power is in the will of the wielder."

Alana looked down at the staff in her hands. Her arms still trembled. She lifted the staff again. This time her grip tightened.

Elranth nodded once. "Good."

He stepped back toward the center of the yard.

"Now," he said calmly. "Again."

She reset her stance and swung again.

~

By the time supper ended Alana's arms ached .Not the dull ache of ordinary work .A deeper one .The kind that lived in the muscles themselves and reminded her every time she moved that morning had been real. The bow staff had left faint bruises along her forearms where the wood had struck during clumsy turns. Her legs still trembled slightly from the running.

She followed the others toward the chapel. No one spoke much in the corridor. The acolytes moved quietly, their footsteps soft against the stone. When they entered, the room had changed. Candles burned along the walls and across the front of the chamber. Their light turned the gray stone warm and golden. Shadows climbed the pillars and gathered high in the vaulted ceiling. The air smelled faintly of wax and smoke. Students and acolytes took their places on the wooden benches.

Alana sat near the back. A small choir stood along one wall. Their voices rose softly, not loud, but steady and clear. The melody was simple, old enough that it felt woven into the stone itself. Alana listened. She did not know the words. But the sound filled the quiet spaces inside her chest in a way she did not expect.

When the song ended an older acolyte stepped forward carrying the Book. He opened the worn pages carefully.

"Tonight," he said, "we remember the story of the Shepherd." His voice carried easily through the chapel. "A shepherd who had one hundred sheep."

The pages rustled softly as he read.

"When one wandered from the fold, the shepherd left the ninety-nine safely in the field…" He continued.

The candlelight flickered across the page.

"…and went to search for the one that was lost."

She stared at the floor.

The acolyte continued. "He searched the hills. The ravines. The dark places where sheep do not belong." He paused. "And when he found it, he did not strike it. He lifted it onto his shoulders."

The choir hummed softly behind the words.

"And carried it home." He finished.

Something in her chest shifted uncomfortably. She could almost feel it. Like a voice she remembered from far away. Calling. Not shouting. Just… calling. Her fingers curled tighter in the fabric of her dress.

The reader closed the Book gently. The choir began another quiet hymn. Around her the acolytes bowed their heads.

Alana sat very still. She could almost imagine the Shepherd walking across the hills. Searching. Patient. Calling for something that had wandered too far. Her throat tightened. She did not understand it. *Why he would go looking. Why he would carry it back instead of leaving it where it had gone? Why would the Shepherd still want it?*

She stared at the candlelight flickering across the floor. And for the first time since arriving at the High Keep. She wondered if the call might be meant for her.

~

The days settled into rhythm. Morning came before the sun. Chilly air in the yard. Running until her lungs burned. Jumping the low beams until her legs trembled. The bow staff in her hands while Elranth watched with patient silence.

At first she was clumsy. The staff caught against the ground. Her feet tangled. More than once it spun from her hands entirely. Elranth never scolded. He simply said, "Again." So she tried again.

Summer warmed the stone walls of the High Keep. Wind carried the smell of grass up from the lower hills. Students trained in the yard until sweat darkened their tunics. By the time the leaves on the lower slopes began to turn gold, Alana's movements had changed. Her feet found the ground more surely. The staff moved faster in her hands.

Elranth watched. Sometimes he nodded. Sometimes he said nothing at all. In the afternoons she sat among the scholars. Scrolls spread across long wooden tables. Gershani case law was dense and precise. Names of judges. Records of rulings. The slow shaping of justice across generations. History was no easier. Kings. Wars. Treaties written and broken.

More than once she found herself staring at the parchment while the others debated quietly around her. But something in her had begun to change. When the instructors asked questions, she thought longer, before answering carefully. She did not notice the way the scholars sometimes turned toward her when she spoke. She did not notice the way her posture had changed when she stood.

But Elranth noticed. He noticed everything. Letters from Tristan arrived when the caravans came up from the coast. Always weeks old. Sometimes more. The parchment carried the faint scent of sea salt.

He wrote simply. Encouragement. Small stories from Caerdis. Reminders that he was proud of her.

Alana read every letter slowly. Then again. Then once more before folding it carefully and placing it beneath the others in the small chest beside her bed. She never wrote long replies. But she wrote.

Perhaps the most surprising change was that Alana began to long for the evening time. When supper was finished and the chapel was lit and the acolytes gathered to read the Book. Alana once more found her heart wanting to hear. Not just to comply.

Autumn crept quietly into the mountains. Cold mornings. Longer shadows in the yard. Alana decided to use the coming winter to design a tapestry for her majesty. A pattern of the Trevano family crest and Gershan's coat of arms.

Then one morning Elranth found her standing at the gate before lessons. Her eyes were bright.

"Visitors," he said.

Alana turned. Two familiar figures climbed the road toward the Keep. Babba walked with the steady strength she remembered. Abbya followed beside him, her shawl wrapped tight against the mountain wind.

Alana did not remember crossing the courtyard. One moment she was at the gate. The next she was in Abbya's arms.

Abbya laughed softly, holding her tight. "Dohita…"

Babba rested a warm hand on her shoulder. "You have grown."

They sat together in one of the quiet rooms overlooking the cliffs. Abbya studied her face carefully.

"You are stronger." She said.

Alana smiled faintly. "They make me run."

Babba chuckled. "Yes. That sounds like training at the High Keep.."

For a while they spoke of trivial things. The market in Caerdis. The fishermen. The early storms rolling in from the Meridian Sea. But eventually Babba grew quieter.

Alana noticed. "What is it?"

He rubbed his hands together slowly. "The adoption."

Her chest tightened slightly. "What about it?"

Babba sighed. "The court has delayed it again."

Alana stared at the floor. "Why?"

"The King is ill," Babba said gently. "Many matters in court have slowed."

Abbya reached over and took Alana's hand. "Do not trouble your heart with it." Her voice was warm and steady. "These things take time."

Alana nodded slowly. She tried to believe it. Abbya squeezed her hand once more. "You are where you need to be."

Alana nodded thoughtfully, looking out her window to the sea below. "Indeed, Yah-Roi sees." She whispered softly and this time the thought was not frightening at all.

Chapter 27

The spring sun warmed Alana's back as she bent to retrieve her staff.

"You were too quick for me, Dula," she said, a twinkle in her eye.

The young woman who had just disarmed her laughed and rested her own staff across her shoulders. "It is the first time I have done it in weeks. You are excelling in form."

Alana brushed dirt from her knuckles.

"Tell that to Elranth," she said dryly. "He just says, *again*."

Dula shook her head. "He wants you to be tenacious."

"He wants me to be humble," Alana shot back.

Dula grinned. "Both."

The sound of hoof beats cut across the yard. Sharp and fast.

Both women turned. A rider came through the outer gate hard, the bay gelding lathered with sweat. A shield hung from the saddle bearing the crest of the royal family.

The yard went still. Acolytes paused mid-drill. Wooden swords lowered. Conversations died. Elranth stepped forward to meet the rider. The soldier swung down before the horse had fully stopped and bowed his head quickly before speaking. Too urgent to mistake.

Elranth listened. He stood exactly as he always did, one hand resting lightly on his staff, his white beard stirring in the wind. Unflappable. The soldier spoke quickly. Once. Then again.

Elranth asked a question. The rider answered. Alana forced herself to breathe slowly.

In.

Out.

The staff felt heavier in her hands. A tight coil began to wind in her chest anyway.

Elranth finally nodded. He gestured for two young men to take the horse. Another pair led the messenger toward the shade of the wall where water and bread were quickly brought.

Then Elranth turned He spoke quietly to one of the senior acolytes. The young man's face paled slightly. He ran toward the tower. A moment later the bell began to toll. Deep. Slow. The sound rolled through the Keep and out across the cliffs. One heavy note. Then another.

Alana closed her eyes. The high bell tolled for only two reasons. The king was dead. Or Gershan was at war.

~

The king was dead. Word moved through the Keep like fire through dry grass. Every time someone said it, they added the customary words after

"Long live the king."

But every time Alana heard it, the words in her mind came differently.

Tristan is king.

Or rather, would be. As soon as he took a wife. In her law class the debate began almost immediately. Scrolls were brought out. Old rulings cited. Students argued across the long table while the instructor listened with folded hands.

"No king has ascended unmarried in nearly seven hundred years."

"That is tradition."

"It is precedent."

"Precedent is not law."

"It becomes law when it is repeated often enough."

Voices rose and fell. Some of the noble acolytes spoke with quiet certainty.

"The court will insist the Crown Prince rectify the matter immediately."

"Immediately," another agreed.

The word echoed unpleasantly in Alana's chest. She had heard nothing about her own case. Nothing about whether the hearings had resumed. Nothing about whether the adoption had moved forward at all. The uncertainty gnawed at her long after supper. Even during the evening reading in the chapel her thoughts drifted. The candles glowed. The choir sang. But her mind sifted through the implications like tangled thread.

After the service ended she slipped quietly out of the chapel and climbed the narrow stairs to the watch tower. The rampart overlooked the cliffs. Far below, the sea moved in and out against the rocks, steady and indifferent to kings and courts. The wind carried the faint scent of salt. Alana rested her hands on the stone wall.

She heard footsteps behind her. No. She felt them first.

Elranth came to stand beside her.

"It has been hard news," he observed.

She let out a slow breath.

"He is king," she said quietly. "And the court will insist he wed."

Elranth stroked his beard. "So you say."

"So the law says," she insisted.

The elder priest said nothing for a moment. The sea wind lifted a strand of her hair and brushed it across her cheek.

Finally he spoke. "The law says his wife must be Gershani."

He glanced toward her. "It does not say he must be wed before he is crowned."

Alana frowned. "But tradition—"

"Tradition is not law, Alana." His voice was gentle, but it stopped her all the same. "Your prince knows that."

She huffed softly and crossed her arms, looking up toward the scatter of stars above the dark sea. "It is a tangle."

Elranth chuckled. "From your perspective."

He was quiet again for a moment. Then he turned slightly.

"Tell me," he said. "Have you finished the tapestry for Her Majesty?"

Alana blinked. The sudden shift caught her off guard.

She thought of the work waiting in her room. The careful stitches she had placed night after night since winter. "It is close."

Elranth nodded thoughtfully. "And the backside?"

Her brow furrowed. "What of it?"

"Is it tangled?" he asked.

She shrugged. "Se. Such things happen. It is not meant for display. The only picture that matters is the front."

Elranth nodded again. "And you know the design of the work?"

"Se," she said slowly. "I am the one creating it."

He smiled. "Then I should trust that you will not send an ugly piece to a woman whom you love."

Alana blinked. The realization settled slowly. "This is not about the tapestry," she said.

Elranth studied her quietly.

"No," he agreed. "It is not."

Her shoulders lowered with a long breath. "It is a safe thing to trust Yah," she said quietly, "with the desire He creates." The words came from one of the ancient texts in the Keep's bibliotory.

Elranth reached over and squeezed her shoulder once. Then he turned and walked back toward the stair.

Alana remained where she was. The stars burned cold above the sea. She lifted her eyes toward them.

"He is Yours first," she whispered. "And You see us both."

The wind stirred the edge of her cloak. After a moment she turned and walked back into the Keep. There was still work to finish on the tapestry.

~

The letter arrived two weeks later with a caravan climbing through the Doreth passes. Travelers brought news with them. Merchants, pilgrims, a pair of scholars bound for Franka, and among the satchels and sealed packets was a letter bearing a familiar hand.

Alana recognized it instantly. Her heart lifted before she even broke the seal. She sat by the window in her small chamber, the afternoon light falling across the parchment as she unfolded it.

My darling Alana,

It is with heavy heart that I report the death of my father, which I am sure you have heard by now.

She paused. For a moment she could see him in her mind, standing in the great hall, the weight of the crown newly placed upon his shoulders.

She continued reading.

I am king, dearest, and as such I seek only the good of my people. One of the unseen ways I believe to aid them is to resume the court process that will allow me to take you as my queen upon your legal adoption.

Her breath caught slightly. She read on.

Do not fear for me, dearest. Simply pray. I firmly believe that Yah is working on our behalf.

The words were steady. Confident. So very like him.

I long for the day I may once again hold you, for on that day I will make you my bride.

Forever yours,

Tristan

Alana folded the letter slowly. A soft smile touched her face. Despite his sorrow. Despite the crown that now rested on his head. He was still Tristan. Still hopeful. Still certain. And somehow his words had settled the restless knot that had lived in her chest since the bell had tolled.

She held the letter against her chest for a moment. Then lifted her eyes toward the dark ceiling beams above her bed.

"Give him wisdom," she whispered.

"Give him strength."

Her fingers tightened slightly around the parchment. "And please… let him feel how much I love him."

The room was quiet. Wind moved softly past the narrow window. After a moment she folded the letter carefully and placed it with the others in the small chest beside her bed. Then she rose. Her broom still leaned against the wall where she had left it. Alana picked it up and returned to the corridor. Dust had gathered again along the edges of the chapel floor. She began to sweep

~

Three days later Alana stood on the mountainside tending the goats with Dula. A pregnant doe stood shaking in the late spring sun.

The labor had been hard, and Alana was uncertain the kid would survive.

She reached cautiously inside the doe, feeling for the issue.

"How long has she been like this?" she asked Dula softly.

"Right after dawn. I sent Gorlat for you as soon as I realized she would need assistance."

Alana nodded.

"You did right."

She felt further. And there it was, a hoof turned back.

Alana gently moved the obstruction and hissed as the doe experienced another contraction. She spoke in soft, soothing tones as the baby, now unencumbered, slid from its mother.

Alana eyed the still form.

"Is he dead?" Dula asked.

Alana tilted her head. "Not until we've made sure. Hand me the muslin."

Dula handed over the soft cloth and Alana cleaned the nose and mouth, rubbing the baby down as the mother turned to lick her offspring.

For a brief, awful moment Alana remembered another form. Too still. Too small. But the image shattered as the goat gave a weak bleat and suddenly pushed upright to stand on shaky legs.

She laughed, her eyes watery. "Praise Yah," she said softly, wiping her hands on her apron.

She had just stood when the gong of the high bell tolled up into the hills. Her stomach sank so fast she thought she might be ill.

Dula looked at her in alarm. "Alana, are you quite all right? You've gone green."

Alana couldn't find the air to speak. She just stared at Dula for one terrifying second, then turned, snatching up her bag and dashing down the trail.

War or death.

War or death.

The continued toll seemed to say with every strike.

She arrived in time to see another official soldier's mount being led into the stable, but the messenger was nowhere to be seen. Neither was Elranth. Alana walked inside the Keep, not even slowing to let her eyes adjust to the dimness indoors. She forced her steps to slow only as she hastened toward his personal study.

The door was firmly shut when she arrived, and the sound of male voices barely carried through the thick wood. Alana paced outside the study for what felt like an eternity but was likely only a few moments. The door opened.

The soldier stepped out, helmet tucked beneath his arm. Her eyes widened. "Pater?"

The man turned to look at her, his eyes narrowing. Then recognition dawned. "Alana?"

She inclined her head. "Se."

He bowed. "Forgive me, lady. I did not recognize you."

She waved a hand. "Never mind that. What word do you bring?"

Pater's eyes softened in pity. "I am sorry, Lady."

Her heart seized. "Is he dead?"

Pater shook his head. "No." A pause. "But he may as well be."

His voice lowered. "His Majesty, the King of Gershan, has been exiled."

"Exiled?" Alana's voice cracked. "What do you mean *exiled*?"

Pater sighed. "The measure is supposed to be temporary," he said carefully. "Pending an investigation into the intentions of the King to marry a foreign woman and make her queen."

The words made no sense, so she asked of Cerwyn. "And the queen mother?"

"Has been placed in the custody of the palace guard until such time as a ruling may be determined into the extent of her involvement with His Majesty's plan." He answered.

He did not look at her. Instead he recited the ruling while staring at a bronze sconce above her head, as though the words were written there.

Cold disbelief poured through Alana's chest. "They mean me."

Pater finally met her gaze. "I am sorry, my Lady."

The title sounded strange in the stone corridor. She pressed a hand over her mouth.

"I have cost him his realm," she whispered.

Elranth stepped into the hall. Alana had not heard him approach. His eyes moved slowly between them. Then he walked toward her.

"Have you?" he asked. His voice was calm. "Or were you simply convenient?"

Alana blinked at him. "Is there much difference?" The bitterness in her own voice startled her.

Elranth crossed his arms. "Only to the One who sees."

She lifted her eyes to him. "I do not see how Yah is in this."

Elranth shrugged slightly. But his eyes held quiet sorrow.

"And yet," he said, "that is what faith is for."

He tilted his head just slightly. "Evidence." A pause. "And substance."

The words were familiar. They had been read from the Book the night before.

Alana stared at him. For a moment her jaw tightened. Then the fight went out of her shoulders. She bowed her head.

"It is a safe thing," she murmured.

Elranth reached out and squeezed her shoulder.

"Se." His voice was warm again. "It is a very safe thing."

Chapter 28

Dust gathered along the edges of the chapel floor again. It always did. Alana pushed the broom in steady strokes, the bristles whispering across the stone. Sunlight poured through the tall windows, turning the floating dust to pale gold.

The chapel was quiet at this hour. Most of the acolytes were in their afternoon lessons. She had nearly finished the last row when footsteps sounded in the doorway. Heavy. Booted.

Alana turned. Gorlat stood there, broad-shouldered as always, his cloak still dusted with road dirt. In one hand he held a sealed letter. Her heart lurched when she saw the wax. The crest of the Queen Mother.

He stepped forward and offered it without ceremony. "For you."

Alana wiped her hands quickly on her skirts before taking it. The wax felt cool beneath her fingers. Her pulse began to beat faster.

"Thank you," she said quietly.

Gorlat nodded once and stepped aside, leaning against the stone wall as though prepared to wait.

Alana broke the seal. The parchment inside carried the careful hand she remembered from the palace gardens. She unfolded it slowly.

My dear Alana,

Elranth has written faithfully of your studies and your growth. I am told you have become diligent in both discipline and humility, which pleases me greatly.

Alana swallowed. She read on.

The kingdom finds itself in troubled waters. You will have heard by now that my son has been driven from the throne by those who fear his intentions.

The words blurred slightly before she forced her eyes to focus again.

I write to you now not as queen, but as a woman who loves her people.

Her hand tightened around the page.

I remain within the palace, though under guard. My movements are watched and my voice is constrained.

A long breath left Alana's chest.

But the people of Caerdis still suffer.

If you have the courage for it, I beg you to come. Help me serve them. There is much that must be done quietly, and I believe Yah has prepared you for such a time as this.

The letter ended simply.

With affection,

Her Majesty

Alana lowered the parchment slowly. Her heart was beating hard now. Gorlat watched her carefully.

"Well?" he asked.

She folded the letter with trembling fingers. "I must speak with Elranth."

He nodded once. "I thought you might."

She found Elranth in the courtyard near the training yard. He stood watching a group of students working through staff drills, his own staff resting easily in his hands. When he saw her approaching he dismissed the students with a quiet gesture.

Alana stopped in front of him and held out the letter. "Elranth."

He read it slowly. His eyes moved across the lines once. Then again. When he finished he folded it carefully and handed it back.

"And what do you think?" he asked.

Alana looked down at the parchment. "My heart says I should go." She hesitated. "But my heart has caused enough trouble already."

Elranth's beard twitched with the faintest smile. "That is one way to describe it."

She shot him a look. Then sighed. "The Queen Mother is asking for help."

"Yes." He agreed.

"She is under guard." She added.

"Yes." He smiled this time.

"And if I go, the court may see it as defiance." She finished her accounting.

"Also yes." He nodded, ever patient.

Alana lifted her eyes to him. "So I am asking you."

Elranth studied her quietly for a moment. The mountain wind tugged gently at the edge of his robe.

Finally he asked, "Why do you think she wrote to you?"

Alana frowned slightly. "I do not know."

"You do." He urged.

She shifted uncomfortably. "She said Yah may have prepared me."

Elranth nodded. "And do you believe He has?"

Alana's fingers tightened around the letter. "I believe He has changed me."

She glanced toward the chapel. "I just do not know if I am ready."

Elranth chuckled softly. "My child, readiness is rarely part of Yah's plans."

She blinked. He rested both hands on his staff. "You have learned to run when your legs tremble."

Her mind flashed to the training yard at dawn.

"You have learned to strike when your arms ache." He added

The bow staff.

"You have learned to think before you speak." He said gently.

The law table.

His eyes softened. "Why would you assume those lessons were only meant for the High Keep?"

Alana stared at him. The wind shifted across the courtyard. Far below the sea moved slowly against the cliffs.

After a moment she whispered, "You think I should go."

Elranth shrugged slightly. "I think Yah-Roi sees further than we do." He tapped the staff lightly against the stone. "And I suspect He did not bring you to this mountain merely to teach you how to sweep floors."

Alana sighed deeply. Her fingers folded around the letter again. The parchment no longer trembled.

Finally she nodded. "Then I should prepare to leave."

Elranth smiled gently. "Se." He turned toward the training yard again. "And bring your staff."

She blinked. "My staff?"

Elranth glanced back at her. "The world below the mountain," he said mildly, "is rarely less complicated than the one above it."

Alana did not realize how many people had become dear to her until it was time to leave them. The High Keep gathered quietly in the courtyard the morning she departed. Dula hugged her first. Hard.

"You must return to us someday," she said, though her voice wavered slightly.

Alana laughed softly through the tightness in her throat. "I will try."

"You will do more than try," Dula insisted, wiping her eyes quickly and stepping back.

Several of the younger acolytes embraced her after that. Others bowed in the formal way they had learned in their etiquette lessons. Even some of the scholars came to offer quiet farewells.

Babba and Abbya had once told her that the Keep shaped hearts as much as minds. Now she understood what they meant. Elranth stood slightly apart from the others. He did not speak until she approached him last.

Alana bowed her head. "Thank you."

Elranth looked at her for a long moment. "For what?"

"For... everything." She said. Gratitude coloring her voice.

His beard twitched with a faint smile. "You swept well."

A soft laugh escaped her despite the tears in her eyes. Elranth placed one hand briefly on her shoulder. "Remember what you learned here."

She nodded.

"Run when your legs tremble." He said.

Her lips quivered.

"And strike when your arms ache." He admonished.

The bow staff rested across her pack.

"And think before you speak." He finished.

She drew a breath. "I will."

Elranth studied her a moment longer. Then he said quietly, "Yah-Roi sees."

Alana swallowed and nodded again. Then she turned before she could lose her courage. Pater and Gorlat waited at the gate with the horses. The road down the mountain twisted through the spring-green foothills toward the coast. Alana did not look back until the High Keep had grown small against the stone cliffs.

~

The journey to Caerdis took several days .Caravans passed them on the lower roads. Merchants. Pilgrims. Farmers driving wagons. The closer they came to the coast, the heavier the traffic became. But something felt... wrong.

Alana noticed it first in the villages. Buildings that should have been freshly whitewashed looked neglected. Market stalls stood half empty. Faces seemed more guarded than she remembered. Pater rode ahead in silence. Gorlat kept a steady watch on the road behind them. No one spoke much.

When the sea finally appeared on the horizon, the sunlight glinting across the Great Gray expanse, Alana felt the familiar pull in her chest. Home. Or what had once been home. The Jewel of Gershan rose along the coast ahead of them. Caerdis. But as they rode through the outer gates, the knot in her stomach tightened. She barely recognized it. The streets near the lower quarter were filthy. Refuse piled along the edges of the road where it had not been cleared away. Beggars clustered in doorways where once there had been busy shopkeepers. A sour smell lingered in the air. Rot. Waste. Despair.

Alana slowed her horse. "What happened?"

Pater's jaw tightened.

"Absence," he said quietly.

They rode deeper into the city. The markets were thinner. Merchants shouted louder, as though trying to drown out the unease that hung over the streets. Near the docks the change was worse. Laughter spilled from taverns even in the early afternoon. Women leaned in doorways calling to sailors. Gambling tables stood openly in alleys where children once played.

Alana stared. This had not been the Caerdis she remembered. The Jewel of Gershan had once been proud. Clean. Alive. Now... The shine had dulled.

"Debauchery follows weak rule," Gorlat muttered from behind her.

Alana did not answer. Her eyes moved slowly across the harbor. Ships rocked in the tide. The same sea. The same walls. But something inside the city had shifted.

She felt it like a bruise beneath the skin. And suddenly she understood why the Queen Mother had written. Caerdis was hurting. And the wound was spreading.

~

Alana had expected the road to climb toward the palace gates. Instead, Pater turned his horse down a narrower street that wound toward the lower quarter where Babba and Abbya lived. She frowned slightly but said nothing. The houses here stood close together, their whitewashed walls weathered by salt air. Some had fallen into disrepair since she had last seen them. Roof tiles sagged. Windows hung crooked in their frames. \

But Babba's house stood as it always had. Small. Neat. The shutters freshly painted. A small herb garden still clinging stubbornly to life along the stone wall. Alana felt a breath leave her chest. Relief.

Pater dismounted first. Gorlat followed. Before Alana could even reach the door it opened. Abbya stood there. For a moment she only stared. Then she moved. Her arms wrapped around Alana so tightly the breath left her lungs.

"You have returned to us." Her voice trembled.

Alana hugged her back just as fiercely.

"Yes," she whispered. "I have come home."

Abbya held her for a long moment before finally stepping back to study her face. Her hands cupped Alana's cheeks. "You are stronger."

"You say that like Elranth," Alana murmured.

Abbya laughed softly through the shine in her eyes and pulled her inside.

The house smelled the same. Bread. Herbs. Wood smoke. But something beneath it felt thinner. Quieter.

Babba emerged from the kitchen wiping his hands on a cloth. He stopped when he saw her. For a moment the big man simply stood there.

Then his face split into a wide smile. "Dohita."

Alana crossed the room and wrapped her arms around him. He felt... smaller. Not much. But enough. When she stepped back her eyes moved over him carefully. His cheeks were leaner. His belt tightened a notch farther than she remembered.

A small knot formed in her chest. "Have you enough food?"

The question slipped out before she could stop it. The room went very still. Babba looked toward the kitchen. Abbya busied herself with straightening the edge of the table. Neither of them met her eyes. The knot in Alana's chest tightened. She had seen this before. Long ago. When villages began to thin and cupboards began to empty and grown men stopped answering simple questions. Collapse rarely arrived like a storm. It crept. Quiet. Slow. Until one day there was simply... less. And people in their prime starved. Her mind flashed to Quinn. She blinked the thought away.

Alana's voice softened. "Babba."

He sighed. Finally he looked at her. "Yah provides." The words were careful. Measured.

But Alana heard what lay beneath them. And her concern sharpened.

~

Night settled heavy over Caerdis. The noise from the docks carried faintly through the streets—laughter, shouting, the clatter of cups. It sounded louder in the dark, rougher than Alana remembered. She sat at the small table in Babba's house, turning the Queen Mother's letter over in her hands. A knock came at the door. Three short taps. Babba opened it. Pater stood outside. Cloaked. Hood drawn low.

"Is she ready?" He whispered gruffly.

Abbya wrapped a dark cloak around Alana's shoulders before she could answer.

"Keep your head down," she murmured, smoothing the fabric near Alana's collar. "And listen to him."

Alana nodded.

Babba squeezed her shoulder once. "Go."

They moved through the streets quickly. Pater said little. Gorlat followed a few paces behind, his eyes constantly moving. The night air carried the sour scent of spilled ale and refuse. Lantern light flickered across narrow alleys where figures lingered too long in doorways.

Alana kept her hood low. They passed within sight of the palace walls. Her heart gave a small jump. But instead of approaching the gates, Pater veered sharply into a narrow side street. He slipped through a shadowed archway and into a stairwell that dropped steeply beneath the city. Alana followed without question.

Stone steps spiraled downward. The sounds of the street faded above them. At the bottom Pater pushed open a small iron door. A narrow hallway stretched beyond it. Damp. Cold. The walls were rough-cut stone.

"Quickly," he murmured.

They moved through the corridor until it widened slightly. Torches burned low in iron brackets along the walls. Alana's footsteps echoed softly.

"What is this place?" she whispered.

Pater glanced back at her. "The city is built on ruins." His voice carried quietly through the tunnel. "One hundred and fifty years ago His Majesty's great-grandfather ordered these passages connected." He turned down another corridor. "In case of siege."

The tunnel sloped gently upward now. The air smelled faintly of the sea.

"They lead beneath the palace," Pater continued. "Hidden entrances. Supply routes. Escape paths."

Alana ran her fingers lightly along the cold stone wall as she walked. "And now?" she asked.

Pater pushed open another narrow door. A stair climbed toward darkness above.

"Now," he said quietly, "we use them to reach the Queen Mother."

Alana followed Pater closely through the labyrinth. The tunnels twisted and forked so often she quickly lost all sense of direction. The stone beneath her boots changed from rough blocks to older, uneven masonry, then back again. She stayed close to Pater's cloak, grateful he knew the way. Left. Down another passage. A narrow stair. A turn so tight her shoulder brushed the wall.

I would never find my way out of here, she thought.

The air gradually warmed as they followed a long incline upward.

The damp chill of the lower tunnels faded, replaced by the faint smell of smoke and cooked herbs. At last Pater pushed open a narrow door. They emerged into the palace scullery. Alana froze. She knew this room. Copper pots hung along the walls. A large hearth smoldered low. The stone counters were worn smooth from years of use.

And standing beside the basin was Suzanna.

The young woman looked up, and her eyes widened. "Alana!"

She hurried forward, then caught herself, glancing nervously toward the door that led deeper into the palace.

"Quickly," she whispered. From a peg on the wall she grabbed a maid's dress and pressed it into Alana's hands. "And this."

A small cap. Pretty enough to pass unnoticed. Alana pulled the cloak free and quickly changed while Suzanna pinned the cap over her blond hair.

Up close, Alana saw the change in her. Suzanna's face looked thinner. Her eyes carried a tiredness that had not been there before.

"The Queen Mother awaits," Suzanna said softly.

Alana nodded. Suzanna pressed a tray of tea into her hands.

"Take this." She pressed.

The tray rattled slightly as Alana lifted it. She drew a slow breath and stepped through the kitchen door. The palace corridors were quieter than she remembered. Guards stood at their posts along the stairs.

But when Alana passed, carrying the tea tray and wearing a servant's cap, they barely glanced at her. One yawned. Another leaned lazily against the wall. Sloppy. Bored. The way men grew when the edge of discipline had dulled.

Alana climbed the stairs steadily. The familiar hallway came into view. At the end of it stood the blue door. Gold inlaid across its panels. Her heart began to beat faster. She knocked once. The door opened almost immediately. Kefira stood there. The lady's face had always been sharp, composed. Now it looked tighter somehow. Drawn.

But when she saw Alana, her eyes softened just slightly. "Come."

Alana stepped inside. And nearly dropped the tray. Queen Cerwyn sat beside the window. The last time Alana had seen her, the queen's hair had gleamed raven-black in the garden sunlight. Now streaks of gray ran through it. The shine had dulled. The weight of months had settled quietly across her shoulders. But her eyes,. Her eyes were still kind. And when she smiled, the warmth in it had not changed.

Alana set the tray down quickly before her trembling hands could betray her. Cerwyn reached forward and took her hand.

"You have returned." The Queen's voice was soft. "An answer to my prayers."

Alana knelt instinctively beside her chair. The queen squeezed her fingers gently.

"Come, my dear." The older woman said. Her smile deepened, though the weariness behind it remained. "We have much to discuss."

Cerwyn did not speak immediately. She kept hold of Alana's hand for a moment longer, studying her face as though measuring what time at the High Keep had done. Finally she released her and leaned back in her chair.

"You must understand something first," the Queen Mother said quietly.

Alana sat opposite her, the tea tray between them.

"This is not an armed resistance." Her tone held no drama. Just clarity.

"I am not gathering soldiers. I am not raising banners."

She folded her hands in her lap.

"I am helping where I can… who I can… with what I can."

Alana listened.

Cerwyn continued. "Food."

She gestured faintly toward the city beyond the window. "Shelter."

Another pause. "Medicine."

Kefira stood silently beside the door, her sharp eyes constantly flicking toward the hallway beyond.

Cerwyn lowered her voice slightly. "There are families in Caerdis who have lost everything in these last months. Sailors who cannot find work. Children who have no bread."

Her gaze returned to Alana. "So we help them."

"How?" Alana asked quietly.

"Through people who still remember what kindness looks like." Cerwyn's mouth curved faintly. "A baker who leaves extra loaves at the back door. A physician who treats wounds without asking coin. A widow who opens her cellar to those with nowhere else to sleep."

"A network," Alana said softly.

Cerwyn nodded. "Community."

For a moment neither woman spoke. Then Cerwyn leaned forward slightly. "I need you to be my eyes and ears."

Alana blinked.

Cerwyn continued gently. "Kefira is confined with me."

Kefira inclined her head slightly in acknowledgment.

"And I need a maid no one remembers."

A faint smile touched the queen's mouth. "No insult intended, my dear."

Alana understood immediately. A maid passed everywhere. Through kitchens. Corridors. Servants' halls. Invisible. The realization settled into place quickly. She was indeed uniquely positioned. And trained.

Cerwyn watched the understanding dawn in her eyes.

"It is not a safe position," the queen added quietly.

Alana reached for her teacup. The porcelain warmed her fingers. She set it down again carefully.

"I did not return to be safe." Her voice was calm. "I came to help." A small breath. "And because you asked."

Cerwyn blinked once. A look of quiet recognition crossed her face.

"Elranth was not wrong about you." She finally said.

Alana bowed her head slightly. "I take that as a compliment of the highest order, Majesty." She lifted her eyes again. "Now please." Her voice was steady. "Tell me how I can be of service."

~

No one remembered her. Even when a strand of blond hair slipped loose beneath her cap. Alana moved through the palace like a wraith. Servants passed her in the corridors without a second glance. Guards waved her through kitchens and sculleries without lifting their heads. She carried trays, swept floors, scrubbed pots, and listened. And listened.

In the quiet spaces between footsteps and whispers, truth began to gather. Morlach. The name surfaced again and again. The vizier had been careful. Patient. It was Morlach who had first seeded the rumor that Tristan intended to marry a foreign woman and crown her queen. It was Morlach who had painted the adoption hearings as the Queen Mother's scheme, an attempt to circumvent the law and place an outsider on Gershan's throne.

The court had swallowed it. In Tristan's absence, Morlach signed orders in the king's name. Orders that left Gershan unraveling. Grain shipments diverted. Trade routes neglected. Tariffs raised and lowered in ways that strangled the markets. Alana watched it happen piece by piece. She had seen it before. In Kuvale. The memory tightened something deep in her chest. Collapse did not always arrive with armies. Sometimes it came with ink and signatures.

During the day she gathered information. At night she slipped into the tunnels beneath the palace to meet Gorlat or Pater. They brought coin. Orders. Names of families who needed help. Bread was delivered. Medicine passed quietly from hand to hand. Cellars opened. The network grew slowly, like roots beneath the soil.

She was careful. Always careful. But two months into the work, the first crack came. Pater was caught. Breaking curfew. He had already been watched because of his connection to Tristan, the former captain of the guard. The trial was swift. Public. Ten solar cycles. The salt mines in the southwest.

The news spread through the network like winter frost. Some left. Quietly. Without blame. Neither Alana nor Cerwyn condemned them. Fear had teeth. And the economy continued its slow spiral downward. Still they worked. Still they helped where they could. Still the network held.

~

Late one night Alana returned through the streets after visiting a family near the docks. Two babies lay in a narrow bed there, their tiny chests heaving with a racking cough. The mother had cried when Alana brought the medicine. Alana slipped through the alley behind the palace kitchens and found the hidden door. The tunnel swallowed her. She lit a torch and began the familiar walk beneath the city. The walls glistened faintly with moisture. Her footsteps echoed softly.

She turned at the narrow wall where the passage bent sharply toward the palace stairs. And heard it. A scrape. Boot leather against stone. Her heart lurched. She was supposed to be alone. Gorlat was days away in the hill country trying to gather support for the network. The sound came again. Alana whirled.

Her hand went instantly for the dagger beneath her cloak. She never drew it. A hand clamped around her wrist. Another slammed over her mouth. The torch dropped and sputtered against the stone.

The man behind her smelled of herbs. Sharp. Bitter. Her head began to swim almost immediately. She fought. Hard. The staff training returned instinctively. She tried twisting, striking with her elbow, trying to break free. But another pair of hands seized her shoulders. A hood dropped over her head. Darkness swallowed everything. Cold iron snapped around her wrists. Then her ankles. The chains bit deep. Her strength faded faster than it should have. The herbal scent filled her lungs. Someone lifted her. The world tilted.

As they hauled her over a shoulder, her final clear thought flickered through the fog closing around her mind.

Yah-Roi...

Please keep the queen.

Chapter 29

The first thing that came to Alana was motion. The slow, rolling sway of the sea. Her body had never forgotten it. The rise. The fall. The subtle pull beneath her ribs that told her she was no longer on land. She forced herself to breathe slowly. In. Out. She would not panic. Not yet.

The irons on her wrists were heavy. Her ankles were bound as well. She lay on something hard wood, by the feel of it. A bench, perhaps. Her head throbbed. Her mouth felt dry and thick, like she had swallowed wool.

She blinked. Darkness covered her eyes, but faint pinpricks of light filtered through rough burlap. A hood. She shifted slightly and a low moan escaped her before she could stop it. Her head pulsed harder.

"She is awake." The voice was unfamiliar. Gruff.

Alana's heart began to pound. The rhythm thudded painfully against her skull. Hands grabbed her arm and hauled her upright. The hood was yanked away. Light flooded her vision. Lantern light. Too bright.

She lifted her chained hands instinctively to shield her eyes.

"Who are you?" The voice that demanded it was deep. Sharp. And so familiar it struck her chest like a blow.

Her hand fell slowly. Her eyes widened. "Tristan?"

The shadowed figure stepped forward into the lantern glow. Yes.

It was him. His hair was longer than when she had last seen him. His jaw was harder, his shoulders broader beneath the dark cloak he wore. But it was Tristan. Her Tristan.

For a heartbeat he simply stared at her. His expression was cold Detached. Then recognition struck. The change was instant. The color drained from his face. Horror followed.

"Get her out of those irons." The command cracked through the small cabin.

He stepped toward her, reaching instinctively for the chains at her wrists. His hands stopped halfway. Shame flickered across his features like a shadow passing over water.

A guard dropped to one knee beside her. A key turned. The manacles on her wrists clattered open and fell away. The guard moved quickly to the irons at her ankles.

Tristan had not moved. He stood there staring at her hands where the metal had rubbed the skin raw. His voice, when he spoke again, was lower. Tighter.

"Alana, You're supposed to be in Doreth." Tristan's voice was thick with confusion.

Alana lifted an eyebrow. "And you are supposed to be exiled." She said it softly. There was no venom in it. Only relief.

He stared at her for a moment, then dropped to one knee in front of her. At last he reached for her hands. "My darling," he said quietly, "I had no idea it was you, or I would not have—"

He stopped. Swallowed. His fingers tightened around hers as though the thought itself made him ill. For a moment they simply looked at each other.

Then something about the absurdity of it struck Alana all at once. Her eyes twinkled.

"You mean to say," she said lightly, "that you make it a regular habit of going about Caerdis kidnapping young women in tunnels?"

Tristan blinked. Then he snorted despite himself. "That is not funny."

She shrugged faintly. "I thought it was."

He stared at her. The lantern light caught the familiar line of his brow as he studied her face, as though confirming she was truly sitting there.

"How are you here?" he asked finally.

"Your mother sent for me," Alana answered quietly. "Pater brought me back to the city." The smile faded slightly from her lips. "He was arrested a month ago."

His head snapped up. "What?"

"Breaking curfew." She confirmed, Her tone was calm now. "Undermining rightful authority." She shrugged one shoulder. "The sentence was ten solar cycles in the salt marches."

The words hung in the air between them. Tristan's jaw tightened. Slowly. Dangerously.

Alana squeezed his hand lightly before the anger could rise.

"How is it that *you* are here?" she asked gently.

He exhaled slowly. "It is a tale I am not sure you will believe." He stood and offered her his arm. "But this is not my vessel." He glanced toward the door of the cell. "Come." His hand settled lightly at her elbow. "I will introduce you to the man responsible for my survival."

Alana rose carefully. Her legs wobbled slightly as the lingering sedative pulled at her balance. Tristan noticed immediately. His arm tightened around hers, drawing her closer against his side.

"Lean on me," he murmured.

Alana smiled up at him. "Gladly."

~

Tristan guided her out into the passageway. The ship groaned softly around them, the slow rhythm of the sea moving beneath the hull. Lanterns swung from iron hooks along the beams, throwing long shadows across the narrow corridor. It was not a passenger vessel. This part of the hold had been turned into a brig. Iron bars rose thick and black from floor to beam. Several small cells lined the passage, their doors locked with heavy bolts. The air smelled of salt, iron, and damp wood.

Tristan walked steadily beside her, his arm still firm around hers. On the left, a shadowy figure leaned against the back wall of one of the cells. His posture was loose. Lazy. As if nothing about his circumstances troubled him in the least. Another man stood further down the passage. He wore the long overcoat of a captain. His back was to them as he spoke quietly with one of Tristan's guards.

As Alana and Tristan approached, the man in the cell shifted.

Chains rattled softly against the floor. Then a voice drifted through the bars. Low. Amused.

A voice she had not heard in nearly five years. "Pet."

Alana froze.

"Imagine seeing you here." Tarren said as he stepped from the back wall into the light.

Her body went rigid. Her throat seized. Time slowed. She did not want to look. Her feet felt nailed to the planks.

The man in the captain's coat turned sharply at the prisoner's words. Alana stared at him now, Something about his face was familiar. Too familiar. He stepped toward her slowly. Studying her with vibrant green eyes wide in disbelief. As if he were looking at an apparition.

Then he spoke. At the same moment the realization struck her.

"Bethan?" The name fell from his lips just as the truth slammed into her mind.

The man looked like the mirror image of Cal Horsgaard. Only older. Harder. Weathered by years at sea. He shook his head slowly. Like a man struggling to believe what his eyes showed him.

"Beaty?" He tried again.

The childhood nickname hit her like a blade. The corridor tilted.

Behind her Tarren clicked his tongue. "How touching a family reunited." His voice full of mockery.

Alana's stomach lurched violently. And she knew with sudden, sick certainty. She was about to be very, very ill. She had the presence of mind to pull her arm free from Tristan. Then she ran. Down the passage. Past the lanterns. Toward the ladder at the end of the brig. Someone called after her. Maybe Tristan Maybe Quinn or Tarren, Maybe they all called.

She could not stop. Her lungs refused to draw a full breath. Her vision narrowed until the world became nothing but the ladder in front of her. She shoved through the hatch at the top and staggered onto the deck. Cold sea air hit her like a wave. Alana dragged in a long, desperate breath. Then another. It did nothing to steady the violent roll of her stomach.

She lurched toward the rail. A hand caught her hair just as she bent over the side. Her body heaved. Once. Twice. Again. Everything in her stomach came up in harsh, burning waves. She clung to the rail as the ship rolled beneath her feet, her hands trembling against the salt-worn wood. Behind her someone held her hair firmly away from her face. Patient. Steady. She heaved again until there was nothing left. Only the bitter taste of bile.

Gradually the tight band around her chest loosened. Her breathing slowed. The sea wind cooled her face. She wiped her mouth with the back of her sleeve and straightened slowly. Her hands still shook where they gripped the rail. For a moment she simply stared out across the dark water.

She turned. Tristan stood a step behind her. Concern written plainly across his face. And just beyond him, another figure. A man she had buried long ago in the deepest corner of her memory. Older now. Scarred by time. But unmistakable. Quinn. Alive.

She turned slowly from the railing. The wind tugged at her cloak. Her eyes moved between the two men. Tristan stood closest, watching her with careful concern. But it was the man behind him who held her gaze. Quinn stepped forward. Slowly. As though he feared she might vanish if he moved too quickly.

He lifted his hands. Took hers gently.

"Bethan." He retreated, The name felt strange on the deck of that ship.

Alana stared up at him. "Quinn?"

A slow smile spread beneath the thick beard that covered the lower half of his face. Years had carved lines between his brows and along the corners of his eyes. But those eyes, They were still the same green she remembered.

Still steady. Still watching her with that same quiet intensity. "It's me, Beaty."

The name landed softly this time. Not like a blade.

Alana blinked. She had spent years believing him dead. Grieved him and buried him in her mind. Her fingers tightened in his hands as though testing whether he was real.

"You… you died, you're supposed to be dead. She said.

Quinn huffed a quiet breath. "Not for lack of trying."

Tristan shifted slightly beside them. Alana glanced at him. His expression had changed. Something in his face now carried a quiet understanding. He stepped back half a pace, giving them room.

Quinn squeezed her hands once.

"You look stronger," he said quietly.

Her laugh came out thin. "I had to run a lot."

His eyes flicked briefly to Tristan. Then back to her.

"Looks like you landed on your feet." He said.

Alana followed his glance. A faint smile touched her mouth despite the storm still spinning through her chest.

"Something like that." Her voice was warm when she said it.

The wind lifted Quinn's coat slightly as the ship rolled beneath them. For a moment the three of them simply stood there. The sea stretched dark and endless around them. And the past, long buried, had just stepped back onto the deck

~

The sudden appearance of her long-lost brother, and her betrothed had her glancing between them.

"This is your vessel?" She asked Quinn.

He nodded. "It is, *The Stormhold*" His voice was full of pride.

She smiled, looking around at the gleaming planking, and polished bells and eyelets that held knots of rope. It was indeed a beautiful and well cared for ship. Which begged the nagging question in the back of mind.

"Why is Tarren in the brig?" Alana's voice had sharpened.

The wind moved between them, tugging lightly at cloaks and loose strands of hair. Quinn and Tristan exchanged a glance. It was quick. Heavy with things unsaid.

Quinn tilted his head slightly, studying her.

"He is my prisoner," he said at last. His voice had gone rough.

"Why?" She pressed.

Quinn's jaw tightened. The muscles along it flexed once before he answered.

"Because I needed to know what happened to you." He finally answered honestly.

The words struck her like ice water. Her past flashed through her mind in jagged fragments. The ship. Chains. The dark cabin. Tarren's voice. Her fingers curled slowly at her sides.

Her eyes flicked toward Tristan. He stood very still. Contained. For now.

"How much do you know?" she asked quietly.

Quinn cleared his throat. He glanced once more at Tristan before answering.

"Only his side." He said gruffly.

The band around her chest tightened again. Threatening to close completely. She forced herself to breathe. Slow. Careful.

"Then you know what I am," she said.

Her voice was steady. But her eyes were on Tristan when she said it.

"We know what he made you to be." Tristan's correction was gentle. But the hand at his side flexed once when he said it.

Alana flinched. The movement was small, instinctive. Tristan saw it. Immediately his posture softened. His shoulders lowered, as though trying to make himself smaller, less threatening.

Her vision blurred. Tears gathered faster than she could stop them.

"I never meant to keep it from you." The words scraped their way out of her throat.

Shame sat there like a stone. Her breath hitched once. Twice. And then the weight of it all, the years, the silence, the memories she had buried so carefully, came crashing down. Her knees gave way.

She sank to the deck with a broken sob. Her strings cut by sheer force of emotion. The wood struck hard beneath her, but she barely felt it. Her hands flew to her face. And she wept. Not quietly. Not carefully. The kind of weeping that came from somewhere deep and long held.

The sea wind rushed past them. Neither man spoke. Quinn stood frozen for a moment, his expression tightening as though something inside him had been struck. Tristan moved first. Slowly. Carefully. He crouched in front of her, not touching her yet. Just there. Waiting.

The lantern light from the stern swung across the deck, casting long shadows across the three of them as the ship rolled beneath their feet. And Alana wept until the truth of her past had finally found its way into the open air.

She cried until the tears were gone. Until her body could give no more. The sobs tore through her until even the strength to make them faded.

She cried for Bethan, for the name she had been born with, For the girl who had been taken. For Quinn. For Colton. For Tristan. For Alana, the maid who had been named by those who loved her. For Pet, and all the pain and memory and heartache tangled together inside her.

When it was finally spent, she found herself nearly face down on the deck. Her forehead pressed against the rough wood. Her limbs heavy. Her body utterly exhausted.

The sea rolled beneath the ship. Somewhere above them the rigging creaked softly in the wind. A hand moved gently over her hair. Tristan. He brushed a loose lock behind her ear.

"Let me help you," he said quietly. "Please, darling."

He reached toward her. But he stopped before touching her. His hand remained there. Open. Waiting.

She blinked up at him through swollen eyes. For the first time she noticed something that made her pause. He was not recoiling. There was no disgust in his face. No horror. Only concern. And hope. Tentative. Careful. Waiting for her to decide.

Her fingers trembled slightly as she lifted her hand. She placed it in his. He closed his grip around hers gently and helped her sit upright. The world swayed slightly as she moved.

Quinn's voice came from nearby. Gruff. Practical. "You need food and water."

Alana sniffed and wiped at her face with the back of her sleeve. "Thank you," she said softly.

Quinn insisted she take his quarters. She was too tired to argue. Someone had pressed bread into her hands, then broth, then water. Tristan had stayed close while she ate, saying little, only watching to be sure she finished. Afterward Quinn led her down a narrow passage to a small cabin. It smelled faintly of salt and cedar.

"There," he said gruffly, pushing the door open.

A feather bed filled most of the small room. Alana had not realized how tired she was until she saw it. "Rest," Quinn added, already turning away. She stepped inside.

The ship rocked gently beneath her feet. For a moment she simply stood there, swaying slightly with the motion. Then she sank onto the bed. The mattress dipped beneath her weight. Soft. Far softer than the narrow pallet she had grown used to at the High Keep, and the small pallet she had in the palace. She pulled the blanket over herself and rested her head on the pillow. Her body felt hollowed out. All the tears. All the memories dragged into the open. The exhaustion wrapped around her like a heavy cloak. Her eyes drifted closed.

Sleep began to creep in slowly. Then— Something struck the wall outside the cabin with a heavy thud. Alana jerked slightly. A scuffle followed. Boots scraping. Another sharp bang. Her eyes fluttered open halfway.

Through the door she heard Quinn's voice. Low. Tight with restrained anger. "No." A pause. "You spent a year keeping me from killing him outright."

The voices dropped after that. Too low for her to make out clearly. But one name floated faintly through the wood of the door.

Tarren.

They were speaking about Tarren. Her mind tried to hold onto the thought. Tried to listen. But exhaustion dragged harder. The ship rocked gently beneath her. The voices blurred. And before she could gather the strength to wonder what they meant... Sleep finally claimed her.

Chapter 30

A gull cried somewhere outside the small window. The sound pulled Alana slowly back to the waking world. The ship creaked around her, the steady groan of timber shifting with the tide. Sunlight filtered through the round glass pane and painted a pale circle across the cabin wall. For a moment she lay still. Her body ached. Not the clean soreness of training. The dull ache of bruises and too little sleep. Her muscles protested when she moved, and her face felt tight and swollen from the tears of the night before.

She stared at the ceiling beams. Had she not woken aboard this vessel she might have believed the whole thing a fevered dream. Quinn. Tristan. Tarren in chains.

Slowly she pushed herself upright. The cabin rocked gently beneath her bare feet as she stood. Her dress was wrinkled and rumpled from sleep. She smoothed the fabric instinctively, trying to press the creases out with her hands. The gesture accomplished nothing. After a moment she gave a quiet sigh and abandoned the effort.

When she reached for the door, part of her expected it to resist. To be locked. It opened easily. The narrow passage outside smelled of salt and tar. She followed it toward the ladder and climbed up through the hatch.

Morning sunlight washed across the deck. Soft. Golden. The sea stretched blue and endless in every direction. Crewmen moved about their work with the easy rhythm of sailors who knew their ship well. Lines were coiled, sails trimmed, barrels rolled into place. Several of them glanced her way.

"Ma'am." Nodded one sailor who wore the creased beret of a lieutenant.

Alana blinked slightly and nodded in return as she crossed the deck.

The word 'ma'am' struck her as odd, Kuvalian, not Gershani.

She was halfway toward the rail before she realized someone was calling to her.

"Bethan." Quinn's voice came over the deck.

She turned. He stood on the raised bridge above the deck. He wore a long overcoat the color of rust, the wind tugging lightly at its hem. His pale hair—bleached nearly silver by the sun—was tied back neatly with a black ribbon.

For a moment she simply stared. It struck her again how very much he resembled Papa. The same height. The same broad shoulders. Even the way he stood at ease against the railing.

She lifted a small wave. And smiled.

"Come up here," he called down.

Her feet began moving almost before she had decided to obey. Step by step she climbed the short ladder to the bridge. He was alive. He was her brother. And he was still very much a stranger.

Tristan stood just behind Quinn. The sea wind pulled lightly at his coat. It was faded blue. Alana recognized it immediately—the same one she had mended once after he and Pater had fenced in the courtyard and he had lost badly enough to tear the sleeve. The memory flickered through her mind.

Tristan glanced at Quinn before stepping forward. He reached for her hand. Alana did not miss the subtle shift in Quinn's posture when he did. Her brother's shoulders straightened. Not aggressively. But not lazily anymore either.

"So," Quinn said slowly. "My Bethan is your Alana."

Alana raised an eyebrow at him. "Still not one to ease into things, are you?"

Tristan straightened slightly. His posture relaxed, but the steel in his voice did not soften.

"You know I love her." The prince said.

He was not explaining himself. Not defending his choice. Simply stating a fact. To Quinn. To the sea. To anyone listening.

Alana wished very briefly that the deck might open and swallow her whole. She cleared her throat.

"Forgive me," she said, "but is there a reason you wanted me up here to witness this display of male posturing?" Her tone was firm.

Both men looked at her. Slightly startled.

Quinn tilted his head.

"He chose you," he said.

Then he looked directly into her eyes.

"But do you choose him?" He had barely finished speaking when she answered.

"Yes." She said

The word came without hesitation.

Quinn opened his mouth. Closed it again. Then glanced sideways at Tristan.

"If you hurt her," he said calmly, "I will personally throw you to the sharks."

Tristan nodded once. "Understood."

Quinn looked between them both again. Then he sighed. Deeply.

"Get off my bridge." He said gruffly.

Tristan's mouth curved into a smirk. He slapped Quinn once across the back as he turned.

"I intended to, with or without your permission." The prince shot back.

Quinn growled under his breath. "You are pushing it, Prince."

Tristan only laughed. Then he offered Alana his arm and guided her down the ladder to the main deck.

~

Alana walked beside him in silence. The deck shifted gently beneath their feet as the ship moved through the slow morning swell. Sailors passed them now and again, giving Tristan respectful space as they went about their work.

She waited. If Tristan wished to speak, he would. For a time he did not. The wind carried the cry of gulls overhead, and the creak of rope against mast.

Finally he broke the quiet. "You are different."

The words were not accusation. Not even surprise. Just an observation.

Alana glanced sideways at him. "In what way?"

Tristan's hand rested lightly over hers where her arm was tucked through his. "You stand differently." He studied her a moment. "Straighter." A small pause. "And you speak your mind more quickly."

The corner of her mouth twitched. "Elranth encouraged it."

Tristan huffed a faint breath that might have been a laugh. "That explains much."

They walked a few more steps. Then he spoke again. "You are stronger."

This time his voice had softened. Not simply noting a change. Admiring it.

Alana looked out across the sea. "The Keep trains more than the mind."

"So I see." He acknowledged.

He glanced at the calluses faintly visible along her knuckles. The ones the bow staff had left behind. For a moment he said nothing.

Then, quieter, he said. "You were crying last night."

The statement hung between them. Not pressing. Not demanding. Just... there.

Alana let out a slow breath. "Yes."

The ship rolled gently. Her fingers tightened slightly around his arm.

"There were things I never told you." She admitted gently.

Tristan nodded once. "I gathered as much."

She waited for the questions. For the hurt. For the distance.

Instead he said simply, "We have time now."

And kept walking beside her.

"I am not sure where to start," she admitted honestly. Tristan walked beside her, his hand resting lightly over hers where her arm was tucked through his.

"How about the beginning?" he suggested.

Alana turned her face toward the sea. The water rolled in long blue swells beneath the morning sun.

"I was sixteen," she said quietly, "when we lost everything." She swallowed once. "Papa. Mama. The farm."

And from there she told him. The words came slowly at first. Then easier. The winter that followed. The hunger. The road. The people she had trusted and the ones she should not have. The slow tightening of the world around her until there had been no choices left that were not terrible.

Tristan did not interrupt. Not once. Only occasionally did he ask a quiet question. A date. A place. A name. He listened.

When she came to the part about the pregnancy, her voice faltered. She watched him then. Waiting. Waiting for the tightening of his jaw. For the flicker of disgust. For the quiet distance that would mean she had finally said the thing that could not be forgiven.

Instead Tristan's eyes filled. He sniffed once.

"I would have liked to have known him." He said softly. His voice was rough with emotion.

The words were simple. But they struck her like a blow. Her throat closed.

"He was my beautiful boy," she said softly.

Her voice thick with tears she had not yet allowed to fall. She stared down at her hands.

"I prayed that Yah would set him free." She whispered.

The words came out tight. As though there was still one small place in her heart where grief had never quite made peace with heaven. Tristan said nothing for a moment. He wiped his eyes with the back of his hand and cleared his throat.

"He is free." He said firmly.

Alana looked up.

"Just not the way you thought." He finished.

She blinked. The words settled slowly. Reframing something she had carried for years. Her prayer. Her loss. The answer she had never recognized.

She stared out across the sea again. For a moment she could not speak.

When her voice finally returned, it was quieter. "I had never thought of it that way." A pause. Then she added softly, "I do not ever want to forget."

One tear slipped free and splashed against the rail. Tristan turned toward her. He took her hand fully in his.

"Then we will remember." His voice was steady. "And he will be to me a firstborn son."

Alana understood immediately. She knew the law. If they married… If Tristan ever reclaimed his crown… Colton would be granted a title. Even now. Posthumously. Her breath caught.

"Why are you so good to me?" she asked softly.

Tristan looked at her as though the answer was obvious.

"Because I love you." He squeezed her hand gently. "And that is reason enough."

~

They stood for a long moment after that. The sea rolled quietly beneath the hull. Wind tugged at the loose strands of Alana's hair and carried the smell of salt across the deck. Tristan's hand was still around hers. She should have felt lighter. She had told him. All of it.

The shame she had carried for years had finally been spoken into the open air. And yet something inside her chest remained tight. Not grief. Not fear. Something unfinished.

Her gaze drifted across the deck. Then down. Toward the hatch. Toward the brig beneath their feet.

Tristan noticed the shift.

"What is it?" He asked.

She did not answer immediately. Instead she watched the hatch a moment longer. As if she could see through the planks and down into the darkness below.

Finally she said quietly, "He is still there."

Tristan's jaw tightened slightly. "Yes."

Alana drew in a slow breath. For years she had done everything possible to avoid this moment. To outrun it. To bury it. But the High Keep had taught her something difficult. Running did not end a storm. It only delayed it.

She let go of Tristan's hand. "I need to see him."

Tristan went still. "You do not owe him that."

"I know." Her voice was steady. "That is not why."

He searched her face. "What then?"

Alana looked back toward the sea. For a moment she struggled to find the words. Then they came.

"Because he is still standing inside my past." She met Tristan's eyes again. "And I am tired of letting him live there."

Silence stretched between them. The ship creaked. A gull cried overhead.

Finally Tristan nodded once. "Then I will go with you."

She hesitated. Part of her wanted that. Part of her very much did not.

"This is not a fight," she said softly.

"It is for me." Tristan studied her a moment longer. Then he stepped back. "But I will be nearby."

Alana nodded. That was justified. She turned toward the hatch. Her stomach tightened as she crossed the deck. Each step felt heavier than the last. Not because she was afraid. But because she knew, with quiet certainty now. The moment she opened that door... Something that had ruled her life for years would finally end.

She reached the hatch. Her hand rested on the iron ring. For a heartbeat she almost stopped. Then she pulled it open. And stepped down into the dark.

~

The brig smelled of salt and rust. Alana paused at the bottom of the ladder. The lantern light swayed with the motion of the ship, throwing long shadows across the iron bars. Somewhere water slapped softly against the hull.

Her hands were steady. That surprised her. For years she had imagined this moment. In those imaginings her heart raced, her breath came shallow, her courage dissolved the instant she saw him. Now she simply felt... clear.

Behind her Tristan stopped a few paces back. He did not crowd her. He did not touch her. He was simply there. Waiting.

The man in the cell shifted. Chains rasped against the wood.

"Good." The word came softly from the darkness. The smirk clear in the sound of Tarren's voice.

Alana's spine stiffened. She had not heard that voice in years, and yet it slid through her memory like a knife finding an old scar.

"Little bird." He spoke his name for her like a whisper.

The lantern swung again, and Tarren's face came into the light. He had not changed as much as she expected. Older. His face was more lined. His hair longer but still kept, even here. He had the same calculating eyes.

For a moment her body remembered before her mind did. The tightness in her chest. The instinct to shrink. To appease. To survive.

She breathed once. Slowly. The moment passed.

"Whose are you, little bird?" The words were soft. Coaxing. Almost curious.

Alana stared at him. Once that question had ruled her life. Once she would have searched desperately for the right answer. The safe answer.

Now she understood what the question really was. A claim. A cage.

She turned fully toward the cell.

"I am Yah-Roi's." She answered. Her voice surprised her.

It did not tremble. But it was tentative.

Tarren's lips curled.

"Yah-Roi?" he scoffed. "The one you abandoned?"

He leaned closer to the bars.

"The one you betrayed when you came to me begging for peace?" His voice softened again. Dangerous. "You remember that don't you, little bird? You came to me." He reminded her, his tone full of accusation.

Alana felt Tristan shift behind her. She lifted a hand slightly. He stopped.

She kept her eyes on Tarren.

"Yes," she said quietly. "I remember."

For the first time something flickered across Tarren's face. Triumph "I knew you would never forget me, Pet."

She took a step closer. The iron bars stood between them now. Solid. Final.

"I remember the lies," she said, ignoring his taunt. "I remember the chains." Her voice did not rise. "I remember the boy I buried because of you."

Something dark flashed through Tarren's eyes now. Anger. Possession.

"You came to me," he warned icily.

His hand reached for her face. "You belong to me."

The old fear tried to rise again. She felt it. Leaning back so he was stopped short by the bars.

"No, I am Yah-Roi's." She insisted this time her voice was stronger. Not defiance. Truth.

Tarren lunged forward. His control finally snapping. His fingers clawed through the bars, reaching for her.

"No!" he shouted. "You're mine, Pet!"

His voice cracked with something raw. "Say it!"

The ship creaked around them. Lantern light swung across the iron. Alana could hear Tristan force his breathing to calm, behind her.

Alana did not step back. She simply looked at Tarren. . Calm. Certain.

"I belong to Yah-Roi, and I forgive you, not because you deserve it, but because He has forgiven me. And now I am finally free" She said simply.

Then she turned. And walked away.

Behind her Tarren's voice rose again. "Pet!"

The name echoed through the brig. She did not stop. She did not turn. She climbed the ladder and stepped back into the open air. And the man who had ruled her past was left shouting at empty space.

~

"You let her do *what*?" Quinn's voice cracked across the cabin like a whip.

His face had folded into a scowl that would have sent half his crew scrambling for cover. Alana flinched.

The reaction came before she could stop it. Her eyes dropped to the bowl in front of her. The stew had gone cold while they talked, a thin skin forming across the top. For a moment the old instinct stirred; stay quiet, let the men argue over her, wait for the storm to pass.

Then her fists tightened against the table. The spoon clinked softly against the bowl as she set it down.

"I went to see him." Her voice was calm.

Not loud. But it cut cleanly through the cabin.

"Tristan did not *let* me do anything." She finished forcefully.

Quinn blinked. The anger on his face shifted slightly, not gone, but redirected. Tristan leaned back in his chair beside her, watching the exchange carefully but saying nothing. Alana lifted her eyes now.

"I am not sixteen anymore," she added quietly.

Quinn's jaw worked once.

"I noticed," he muttered.

She continued before he could launch into another protest.

"I needed to face him." She insisted. Her fingers curled lightly against the table. "And now it is done."

Silence stretched across the small cabin. The ship creaked around them. Finally Quinn exhaled through his nose and scrubbed a hand down his beard.

"You could have been hurt." He muttered.

Alana met his gaze steadily. "I was."

That stopped him. For a moment the only sound was the slow slap of water against the hull. Then Quinn leaned back in his chair with a heavy sigh.

"Next time," he grumbled, "at least warn the captain before you go confronting prisoners in his brig."

The corner of Tristan's mouth twitched. Alana reached for her spoon again.

"I will keep that in mind." She promised saucily. The closest her tone had come to matching that of her younger self from a time when they argued.

"He doesn't deserve anything from you, Bethan." Quinn's voice had lost its edge now. Still rough. Still protective. But calmer.

Alana nodded slightly. "I am aware." Her voice was soft. "But I did not go for him." She lifted her eyes. "I went for me."

Quinn studied her face. Longer this time. As though trying to measure the woman sitting across from him against the girl he remembered.

Alana folded her hands together on the table. "He trained me," she said quietly. "Like a dog." The words hung there a moment. "To answer him." Her fingers tightened once before she continued. "I am not that woman anymore."

She lifted her chin slightly. "I am Yah-Roi's."

The words came the same way they had in the brig. Certain. Steady. "And I am free." She finished firmly.

Quinn's jaw tightened. The muscles along it flexed once. "You won't go see him again?"

She shook her head. "No."

The answer came without hesitation. For a moment neither of them spoke. The cabin creaked softly around them as the ship rocked. Alana felt the weight settle in her chest again. Not from fear. From something quieter.

Quinn had not asked what she meant. Not about Yah-Roi. Not about freedom. She knew that look. Knew the closed door behind it.

Quinn leaned back in his chair and dragged a hand through his beard.

"Good," he muttered.

Alana lowered her gaze to her bowl again. Her heart felt unexpectedly heavy. Not because she doubted what she had said. But because the God they had both been raised to serve now seemed to stand between them like a wall neither of them quite knew how to cross.

Tristan cleared his throat. The sound was deliberate. Careful. As though he were trying to ease the tension without drawing attention to it.

"You have many names, Darling," he said lightly.

The comment seemed almost pulled from thin air. "He calls you Bethan. I know you as Alana." The prince continued.

He glanced between her and Quinn.

"Which would you prefer?" He asked gently.

For a moment no one spoke. Alana's eyes moved between them. Quinn. Tristan. Two men from two different chapters of her life. The moment felt heavier than it had any right to be. She folded her hands together loosely on the table.

"I think..." she said slowly. "...that my name does not matter so much."

Quinn's brow creased slightly. Tristan watched her quietly.

"I can answer to both," she continued.

A faint smile touched the corner of her mouth.

"I have had to learn to." She said with certainty.

Her gaze drifted briefly toward the small window where the sea stretched wide and blue beyond the glass. Then she looked back at them.

"I think the only thing that truly matters..." She paused. "...is that I am a daughter of Yah-Roi."

Her voice was soft. But steady. "He sees me."

The words settled quietly into the space between them.

"And that is more than enough."

Tristans Reckoning

Coming June 30, 2026
A king bound by duty
A choice that will cost him everything

Crown Prince Tristan's chest heaved. The wooden sword in his arm seemed to weigh more with each swing and blow. Sweat ran down his face and neck. His father's sword swung in a blur of motion, striking his forearm. Tristan yelped in pain, and he lost his rhythm. His father's sword came to rest over his heart.

"You are dead," King Aurelio said seriously. "However," the king continued, "you held well, my son."

Tristan's heart burst with pride. He had been learning the sword for months, and this was the first time his father had acknowledged him with approval.

"You really think so, Father?" The prince winced as his voice cracked on the last word.

"Se," Aurelio replied. "That was a good match."

Tristan looked at his father in surprise.

"You are becoming a man," Aurelio said.

Tristan beamed, but the moment broke when a courier stepped into the quiet arena, his footsteps shuffling over the sand.

"Your Majesty," the courier said.

Aurelio turned to the man. "Se? Speak."

"I came to inform Your Majesty of dire news," the man continued stiffly.

Aurelio's brow furrowed. "Say on."

The courier shifted his feet nervously before continuing. "Your Majesty, the First Earl of Nico has fallen ill."

Aurelio fully turned his attention to the man. "You are certain?"

"Se, Your Majesty. The fever took him yesterday. The physicians say there isn't much hope."

Aurelio waved a worn hand in front of his face and sighed deeply. Turning to his son, he studied him for a moment, something unfathomable in the king's brown eyes. Then he turned back to the courier and spoke in a low voice, sadness edging his tone.

"Very well. Yah-Roi's will be done. Bring me word if there is any change."

The courier nodded and withdrew.

Aurelio turned back to his son, already handing off the practice sword.

"The world changes quickly," he said, almost to himself. "This will be a turning point for the kingdom. I will have to choose a new vizier."

Tristan twisted to look up at his father, who still stood a head taller than he.

"Must you have a vizier?" he asked.

Aurelio's mouth tightened. "A trusted set of second eyes, Se. It is for the good of the realm."

His gaze had already left Tristan, and the boy resisted the urge to call after him. Aurelio was already walking toward the archway.

"A king must always look to the affairs of the realm. You will be king, Tristan, as my heir. You must be aware your life is not your own, it belongs to Gershan." Aurelio had said this for as long as Tristan could remember.

Tristan placed the swords back in their holders and took in the empty arena for just a moment. The sand still displaced from the match.

Father made time today, at least. Tristan thought.

He sighed, then turned to follow after the king

Chapter 1

Aurelio chose his new vizier from the list of appointees put forth by the nobles.

"Morlach is a man who reframes what I cannot see, Tristan," the king instructed his son. "He is aware of the opinions of the common populace and never fails to help me see a way to strengthen forward progress in economics and diplomacy."

Tristan had watched for a year.

His mother, Queen Cerwyn, did not like the vizier personally. Tristan only knew that because he had once walked in on her speaking with his father.

"He manipulates the court, and respectfully, dear husband, I fear he manipulates you," she had said boldly.

Tristan's mother never failed to speak her mind to his father, and Aurelio had always taken her opinions under advisement.

Until that night.

"You would do well to watch your tongue, wife. To question Morlach is to question my judgment as a leader." Aurelio's voice had been low with warning.

Tristan had watched from the crack in the door, his parents silhouetted by the fire. His mother had stiffened. Then he saw her shoulders slump.

"You have already changed, and you do not see it." Her voice had been so soft Tristan could scarcely hear it.

He had not heard his father's reply.

After that, his mother had become quieter, less apt to share her mind, more careful of his father's moods.

Tristan had done the same.

On this day, he stood to the right of his father's throne, listening to the buzz of court. Women in gaily colored gowns and men in coats and breeches all petitioned for a portion of his father's time and opinion.

His father listened to the Duke of Vershan explain why the Duke of Uebla was in danger of breaching national security—something about salt and sailors. Tristan was not entirely sure. To his shame, he had been watching the feather bob in Vershan's hat for the better part of an hour.

That was when Morlach appeared.

It seemed to matter little who was speaking or what the topic was. As soon as the vizier entered, Aurelio's attention shifted to him alone" Report," Aurelio commanded.

Morlach stepped forward, brushing past Vershan.

"Your Majesty, as you are aware, Morocan has been pressing their quarter along our southern border for nearly three months. The agreement was that they would hold only the southern half of the strait. However, their ambassador now asks for concessions along our shores for mutual aid." The vizier sneered.

Aurelio frowned. "And the other matter?"

Morlach's eyes fell on Tristan, and the boy was suddenly no longer interested in the feather.

"Your command has been relayed to the elders of the High Keep. The crown prince leaves within a fortnight of his birthday," Morlach said, his voice smooth and cunning.

Tristan's heart lurched.

"Father?" he asked, his voice cracking as he turned toward the king.

Aurelio looked at him.

"You are the same age I was—indeed a year older. All kings are trained at the High Keep. Your mother as well." Aurelio gestured to Cerwyn, who sat stiffly on her own throne.

She knew this was coming, Tristan realized.

His eyes moved between his father and his mother. Truly, he had known it too. His mother spoke fondly of her time there.

But to leave Caerdis…

He straightened.

"As you will, Majesty," he said.

He bowed then, politely, to both his parents, already mapping the journey to Doreth in his mind.

~

Tristan was determined to treat the journey to Doreth like an adventure. His father's elite Kingdom Guard traveled with him to the High Keep.

The first night they camped under the stars, field tents, and game from the woods. Tristan sat by the fire and listened to the men banter. The embers turned orange. The shadows grew. The talk became story.

"The battle at S'lmancha," Dolfo said, slapping Toval on the back. "Now that was fight, Se?"

Tristan leaned forward as Toval raised his drinking tin. "Se, though as I recall, you hid under a rock while I took out that lead archer with my own bow."

The prince blinked, watching Dolfo's face closely, waiting for the bigger man to react.

The circle around him however burst into laughter, and the captain of his father's guard, Fernan raised his own tin. "Next you'll be telling how you took out an entire mounted archery unit with that bow of yours."

Toval's eyes twinkled. "Se, the story gets better when I tell it."

Dolfo huffed, but his lips twisted into a wry grin.

The boy sat back, watching the ease and camaraderie.

They are like brothers. He thought. I want that.

He was startled by the idea. He was a prince, not a warrior, but still, something in the easy way these men carried themselves, despite their capacity for violence, called to something in the boy.

Father is a warrior, but not like this. Tristan thought of the kings in Yah-Roi's Book. They had been warriors too.

I will be a warrior, and I will be a king. And I will be good at both. He decided.

~

The High Keep rose on the cliffs overlooking the crystalline waters of the Medrian Sea. Its white walls and gold-capped towers shimmered in the late spring sun.

Tristan rode in the middle of the Guard's formation. Fernan rode beside him.

"Have you been here before?" Tristan asked the captain.

Fernan nodded. "Se, but not recently."

Tristan knew better than to wait for more. After six weeks of travel with the man, he had learned that Fernan rarely spoke unless it was to give an order or tell a joke.

The gates loomed closer as they approached. Tristan drew courage from the ease of the men around him.

When they arrived, a man with a beard that had once been coal black came to meet them. He carried a staff and wore the rough linen tunic of the priesthood.

"I am Elranth," he said simply.

The elder had spoken softly, but even the guards sat a little straighter.

"We welcome you, Highness, to the Keep." The man bowed in respect.

Tristan swallowed, certain he was the one who should be bowing. The boy dismounted and bowed in return.

"I am grateful for your hospitality," he said, in an attempt at diplomacy.

Elranth's lips twitched. "We will see if you are grateful after I have made you run for six spans, Se?"

Tristan tilted his head, unsure if the elder was joking or if this was a test.

Behind him, Toval coughed.

"You will learn here, Se?" Elranth asked. "It is why you came."

Tristan swallowed again, then nodded. "Se, I will learn. Even if I must run."

Elranth did smile then. "Praise Yah. A humble prince."

This time, the guard did not stifle their laughter.